WIDOW
WALK

WIDOW
WALK

GAR LaSALLE

Widow Walk is a work of historical fiction. Apart from some well-known actual people, events, and locales that are part of this narrative, all names, characters, businesses, organizations, places, events, and incidents are either a product of this author's imagination or are, in all cases — are used fictitiously. Any resemblance to current events, locales, or to living persons is entirely coincidental.

ISBN: 978-0-9978436-5-1

Published by Solipsis Publishing Seattle, WA
SolipsisPublishing.com

Editor: John DeDakis

Design: Maps and Widow Walk Medallion — Randy Mott (MottGraphics.com)

Cover Design: Neil Gonzalez (Greenleaf Book Group - (GreenleafBookgroup.com)

Interior Design: Alex Head (TheDraftLab.com)

Social Media and Marketing: Scott James

Web design: Archana Murthy and Scott James

Audio Book Production: Mike McAuliffe, Tom McGurk, Wendy Wills (Bad Animals.com); Narrator: John Aylward

SOLIPSIS PUBLISHING

To the Epiphany Bringers

TABLE OF CONTENTS

DRAMATIS PERSONAE

On Whidbey Island (in Puget Sound, U.S. Territory):

Emmy O'Malley Evers - Wife of Isaac Evers
*Colonel Isaac Neff Evers - Prominent Pacific Northwest Settler
and regional judge and tax collector*
*Sarah Evers - 10 year-old daughter of Emmy and stepdaughter
of Isaac*
Jacob Evers - 6 year-old son of Emmy and Isaac
Winfield and Corrine Evers - Isaac's younger brother and sister
Ben and Missy Crockett - Neighbors
*Tom and Rebah Iserson, Major Robert and Thomasina
Anderson - Visiting guests*
Dr. Joseph Edwards - Prominent Whidbey Island physician
Sam - Salish native guide and employee of Isaac
*Jim Thomas and Princess Susan - Salish natives,
Whidbey locals*

In South Puget Sound, (U.S. Territory):

*Captain George Edward Pickett - U.S. Army commander
stationed in Bellingham*
*Lt. Colonel Rufus Ingalls - Quartermaster General of Oregon
Territory, close friend of Pickett*

In North Puget Sound, (U.S. Territory):

*Anah Nawitka Haloshem (a.k.a. "Black Wind") - Haida tyee
of Raven Clan (Queen Charlotte Islands)*
Little Raven - Anah's father, aging Raven clan leader

Klixuatan - Shaman of Raven Clan
Vladimir Varienko - Captain of the Pietrevos,
a Russian cargo ship
René Marté - French-Indian (Metís) Trader and smuggler
Eban Cull - Marté's companion smuggler
Antoine Bill - a Metís guide and interpreter employed by the
Hudson's Bay Company
MaNuitu'sta (a.k.a. "Patient River") - Bella Coola Nuxalk
clan tyee, father of Pickett's second wife
Na'Pen'Jo (a.k.a. "Jojo") - MaNuitu'sta's son,
Emmy Evers' guide
Morning Mist - Pickett's deceased second wife, daughter of
Ma'Nuita'sta
Marano Levi - Wandering unordained priest
Ksi Amawaal - Tsimshian tribe grand tyee

MAP ONE: THE HOMESTEAD

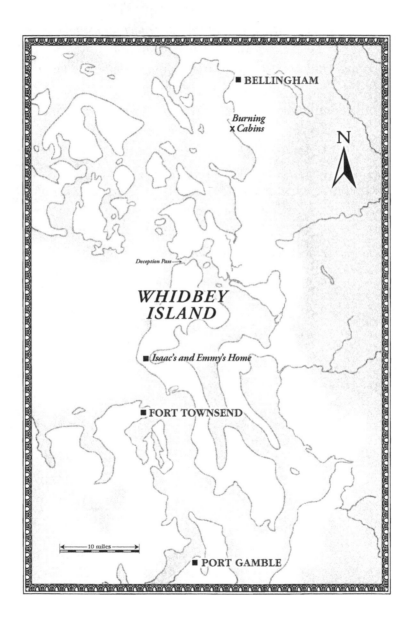

BELLINGHAM

Burning
x *Cabins*

N

Deception Pass →

WHIDBEY ISLAND

Isaac's and Emmy's Home

FORT TOWNSEND

10 miles

PORT GAMBLE

MAP TWO: A LAND IN CONTENTION

MAP THREE: THE HAUNT OF
THE NORTHERNERS

PROLOGUE

◇◇◇◇

Emmy

When she and her husband staked their claim on this alluvial plain, they did not know it had been haunted for thousands of years, first by long-gone bottom feeders who had dwelled in the vast lake that had been scraped out by retreating, massive, growling sheets of glacier ice, and then later, when the water finally receded, also by the beasts and aborigines who had looked upon the deep rich soil as *their* own.

Emmy Evers found a small gray arrowhead in the first week she walked the square mile that was now theirs, hers and her husband Isaac's, the rights to their stead conveyed on a thin piece of paper by other new settlers, ones with government-given titles. Her young children, less reverent of the land than she, would later uncover several more ancient hunting tools as they played and worked the farm. And each time she again fingered that first, sharp treasure-find, the arrowhead pried away from a clod of moist black soil, she wondered where the makers had gone...the ones who had first chipped tools like this out of flint...and why they had left the richness of this land.

And each time she felt the prick of its sharp edges, she wondered whether they really ever *had* left, for in the few years she owned her fertile prairie mile, she learned that spirits lingered. She sensed they walked her plowed fields on certain nights, the patterns of their visitations incomprehensible to her and other mere humans.

Seven years into her stay there, her family gave of its own, in a way she had long dreaded and forever mourned. The Northerners had visited. They were emissaries of the Dead.

CHAPTER ONE

<><><><>

Emmy

*He is away again. I fear the Northerners are about. I am
concerned for him and for us.*

— *Emmy Evers' Diary, October 1ˢᵗ, 1857*

D awn, almost. So Emmy pushed herself up and out
of bed. She wouldn't pamper herself, nursing a
cold. Too much to do every day now.

Her husband, Isaac, had departed in the darkness
without saying goodbye. They had talked enough the evening before, she supposed. But she was alone again now
with her children and her work. Alone again.

She pushed herself away from that thought, too.

Her daughter Sarah was already up puttering, dawdling a bit from starting her outside chores. Jacob would have to be chided up again. She would have Sarah do that for her.

They were so different, her two. Jacob worked hard for a lazy six year old, prone to discharging his duties in spurts of blind fury, whereas his step-sister Sarah, almost five years older, was the steady one, intensely stubborn, quiet and self-absorbed so that she seldom needed any attention, or so it seemed.

Sarah protected her slower little brother in a tender, defensive way that gave Emmy some reassurance that, should anything ever happen to her and Isaac, Jacob would have someone to care for him. That could happen, Emmy knew. She and Isaac could become ill. Isaac's first wife had died of a cancer, after all.

And out here, things happened. Emmy had lost her first husband in a logging accident. Whipsawed down.

And Emmy also knew of several settlers who had been murdered in the past year by the Northerner marauders. Some had been carried off by them. The slayings had been gruesome and cruel. The kidnapped victims, if ever recovered, told stories of terrible outrages they had endured while they'd been kept. Emmy personally had known a few of the ones who had been killed early on — spared the ordeals.

As she thought about that, she realized it was always present, that fear — the possibility of the Northerners' sudden appearance. She had accepted that risk, of dying that way, she knew. But it was a reluctant acceptance - a resignation. It put an edge on everything, on every plan she made, every step she took.

◇◇◇◇

Emmy walked to the barn, a crisp early frost holding to the grass, crunching beneath her footsteps. She had, during her childhood in Boston, loved the sound and feeling of that, but knew that here it meant that the October rainfall would start soon, and when the rain started on Whidbey, it got cold fast, the island's winter roughly brushing aside any lingering colors of the fall; muddying it all. So, as much as she loved reminders of her childhood, the frost here was a disappointment at the same time.

She had weathered here long enough to hate the gray, drab skies that would settle in soon enough, moving from intermittent warm showers into a bitter, soggy, constant drizzle, keeping her inside the small house and, with that, inside with her fears and suspended hopes. Looking to the windows for whatever was outside.

Seeing the leaves falling, dissolving with the rain into the Northwest muck that seemed to attach itself to everything, aggravated her sense of an always-looming despair. She had lost two previous pregnancies in October just like this one. *Would she lose this one too?* she worried. The gloom, that depressing, weighty sadness, pulseless and leaden in its countenance, could then settle heavily onto her, she knew.

If she let it.

So pervasive was that impending winter darkness, the potential of being overwhelmed by sadness, that it forced her at this time every year to search deeply to remember the freshness of light and color. By now she had learned the value of that necessary exercise, one that would help her forbear again until spring arrived. But she still had to discipline herself better, she had decided. She had to set an example for Sarah and Jacob.

She hitched her mare to the buckboard, then rode to the orchard to pick up the apples that had fallen in the night's wind —there would be at least a few bushels — before the deer found them. She cinched her rubber rain cape tightly to cut the wind. It always bit through the seams, however, turning her cheeks red and her fingers a faint blue.

Somehow, protected as she had been during her childhood by the warm softness and refinery of the cozy Boston hilltop brownstones, she knew she needed to learn all of the nuances of the Northwest cold seasons once and for all. It would help her outlast them. She knew she had to maintain a strong demeanor in the face of it all if she were going to continue as the respectable wife and mother that her husband, Isaac, expected. But the pain in her fingers from the cold added a bitter dimension to that discipline. She would outlast that feeling too, she told herself.

There *were* little breaks, little surprises before the first days of winter that brought hope, she reassured herself, as she picked the windfall around the apple trees. Assuming Isaac did not run into Northerners and get himself killed on this trip, she knew he would return in ten days with provisions from his stay in Bellingham.

She brightened a bit, thinking about more surprises that would come in right after that, when her neighbor, Ben Crockett, Missy's husband, returned with his canoes stringing behind him from his trip down south to the Elliott Bay settlement, now called "Seattle," after the settlers there decided to honor one of the prominent tyees by naming it after him. Ben would bring more jars and paraffin for preserves, perhaps a bolt or three of practical cloth, some cinnamon and cloves, and *lots* of pepper, if it lasted. So many settlers had come into the area that new provisions didn't last long before they were redistributed across three counties.

And maybe Isaac or Ben would think to bring something pretty — sashes or soft ribbon or even tiny pearl buttons if a British or Spanish ship or a fast one from San Francisco had arrived in the Puget Sound area in the last week.

She needed so much to be complete, to make this small house into a respectable home. And she wanted the baby to see some softness and color when it came into the world. She needed another girl.

Emmy lifted the heavy baskets of late harvest apples onto the buckboard. Doc Edwards likely wouldn't approve, even though he knew she lifted with her legs and used a plank to push the bushels into the buckboard. She knew her limits. Edwards didn't.

She thought about Jacob and Sarah's dawdling this morning and their response to her chiding. Where did her children get their blue eyes? she wondered, as she rode back down to the house. Where did they learn to wear expressions that made them appear as if the things they saw just disappeared inside their heads and stayed there unprocessed? It *had* to be from their fathers' lines, the Terns and the Evers, because she had *no* recollection of blue eyes on either side of her own family. And as smart as he was, it *was* Isaac's habit to sometimes keep things unprocessed in his head.

"Patience, Woman...I'm mulling it over" he would respond when she challenged him at times to make a decision on business matters.

But was it "mulling" or rather, really his excuse for procrastination? She again laughed to herself, thinking about their dissimilarities.His hesitancy. Her directness.

His blue eyes; her brown ones.

She, herself had always been told that the intensity of her own brown eyes burned deeply into every person with whom she interacted, as if she had the ability to disinter a person's buried emotions with a single focused stare. She had always assumed that was because she had been told as a little girl that dressing down someone with your eyes was a rude habit. And so, minding her elders, she had taught herself to take in everything about a person without wandering her focus up, down, or around the way others did when they bothered to pay attention to something or someone.

And that had become useful, she realized, because she had always believed everything was important in its own way and therefore valuable, with bits and pieces to store away for understanding later as necessary. Everything.

Isaac had said he was smitten from the first time she did that to him. But she didn't understand that because she had just been looking at his soul and she thought "smitten" was a funny word for anyone to use when regarding her.

As she drove the buckboard back to the house, she looked over the high bluff on which it stood, to the sea below.

What was out there that she couldn't see?

She hoped Isaac was taking care of himself.

CHAPTER TWO

◇◇◇◇◇

Isaac

To Bellingham. Adjudication. Knifing over some native's cut fish nets. Citizens want a hanging, for God's sake.

— *Isaac Evers Diary, October 1st, 1857*

Isaac smelled its sweet smoke several minutes before he saw the colors of the fire. Cedar and firs; a late summer forest flare-up, caught in the tall trees crowding the shoreline in the distance. As he and Sam pushed their way closer to it, up the late September coast, paddling from Whidbey Island toward Bellingham, the salty air burn-reddened his cheeks and the smoke wakened him fully again.

He inhaled deeply. The big Northwest giants carried so much more pitch than the evergreens he had known in Ohio, so when they burned, the smoke was pungent - like a perfume, almost. He had always liked that. Indians thought the trees were sacred, he mused. Perhaps that was one of their reasons. He inhaled deeply again.

It wasn't a big fire. The constant drizzle kept the fire from turning into a big one, he thought, not like others he had seen over the years. Autumn five years ago had been dry enough that it took two months for the fires on the peninsula to burn out. But the trees were wet now from a steady, damp, disappointing summer. That had ruined half of his harvest.

He hated the rain as much as Emmy did. He often wondered whether the mold he found on everything at home caused the dark green in the forest canopy, too.

He hadn't expected it to be so when he moved west for his life's big chance. He had heard this rocky sound was clean with life and land was virginal and free—harder than in Ohio and Missouri, but in a different way. More people to mourn his losses and mark his milestones back there, but more things to test himself against here. Now, it was the land itself, and the natives of this region - damned childlike to him - that he always seemed to be protecting. Or fighting.

But, as he thought about it, he had no regrets. He'd made his name here, marked the land as his own.

Paddling slowly as he watched the fire on shore, he almost forgot the weariness and ache in his shoulders and neck. Shoving off in the darkness after a long night at home had become harder each time, he realized. But he couldn't complain. He had accepted the job.

They had to get north quickly because he had to try the case at the Bellingham mill and get back southwest within six days to preside over another one in Port Townsend. Going along the coast by canoe with Sam, a competent but taciturn traveling companion, was the fastest way, if the weather was with them.

He hated leaving again. Too many things to do back at home. Emmy was fighting a fever, and he knew she might lose this pregnancy, too. She hadn't seemed to take as well after the quickening this time. He wondered whether the two recent failed pregnancies, both early losses, meant she might not keep this one also. He didn't know about these sorts of things.

He was pleased that Emmy had kept her figure, as hard as she worked, and it surprised him she had gotten sick again because she carried herself so ferociously in all she did, and moved so fast in this world. She had always seemed unstoppable, and no matter how tired she was, she seldom complained. He knew when he returned from this adjudication chore, he'd find she'd been working long hours doing a hundred tasks, doing many things he didn't pay much attention to but needed to be done.

She was *so* blessed full of fire. That always gave him hope. She was the home. More and more, he had started to realize that he just tended the fire.

He was staring at Sam's back, and it took Isaac, as full of Emmy as he was, four full strokes to notice that Sam had stopped paddling. Getting his bearings, he figured. They had covered about forty-five miles, still far south of Bellingham now but passing several reef net setups. So there were Lummi nearby. Strange that their nets weren't being tended, which meant either the fishing was bad, odd for this time of year, or they'd gone ashore for some other reason.

His eyes weren't any way as good as Sam's, or of any of the other natives he knew, so he had to cup his hand to his forehead, squinting to see the source of the smoke on the beach. It wasn't the trees alone; the remains of cabins—white-washed settler cabins—were on fire at the base of the small forest fire.

They drifted without paddling and watched for a few minutes until Sam grunted and pointed to a spot on the beach about a half mile north of the cabins. Isaac started to protest then saw what Sam was watching.

It was a long boat. Northerners.

It rested high on the beach not far from the cabins. Medium size, high gunnels, large enough to hold fifteen or sixteen. Isaac couldn't make out the markings from here, but a raiding party, almost certainly. The boat was unattended, so that meant the cabin folk had likely fled into the forest and the raiders were hunting them.

Isaac felt for his musket but kept his eyes on the long boat. Wished he'd brought more powder than what he thought he would need for hunting and bear. Wished Pickett and the federals would finally get their steamer gunboat stationed up here to help put a stop to this type of butchery. If the Brits had gunboats, why couldn't the Oregon territory get one for its citizens?

They had to make their decision quickly. If they turned to run against the incoming tide or put up their sail to tack against the wind . . . they couldn't outrun a long boat. They had to reach shelter.

Without waiting for Isaac to react, Sam set the pace, fast and smooth and Isaac knew what he was thinking. No time for talking it over. If they moved swiftly, they might make it to the shore undiscovered then wait for the raiding party to leave. No time for anything but hiding, as had the settlers, hopefully.

Isaac chided himself as he rowed. Should have known who the cabins belonged to, being the appointed tax collector and circuit judge for the region. But settlers were showing up all the time nowadays, drifting up from the gold fields in California or coming overland from Missouri and the Midwest; too many to get to know anymore.

The folks in those cabins had found themselves a smooth-stoned beach and built a place close to the salmon and clams. "When the tide goes out, the table is set," they'd likely heard. They had settled onto the beach and gotten lazy, typical for whites. They didn't know northern raiders had never really stopped their slaving runs. You just didn't hear about them as much because so many natives had died of measles and smallpox north of the Vancouver Islands.

But the raiders hadn't changed their ways, and new settlers brought a lot of useful things with them that drew thieves out from their protected coves—Kwakiutl, Tlingit, or Haida, likely. Sam would know. His Salish tribe had to fight them all the time. Headhunters all, he'd said.

Isaac and Sam pulled up on a short spit that jutted out just far enough that a casual look up the beach wouldn't reveal them.

Sam was out of the boat and up to the crest before they landed. As cautious as Sam was about everything, Isaac had never seen him scared this much, and his quiet, crouched movements told Isaac that Sam was close to panic.

Faster now, Isaac secured the boat and joined Sam. They could see the long boat and part of the closest cabin, still smoldering.

"Haida...Raven markings. Maybe ol' Black Wind, hisself," Sam whispered.

That sent chills down Isaac's spine. He had heard about Black Wind for years. Everyone had. But no one knew if the infamous Northerner predator was real or a myth. Isaac decided he didn't want to find out. He tried to push himself into the sand to lower his profile.

It was getting dark. Isaac looked behind him and saw the little beach wouldn't give them much protection if they had to fight, and the flat between the cabins and where they hid, covered by brambles right up to the tree line, would make it difficult for him to detect anyone trying to flank their position.

Sam would have seen that too. Even if they had reached the spit unobserved, if the Northerners headed out moving with the tide, they would pass right by the spit. It all depended on what they brought out of the burning forest.

If their boat was full, they wouldn't stop. They would stay away from Bellingham where he was headed and likely keep their heading west of Whidbey where he and Emmy lived. They'd just slip back up north quietly through the small islands and up past Vancouver—if their boat was full. Otherwise they would continue looking for plunder — and captives.

Still three hours until complete darkness. Isaac wondered if he would be tested before the night was over.
The Bellingham trial for which he was to be the judge
would have to wait. Isaac knew God would be presiding
over this one.

CHAPTER THREE

<><><><>

Emmy

Emmy unhitched her mare from the buckboard and as she led her old horse to the front yard, she looked out again at the cold gray water of the sea below the bluff. A low-lying fog hovered over the strait, obscuring the lights of the small settlement surrounding Fort Townsend. For a moment, she thought she saw a long black object in the water - perhaps large enough to be a vessel - a fishing canoe? A long boat? - But the fog hid it almost immediately. She shivered, thinking about what the appearance of long boats would mean.

She remembered that five years ago, as later recounted in the *Colonial Herald*, a Northerner raiding party descended on a Lummi tribe settlement near the Bellingham mill. The Lummis, always resourceful, frequent victims of

Northerner predatory raids, had practiced a strategy to defend themselves. The visibility on that day happened to be good. The Lummi saw the marauders approaching well in advance. As the Northerners left their long boats and moved through the woods towards what they thought was a sleeping village, Lummi warriors, hiding high in the woods' evergreens, descended and then destroyed the unguarded long boats on the beach. They then surrounded the small war party and killed every Northerner warrior.

But that much-celebrated victory had been an anomaly. The war party had been small, with less than twenty men in two long boats. The Lummi had seen the predators and had been prepared, Emmy knew. She had heard many stories about the Northerner predations of native tribes and isolated pioneer settlements. Like the one in which she lived. Her home was undefended with Isaac gone. The blockhouse that Isaac was building on the bluff was still unfinished.

The fog cleared enough that she could see across the strait. No craft on the water.

She went back to her chores, trying to put that out of her thoughts.

As she, Sarah and Jacob carried the bushels down to the cellar bins, she watched how each of her children approached the chore. Sarah, she knew, would carefully separate the bruised apples from rest, put them in a smaller basket, then, before her stepbrother could escape, hand it to him with instructions.

Sarah did exactly as Emmy predicted.

"Little Brother, please take this to the kitchen so mother can use them," Sarah said to Jacob, who was already heading up the cellar steps to play outside.

Emmy shook her head, smiling to herself. Sarah was like her, she realized, and, in his impulsivity, Jacob was so much like his father, Isaac.

That made her think again about Isaac. Now that he was back on this side of the mountains from the inland war with the aborigines, she had found herself searching his soul again. What was it that was different about him now?

He had changed, but she wasn't certain fully how yet. He seemed sadder and resigned, somehow. Whatever he had seen east of the Cascades when he had led his volunteers to fight the Walla Walla and the Palouse tribes had stooped his shoulders a bit, too.

It didn't seem fair to him, she thought. Isaac came back commissioned as a militia colonel, but he had traded something precious for that rank.

She felt it in so many ways, when sleeping next to him and even when they had the privacy to be intimate, when the children were over at his brother's home. It was in his hands and all up and down through his back now. They had never before been stiff and tentative like that, before he went east. His intimacies were vacant and roaming, during those private moments, it seemed. The private moments were further and further apart.

And later, awakening with him gone, she knew he was wandering the shore on moonlit nights again, coming in before dawn, but then getting up out of bed early, throwing himself at this job or that obligation, never saying no to any task, official or neighborly. It was as if he were filling every second with work so that he didn't have time to ponder. If he "mulled," using his own word — he didn't understand the necessity of truly thinking something through. Isaac jumped into projects, but was terribly indecisive about completing them, she realized. It was if he had become a gambler, trusting instinct and luck instead of real deliberation and discernment to weigh a project's worth. More and more, it seemed he needed her to manage his "inspirations." Was she perpetuating his impulsivity by aiding him in his projects? Or was that what she was supposed to do as a married woman - be an accomplice in an unequal partnership?

She picked a half dozen eggs for a late breakfast for the children. It was already almost seven o'clock.

Breaking the eggs carefully, one at a time into the skillet, hearing the sizzle, she realized that her sense of loneliness had worsened after Isaac returned from the Indian war, more than when he had been on long trips doing his legal work in the first years of their marriage; more than when she was married to Sarah's father, Jervis Ternbull, a rich husband she had hardly known; more than when she had been a young teenaged girl not that long ago in Boston.

Emmy called Sarah and Jacob to the table for their breakfast. She watched them eat, Jacob bolting his food as usual. She wasn't hungry, however. Her morning nausea had worsened over the past few days.

What would happen with her third child? What would become of Sarah and Jacob? Could she give them what they needed?

She understood that Isaac knew his long absences were not good for the children, that she wanted Isaac to spend more time with them. But he had pushed that aside. He told her he thought Jacob was just too young to accompany him, even on short trips to Olympia, and he didn't think it safe to bring Sarah on trips either, as feisty a young girl as she was, because even the friendly people were rough. Emmy knew that most carried some ready weapon at all times, even when using the courthouse privy, so she accepted Isaac's refusal.

That said, Emmy reminded herself that the children needed more. She had saved enough for them to travel with her to New England last year, to meet their grandparents before they passed on, meet cousins and aunts from both sides, experience and learn the most diplomatic ways of contending with her sister, their aunt, Kathleen.

But Isaac's departure for eleven months to fight in Eastern Washington had stopped those plans short. So she stayed here on Whidbey. Dutiful. Waiting.

◇◇◇◇

After breakfast, as she scrubbed the frying pan clean, she again thought about the disruption to their lives that their participation in the Palouse expedition of General Steptoe had imposed.

It was frustrating. She and Isaac had outfitted an entire company of men, even supplying some of the poorest with shoes and weapons. The government, by the verbal oration of the territorial governor, Stevens, had promised to compensate them for their patriotic service, but no payment had come, and it had already been over a year since that bloody affair. It was a disgraceful abrogation of a promise, she believed.

It wasn't that they were poor. She still had something left from the sale of her property in Olympia she inherited after the death of her first husband. Isaac was paid well for his legal and tax-collecting work. They had claim to over a square mile of prime fertile farmland bordered by waterfront. They had hired hands farming it and were selling the beef and produce to the military and to every ship that came by way of Bellingham or Port Townsend. The narrow slice of land they owned controlled easy ports to both sides of the island and the straits that reached down to Seattle, up to Canada and out the Strait of Juan de Fuca to the Pacific.

It was just that they had to work all the harder now because the government *hadn't* paid its debts. They were barely beyond a break-even, despite all the projects underway. And whatever Isaac had seen on that expedition had changed him and their relationship.

The prominence he had attained from that expedition - he was widely regarded as a hero now - had gone to his head - not as it might have with other men, as it would most certainly done with her first husband, who was prone to arrogance.

Isaac, instead, had become almost recklessly ambitious and frantically impatient. It was as if he were trying to get everything done immediately - as if he believed his time on this earth had been foreshortened somehow.

And the enormous amount of extra work they had taken on as a result, put them even farther apart from each other, it seemed.

She called Sarah into the house.

"Sarah, I will need you and Jacob to go to Missy and Ben Crockett's and then over to Doctor Edwards. Give them their mail that arrived yesterday. And ask if either of them will want to order a side of beef. We will be butchering next week when Isaac returns."

From the window, she watched Sarah mounting the mare, and after pulling Jacob up behind her, slowly trotting off to the neighbors. Jacob's dog, Rowdy, followed.

◇◇◇◇

The stove was getting cold. Emmy stepped down to the back yard and picked up an armful of wood from the pile next to the barn. She would need to chop some more alder - enough for a week at least. Isaac had left without finishing that task before he set off that morning.

That prompted her to think again about the balance within their relationship. Something else irritated her when she thought about the cost of Isaac's participation in the Palouse war. When he was away, *she* had run the farm in her *own* way. She enjoyed the challenge and had done quite well by it, increasing the production even without the hired hands and farmers he had taken with him.

Now that Isaac was back on this side of the Cascades - as he, his family and everyone else, it seemed, expected - she had stepped to the rear, and returned to the subservience of a wife. She had done so, whether she agreed with his actions or not, as she had been taught was her duty.

And it was her sense that Isaac hadn't even noticed that she had carried everything on her back in his absence, his risky gambles that she squared, as well as the new, more certain projects she had initiated.

On his return, Isaac had picked up everything as if he had been in charge all along. He moved her aside, took over her projects, like completing the huge, long landing dock on their waterfront property so that deeper draft vessels could off-load without fear of grounding during all but the lowest of tides. That dock immediately increased their income. Substantially.

But despite their near-prosperity and the pride she had in Isaac's various accomplishments — *their* accomplishments — she felt like something had been taken away from her when he returned.

And, during her worst of times, weathering the depression she felt in this time of year - a forlornness, magnified so intensely by the dark dampness of the region — she wavered in her resolve to endure. When she was again alone - as she was now, managing *all* of the business projects and caring for her family as if she were a single mother, she had to fight an enormous, perplexing frustration.

Despite recognizing that brewing hard feelings was a useless exercise, she feared she was starting to resent him.

It was on days like this that she faltered, wondering whether she should feel sorry for herself, or blame herself for not protesting some of Isaac's foolish risk taking, or let herself drift away from a hard love. It was on days like this that she wondered whether she should delude herself and pretend that the potential rewards of *future* prosperity might actually outweigh the loneliness she knew she easily could fall prey to on the worst of days.

Recognizing that, she reminded herself that long ago she had decided she would avoid indulging in either delusions or negative feelings about others.

And the prosperity wasn't all that important to her, in any case. She had been on both sides of the convenience it brought, so she knew she would survive without it. She knew she could — and would — endure most anything and do the right thing. Isaac's absence, and her resourcefulness in raising her children — so often by herself in that hostile country, really had given her the reassurance that she possessed a wherewithal more important than any contrivances money might buy.

That realization, at least was a fair compensation.

And such self-appraisal was not an overestimation of her abilities, she hoped. She knew that many who dealt with her during Isaac's long absences had learned to respect her. She heard one person had even commented that "the steel in her tiny frame had a spring-like memory." That gave her hope for better days to come.

Despite all of that, on *this* day, as the fog moved back in over the strait, she again found herself looking out the kitchen window, towards the sea, watching for whatever might come. Friends or strangers. It was a habit now, an important one, she realized.

Friends or strangers.

CHAPTER FOUR

◇◇◇◇◇

Anah

CONTINUED ASSAULTS!!!
Fourteen savagely murdered; Six missing
Officials at the Hudson's Bay Company reported the tragic loss of another contingent of coal-miners on its Campbell River Coal Mining operation.

The Vancouver Colonist - August 15th, 1857

To know him was to fear him, whoever he was, the one they called "Black Wind." Few outside of his small clan, however, really could identify him beyond a vague description as that of a tall, well-muscled, heavily tattooed warrior with an aggressive bearing and disturbingly dark presence. No one, neither non-native settlers nor the peaceful peoples along the coast, was safe from his predation. He and his clan seldom left tellers behind.

Hlgahlas Tatsu ("Black Wind") in Haida, Anah-nawitka-halo-shem, ("Has No Shame,") as he was called in Chinook trading jargon by tribes up and down the British Columbia coast, had been raised by his father's aging aunt. She took him on only at the insistence of a father grieving for his young wife.

Anah's mother had been lost to measles in the first wave of disease that hit the Haida after Protestant missionaries passed through the Charlottes, attempting conversion and, when that failed, bartering for specimens of tribal artifacts for sale to collectors in New York and London.

The Haida and the Bella Bella called the malady "Tom Dyer," after one of the sailors on the missionaries' vessels. Thousands perished along the coastal areas over a two-year period before the epidemic burned out.

Anah's only siblings, two older sisters, had been taken away by "the Boston Men" when his father was away one spring hunting in the far north. The American fur traders had come to the village talking about buying small black shale totems that some women and older men carved during the winter months when they had to stay in the long houses. But instead, the traders took the pieces that had been displayed and then grabbed the two girls.

Anah watched the entire event from the beach, the Bostons pulling his screaming younger sister by the hair into their boat and paddling to their big boat with sails anchored offshore. They didn't take him, as sturdy a child as he believed he was, just the girls.

When his father, Little Raven, returned, he was angry. Howling like a wolf, he beat Anah every day for a week. No one ever saw the girls again, although Anah saw them in his dreams, on the beach, running away from him.

As he grew older, Anah became sullen and quick to hurt others for perceived wrongs, prone to long rages and howling violent demonstrations.

By the age of twelve, he had killed two grown men in retribution raids against the Bella Coola along the inland straits off the big Island of Vancouver.

Because he was tireless and accurate in his hunting and trapping skills, Anah was allowed to accompany his father and the elders of their small clan on a slaving run down into south Puget Sound, a coming-of-age honor that was not accorded other young men in that region. That caused some enmity between Anah and the young men who were not given the same privilege, but everyone already understood he was unique in a strange way that needed to be respected and, as well, given distance.

To move as a man in the long boat, one had to push the oars fast in concert with warriors seasoned to successfully chase wounded prey and outrun the lumbering ships of the Brits and Russians.

Taunting the Brits by paddling ahead just out of range of their cannons, in particular, was a great coup, and the Royal Navy had never caught a long boat with any of its sailing vessels stationed in British Columbia. The Haida, masters of the tides and currents all along the inland coast, loved to tell how they outwitted the King George Men and the Bostons, just as all neighboring and distant tribes had lore about how they had outwitted the Haida.

The Brits, however, simply brooded over this frustration and requisitioned for improvements in their Northwest fleet, bigger cannons and faster ships, to finally catch the insolent marauders.

When Anah was thirteen years old, in 1842, off Maury Island, on an early summer run deep into south Puget Sound, his clan's long boats set upon *The Pigeon,* a small two-mast schooner caught in the morning's windless drift five-hundred yards offshore.

Anah was the first to board the hapless vessel, whose crew had been alerted to the Haida's approach by their syncopated, grunting war song. The prows of the long boats had ornate, frightening clan carvings, and, standing behind the big-eyed figure-head on the lead boat was the shaman of the clan, Klixuatan, dressed in bear skin and capped with a huge, monstrous, long-beaked raven mask. Klixuatan stomped his spear onto the deck, blowing a whistle and singing in a high-pitched whine.

The oarsmen pulled the boat forward, paddles dipping the water in synch with the stomping beat.

No shots were fired because the schooner crew carelessly had left their powder to molder outside over night in a wooden bin.

Because the sound carried well across the still of the morning, the terrified men had had at least five minutes to prepare themselves for the onslaught, and a ferocious knife fight ensued on deck, seven desperate men against two large converging long boats, each carrying twenty-five warriors.

Anah killed two more men that morning and took a head, his first ever, as a prize, that of his biggest opponent, an orange-bearded, long-haired man with a knot braided in the Chinese style. For the first time, Anah saw the difference between the angry, terror-filled eyes immediately before an opponent's death and the flat colorlessness caught in those same eyes when all life had drained away.

The dead eyes on his prize were different than those of one who had simply given up living, as he had seen on his hobbled aunt the year before. He thought about how her eyes had become bottomless black holes — tired, taking in no more. The eyes of this sailor, however, were without color, as if the spirit released with the beheading had carried their hue away with it.

After the killings, one of the long boats stayed behind to ransack, then set the sloop on fire while the second boat proceeded southward.

Anah crowed his pride for an hour after the killings.

Maury Island, a triangular land mass roughly three miles across, was separated from adjacent Vashon Island by a small waterway, passable during a medium tide, which led into a natural harbor bordered by each island.

Vashon, the larger of the two, had recently been swept by a seasonal forest fire, so the local Suquamish natives who remained had moved their encampments onto the higher northeast bluffs of Maury, to positions that presented easy access to the beaches below, as well as a 280-degree view of the entire sound. From their huts they could see all the way from the big mountain "Tacomat," later called "Rainier" by the explorer Vancouver, up along the Cascades and the white-haired woman mountain called "Kulshan" by the Lummi, over to Whidbey Island, and then westward to the sacred peaks of the Olympic Mountains.

The Suquamish watched the brief, bloody battle below between the Northerners and the schooner's crew. They knew about the Northerners and, for generations, had heard verbal renditions from elders who, like many tribes along the Puget Sound, also had contended with them.

The Suquamish women, fearing a landing by the marauders, spread out into the dense forests of Maury, looking for hiding places for their children and for their settlement's few valuable possessions. However the men of the clan, encouraged that this was a small war party moving in only two long boats, plotted an ambush.

The leader of the Suquamish clan, Na ma t'shata, argued that they outnumbered the raiders and had many more craft, and because their own boats were smaller than the raider's boats, they were much more maneuverable.

He noted that the smaller of the raiders' two long boats had passed through the narrow channel on an outgoing tide, while the larger one lingered, its warriors busy dismembering the stricken ketch. All the Suquamish knew that the tidal flats between the two islands extended for almost a mile, and when the tide moved out, it did so swiftly, leaving all but the smallest of craft attempting to pass through stranded and immobile for hours.

Na ma t'shata argued that an attack against the small lead Northerners' boat in the deep harbor by several of the Suquamish craft would easily overwhelm it, especially if they could hurl the large boulders they had collected for a purpose like this into the Northerners' canoe.

Over the previous four years, since the last time Northerner raiders had passed through, the Suquamish elders had carefully selected the stones. Anticipating a return by the Northerners in the future, they had conferred on each huge stone a name for incantation during the dangerous approach to the marauders. Heaved by two men from a smaller canoe, they reasoned that the stones would punch holes into the bottom of the war canoe, then the Suquamish, from their smaller craft would be able to surround and spear or drown the Haida warriors in the water. Then, Na ma t' shata predicted, they could go back and finish off the remaining warriors in the larger boat immobilized by the outgoing tide in the shallow channel.

Observed by Suquamish who remained on the shore, the fierce battle in the harbor lasted less than fifteen minutes.

Anah was in the first Northerner boat through the channel, carrying his war trophy still dripping the blood of the beheaded sailor. In the same long boat, his father, Little Raven, had directed the warriors to head toward the south shore of the harbor, where several years before they had found a rich Suquamish village with racks of drying salmon, some metal utensils and axes, and stores of fresh water. They reached the shoals but saw that the village was gone, so they started moving into deeper water out of sight of their second boat that was dismembering the schooner. As the Haida moved around a small peninsula, the Suquamish attacked, fifteen small four-man canoes moving in on the longboat from three sides.

Anah, seeing two warriors in one of the approaching canoes struggling to stand up with a massive stone, immediately understood the tactics being advanced. Ducking arrows and spears, he barked to the warriors in his boat to stop paddling and instead commanded them to use their long oars to stave off the smaller canoes.

As they did so, Anah impaled his severed trophy head onto a pike and pushed it into the faces of the oncoming attackers in the closest boat.

Anah knew the Haida were great swimmers. He ordered several of the warriors to leap into the water and pull on the gunnels of the lead Suquamish boats, which already were rocking unsteadily as their occupants struggled to stand with the large stones.

Three of the Suquamish canoes tipped, including Na ma t' shata's, and the rest of the tribe, seeing this, broke off the attack.

Anah and Little Raven's long boat moved back to the shoals where the other Northerner long boat was wallowing in the mud.

The Suquamish made no further attempts. Na ma t' shata, untouched but very dead, washed up on Maury two days later.

By the time the Haida raiding party returned to its small village on the Queen Charlotte Islands three weeks later, the thirteen-year-old Anah had acquired three more heads and a reputation for mutilation of the dead.

This form of barbarism was not the custom of his clan, and it embarrassed his father, Little Raven. But it did not matter, for everyone understood thereafter that Anah had a brilliant dominating presence that made him special in the tactics of war and survival. Klixuatan, who had witnessed Anah's actions during the battle with the

Suquamish, pronounced that the vigor of the clan was with the young teenager.

Although his aging father, Little Raven, remained chief, Anah became the resonant leader of the Haida Northerner clan. His reputation among the numerous Haida and other tribes grew over the next seven years, rivaling the formidable tyees, the chiefs of the Tsimshian and coastal Chinook tribes, whose warriors numbered in the thousands. And, because of Anah's proclivity for rape and occasional cannibalism, even the Spanish and Russians, who rarely sailed this region anymore, knew his name and steered alert in the Hecate Strait that ran between the Queen Charlotte Islands and the mainland. Only a few of the Portuguese ships, those that bartered for slaves bound for the brothels and mines of Brazil, ventured into the Queen Charlottes.

The British Hudson's Bay Company, given exclusive domain over the area by the Crown, soon put up a bounty for Anah and raised it twice, but no one was foolish enough to bribe his way into the Charlottes to go after it. Anah's mobility on and off the Queen Charlotte Islands kept him out of the grasp of the frustrated Brits.

In 1850, at the same time the territorial British governor, Douglas, was personally leading retribution excursions against dormant and well-established Nootka and Bella Coola clans, he also dispatched three survey expeditions out of Esquimalt with accompanying contingents of Royal Marines, expressly for the additional task, should the opportunity present itself, of capturing and hanging Anah.

Each time, though, he and his most loyal accomplices had enough forewarning from Tlingit allies along the coast to move out of reach, abandoning villages and then taking new ones if the Brits found their winter encampments.

Anah's elusiveness made a mockery of the Brits' efforts. He continued his predation, occasionally even raiding the tribes protected by British garrisons.

Slaving was profitable for Anah, more so than the miscellaneous pickings from the Qualicum, Suquamish and Bella Coola villages he ravaged.

As the fur trade died out by midcentury and increased pressure was brought to bear by the Brits against slavery, Anah learned the value of selling women for other purposes than labor. He found ready buyers for his healthier captives from the Portuguese and Russians, and also from a few American ships venturing up from Oregon.

And his personal appetite was voracious. It was rumored that he kept several women, fair and dark-skinned, red- and raven-haired in his own entourage. Few slaves sold by his clan escaped his mark, especially the young women and boys.

◇◇◇◇

In 1853, in the twenty-fourth year of his life, Anah traveled with his father and a huge raiding party—composed of several Haida, Tlingit, and Skidegate clans—far, far south along the coast into northern California.

When they returned, they had acquired an immense amount of wealth with miscellaneous trading items, including over one hundred captives: young women, children, and a few healthy male teens, many of whom had fair hair and complexions. They had been snatched in quick raids on six peaceful, unprepared Umpaqua and white coastal settlements between the Rogue River and Mendocino.

Anah kept two young Scandinavian twin sisters for himself, kidnap bounty from a Coos Bay emigrant settlement, and distributed half of the other captives to his followers. Anah was fascinated by the twins—not with the respectful reverence many aborigines held for such children, who were a rare occurrence among Northwest Indian tribes, but with a defiant contempt for the powers that created this anomaly.

The girls, ravaged repeatedly by Anah, were both pregnant within a fortnight.

One week later, he traded the rest of the exhausted captives for a small mountable cannon and several breech-loading rifles to an enterprising Portuguese slaver, who sailed south again profitably depositing the remaining victims with buyers in Panama, Chile and Brazil.

By this time, Anah had collected six wives, none who were Haida, and from them, twenty children. With the cannon mounted on his largest cedar canoe, he began waging war on anyone who wasn't Haida or Tlingit, attacking several villages the next year.

The terror was great enough that the Qualicum and even the fierce Kwakiutl moved their long houses far away from the shore so the distance between these dwellings and their previous location came to be called "Madman land." Still, armed as he was with his own cannons on a fleet of eleven long boats, Anah was wise enough to continually evade any confrontation with the Brit navy ships.

The prestige he gained from his predation, measured in part by the fear he read in other men's eyes, stimulated an insatiability. Anah continued his raids well into the winter when other clans had moved to their winter long houses. His Raven clan was the first out in the early spring.

In Victoria, as the terror along the coast increased, the Hudson's Bay Company's balance sheets reflected the impact of Anah's raids to the company's mining and trading operations. By 1852, emigrant settlers and indentured operatives, protesting for the safety of their lives, increasingly refused to move to remote coastal outposts. These events did not go unnoticed by the company's London investors and insurers.

CHAPTER FIVE

✗✗✗✗

Pickett and Ingalls

We have increased the vigilance in our patrols of the region, due to the thwarted attack on the Elliot Bay settlement by a loose coalition of aboriginal people, and also due to fears from local citizens about similar raids planned against this Bellingham milling community....

Regarding the request by the regional tax collector, Isaac Evers, urging the territorial government's subsidization of settlers onto San Juan Island to bolster our claim to that strategic location, the rumors persist that the British covet the same and may increase their efforts to secure it. Plan to investigate further.

— 1857 Report by Captain George E. Pickett to General William S. Harney, Commander, U.S. Army, Oregon Territory

T he swell and chop pounded the small sloop, turning his stomach into an inelegant distraction. George Edward Pickett wondered why he hadn't left the espionage to others and instead, had let himself be talked into the trek across the strait into Victoria again.

Accompanied by his best friend, Lt. Colonel Rufus Ingalls, Quartermaster General for the Department of Oregon, and two of his casual companions, the brothers Will and Darby McIntyre, Pickett had made the trip again in civilian garb. But this time he was immediately recognized by two of his officer counterparts in the Royal Infantry Brigade stationed in Victoria.

Despite their reassurances that he could enjoy the boom town without exposure, by the third night, he was certain he had been saluted by a few drunken noncommissioned officers he passed on the streets. His attempted espionage, his ruse to disguise a junket, had been thwarted.

Pickett had other reasons to be concerned. Although none of his own superior officers was likely to hear about this trip, Ingalls being exceptionally discreet, Pickett had reason to be concerned about the ill effects of nasty gossip. Despite the protection from hostiles that the fort afforded to the Bellingham community, because of repeated episodes of disorderly conduct by the soldiers under his command, the county's townspeople already had a substantial contempt for the military establishment stationed there. So, even unfounded rumors about the drunken or wanton behavior of the officer in charge of the outfit would make it all the more difficult for him to get the cooperation necessary for the sturdy challenge of maintaining peace between the white settlers and the natives in the region.

They were always at each other's throats, each using the slightest of incidents as provocation for escalated violence. He hated the mess the violence created.

Pickett fretted about that during the long heaving ride back south and debated whether the small pleasure he had found cavorting in the makeshift pubs was likely to do much harm to his reputation. He thought about his comportment and decided it had not been scandalous.

He was an officer and a gentleman, after all.

He had learned to hold his liquor in a genteel manner as a young West Point plebe, and he had practiced that control in the lonely years after the death of his first wife and daughter while stationed in Texas several years before his commission to the Northwest. Thus, the gossip in Victoria, at least, would not be based on any public displays of rowdiness on *his* part.

He realized during the crossing, however, much to his chagrin, that the McIntyre brothers' antics in the main street bordellos might be confused with his own more civil behavior. At least they hadn't been arrested. But he knew they were loud, and grew louder still if drinking in each other's company.

He would hear about it soon enough, he decided, because gossip from Victoria and Olympia was a favorite pastime for all the citizens of the region.

Victoria, a town whose rowdiness would have embarrassed the Queen, its royal namesake, had outgrown order after gold had been discovered near the Fraser River in '56. Within a few months after the rich find, the town's population had quickly reached five thousand, swelling to become an international tent city whose population equalled that of the entire Puget Sound to the south.

In less than a year of the Fraser strike, thirty thousand travelers had passed through Victoria, and the town's promise of sexual favors, gambling, and instant wealth, built on rampant speculation, had seduced the naïve and stripped the foolish. The desperate hunger of the wayfarers passing through made it dangerous for anyone not adept at defending himself.

Pickett, trained in pugilistic and knife fighting, knew he could handle himself well, but kept a small six-barreled pepperbox pistol concealed in his vest, nevertheless.

On this trip, he'd only used it on one occasion, while into his spirits and departing from a large tavern tent. He had brushed against a surly drunkard who took offense and pulled a knife. Pickett had reached for the pistol's reassurance. Fortunately, the Brits kept good order and enough sober military presence that a constable intervened before Pickett had to put the inebriated aggressor down.

He hadn't gone to Victoria for female companionship, despite the prodding of Ingalls, who had often expressed that sexual intercourse was the solution to everything.

Pickett was over women for now, feeling a bitter unluckiness. The two times he had fallen in love and committed to marriage, each wife had passed on a few months after childbirth.

The thought of that happening again to him, such an emotional toll with all the unmanly weeping that transpired afterwards, overwhelmed him.

And despite a powerful ache from his groin up to his stomach, his heart just needed peace.

He could not bring himself to play undignified games without love in sight; nor could he condone the thought of paying for the discharge of his baser passions. So, on this occasion, he behaved as he usually did, drinking with his companions to lighten, for a bit, the duty of his office, but keeping to himself mostly, a decorated knight without a Guinevere in a savage land.

A few years before this trip, in the late winter of '55 and several years after the death of his first wife, George Pickett had found the person whom he considered his love of a lifetime. She was a slender thing, slight enough that his round, robust features dominated the visage of the two of them when they stood side by side so that she almost disappeared, it seemed.

Perhaps that is why the quietly performed marriage between a U.S. infantry captain and an Indian teen largely went unnoticed in the Bellingham community. Or perhaps it was that Pickett normally kept to himself anyway, guarding his privacy and rarely staying at the fort he had built.

In the winter of '56, within ten months of marrying his "little Indian savage," as he liked to tease her in the Chinook jargon with which they communicated, she delivered a healthy, slight-framed boy. Four months later, she died in one night from a convulsive fever that followed a fit of dyspepsia.

Leaving the baby with a family living close to the home he had built for his family, Pickett wept repeatedly for days on a self-granted leave.

Ingalls and other friends couldn't console him.

When he returned eight weeks later, he was sober and resolute with a sense of duty that stayed with him during the remaining time he spent in the Northwest. Those who served under his command knew him to be gentle and serious, carrying a grave sense of purpose devoted to maintaining peace while following orders with enough flexibility that it was sometimes misinterpreted as permissiveness by those prone to pushing their luck.

In April of '57, after reporting rumors to the U.S. Commander, William S. Harney, of a possible move by the Esquimalt-based British Navy, Pickett received orders to make preparations to move his command. The dispute between the Brits and the United States over Puget Sound border territory seemed to be intensifying again.

With the Oregon Treaty of 1846, a prolonged and bitter international and presidential election dispute over the U.S. and British North American borders had been resolved, or so it seemed. But immediately after the signing of the treaty, Northwest and British Columbia residents found an ambiguity in it that established one new point of contention: the wording in the document had not named the boundary waterway to which the term "strait" referred. The Brits claimed it meant the *Rosario Strait*, which would have included San Juan Island with Vancouver Island as British territory.

But the Oregon territorial citizens believed it had meant the *Haro Strait*, which would have placed San Juan Island in U.S. possession.

Recognizing the strategic value of controlling by fort and gun the most direct pathway into the harbor-rich Puget Sound, Harney ordered Pickett to maintain the

Bellingham garrison, prepare to take command of troops from nearby Port Townsend, and upon further orders, establish a new position—robust fortifications on this northernmost of a chain of islands that ran down the Puget Sound as far south as Tumwater.

In addition to maintaining an advantage over the British, Harney reasoned, hostile indigenous people, loosely aggregated into various tribes, occupied every one of the many islands. The five thousand United States citizen settlers who had moved into the Puget Sound area over the past eight years needed protection from the marauding Northerners who, in recent years, had raided white and native settlements as far south as Olympia. Harney knew that control of San Juan Island would be important to the success of that responsibility as well.

The British Hudson's Bay Company had abandoned its outpost in Steilacoom, one hundred nautical miles south, twenty-one years earlier, but it still maintained a presence on San Juan, which was immediately across the Strait of Juan de Fuca from Vancouver, most certainly for the same strategic reasons that Harney had recognized.

The establishment of the fort might likely infuriate the Brits, but Harney believed the issue needed to be resolved. The venerable Harney had never been afraid of confrontation or controversy, whether from an enemy or a superior officer. He also knew that Captain George Pickett would discharge his duty with honor.

◇◇◇◇◇

While in Victoria, Pickett had listened in the taverns for discussion from the Brit marines about the San Juan controversy, or for any signs they were preparing for any new expeditions. But neither he nor Ingalls had heard any rumors, so he surmised that perhaps the dispute was dying down. Perhaps he would not have to move his garrison after all, he speculated. And further orders from Harney had not arrived.

Lost in thoughts as they traveled back to Bellingham on this late fall day, he briefly noticed the waters south of Vancouver were full of life that just was not present in the Chesapeake he had known back home in Virginia.

He observed in the distance, hundreds of sea lions chasing salmon, and boiling pockets of dogfish furiously feeding on squid. Seagulls and cormorants hovered over the tumultuous feeding.

It was beautiful, he thought, a rich, endless, beautiful bounty.

As they neared port in Bellingham, Pickett briefly turned to Ingalls and thought about their friendship and the events of the past few days. He wondered if he had diminished Ingalls's regard for him in any way. He always worried about things like that.

◇◇◇◇

Ingalls, who sat on the starboard side of the rig, had been observing Pickett staring off into the distance. He knew his friend Pickett well and also how difficult the past year had been for him. Ingalls had cajoled the young captain into this trip, hoping it would pull the man out of his doldrums. And Ingalls knew what was troubling him. He was still in mourning.

George Pickett and Rufus Ingalls had been friends since their days at West Point. Ingalls, three years older than Pickett, had the privilege of seniority at the academy and the opportunity to discipline Pickett and other plebes during the hazing that accompanied initiation.

Observing the accommodating manner in which Pickett responded to the top-down pranks the upper classmen bestowed on frightened newcomers, Rufus marked him to be a good fellow. Thereafter, he always enjoyed Pickett's company and jollity, in comparison to the stiff responses and self-important strutting of most of the other plebes.

And, although Pickett's playfulness and casual attitude earned him demerits, pushing his ranking down to dead bottom in his class by the time he graduated, it made the rigidity of the environment tolerable for fellows like Rufus Ingalls, who at that time looked upon military professionalism as a secure convenience rather than a calling.

Over time, he grew to admire Pickett's ability to always balance levity and abandon with a sense of gentle propriety. And Pickett never seemed to lose that sense of playfulness.

In the '46 Mexican War's battle of Chapultepec, his regard for Pickett was forever solidified after witnessing Pickett rescue the U.S. flag from a wounded colleague, the young Captain James Longstreet, and, under fire from both Mexican Army regulars and desperate young men from the regional Mexican military academy, Ingalls saw Pickett climb a ladder up the bell tower of the fortress, tear down the enemy's colors, and replace it with the Stars and Stripes.

That rallied the Americans and seemed to deflate the Mexicans. In the midst of the wicked fight, Pickett, still waving the flag furiously, had turned to Ingalls and winked, saying, "Some fight, eh, Rufus?"

Ingalls always remembered that.

He thought about just how serious everyone had been in Mexico, seeing this as the opportunity for combat honor, overrating Santa Anna and the Mexicans, and underestimating themselves and the resolve that came from their conscious participation in the expansion of the country's borders, the destiny of a righteous nation.

He thought about the days in Mexico City, after they took Churubusco, all the young men in the cantinas; the happy Pickett, sporting his new bars from the field promotion he'd received from that flourish; the flush and swell of all the stories still running through their minds.

Ingalls had kept in touch with Pickett after that, and when he found himself appointed Quartermaster for General Harney in Astoria, Oregon, he sought out his friend who had been assigned to establish the distant Bellingham fort.

They sported together, Ingalls always enduring Pickett's playful teasing, and had shared a few unsuccessful expeditions against the more hostile natives of the region.

Ingalls had been there when Pickett met his second wife, a pretty brown thing called Morning Mist.

On that occasion just two years ago, Pickett and Ingalls had accompanied a British foray into the eastern side of the lower Hecate Strait, to observe how the Brits conducted their military business with the aborigines of that region.

The British territorial governor, Douglas, had arranged treaties with several clans, but ultimately had abandoned any form of negotiation. Instead, he had employed the same tactic as had his British counterparts with the aborigines in New Zealand—expropriating large tracts of land as white settlers moved in.

Ingalls, appalled by this practice, had nevertheless been intrigued by the interactions between the British and the northwest natives because he had personally witnessed a distinct variation in the behaviors of the aboriginal natives and wondered how the Pacific Northwest natives might react to such scurrilous behavior.

Both he and Pickett shared the belief that such actions would only increase the resentment of the natives against the whites, possibly provoking more Northerner raids. The tactics reminded them of the worst diplomatic mistakes they had witnessed earlier in their careers.

So many broken treaties and misplaced trust in promises, he rued. The pattern hadn't changed in years. The violent reactions of the aborigines to the expropriation of their homeland was almost always the same and predictable.

While stationed in Texas after the Mexican war, for example, both he and Pickett had encountered southwestern native ferocity in the Arapahoe, Comanche, and Kiowa and had chased them across dry plains in various actions after particularly terrible atrocities against the whites.

But this situation seemed to be different in so many ways.

Both he and Pickett shared the view that on the balance, in the Northwest at least, most of the abuse went from white to red, rather than the other way around. Ingalls had marveled at the difference between the scruffy, lean, and vicious Apache from the Northwest Coastal Indians, who were mostly fat and docile from the ready and rich food supplies that their fishing and foraging presented to them. It was as if the Northwest Indian's placidity had made them easy marks.

Because of their past experience in the Southwest, it surprised neither Ingalls nor Pickett that at least a few bands of Northwest Coast Indians, the Haida and Kwakiutl especially, responded to the British and American incursion into their territory distinctly differently than that of aborigines from many other more peaceful Northwest tribes.

The destructive acts by the Northerners they had witnessed seemed consistent with their own understanding of what they, like most of the whites they knew, considered the primordial spirit of aborigines — violent, child-like and instinctive.

When he or Pickett confronted natives around Bellingham and Astoria with stories of raiding, rape, and savagery, which only served to provoke the whites into further harsh retribution, the docile ones, like the Lummi and Nooksak, always pointed northward, blaming Alaskan and Russian aboriginal "Northerner" outlaws for descending into the softer south for prey and plunder.

On that particular Vancouver expedition with the British, he and Pickett observed British negotiations with the peaceful tribes of the Tsimshian and Stikene. The tactics used by the Brits were particularly interesting and ultimately disturbing.

The Hudson's Bay translator, a Metís half-French half-native, named Antoine Bill, whose Suquamish mother's clan had no fondness for any of the northern coastal tribes, seemed to be telling the native "tyee" chieftains that their "X" marks on the treaty documents were simply a sign of friendliness to the Brits, who were there only to keep order and safety for all people.

Both Ingalls and Pickett spoke enough Chinook to know what was being said, however. Antoine Bill was omitting the fact that the tribes would have to move from their land. Did the aborigines understand what was happening, he wondered?

Yet neither he nor Pickett, guests of the Brits, had the authority to interfere in the negotiation, so they remained silent. It was God's will, he concluded. Survival of the cleverest.

And then something else happened to mark that occasion.

As Ingalls observed one "tyee" after another walk up to the table to place his mark, he saw a pretty face in the crowd of onlookers staring over at them.

At first, he thought she was looking at him, and straightened himself in anticipation of a possible covert liaison with the girl. But then he realized she was looking directly at Pickett, who like he, had dressed for the occasion in his uniform, complete with epaulettes and sword.

After a moment, he elbowed Pickett, who turned to see the young girl.

Her name was Morning Mist.

Ingalls recalled that Pickett seemed fixed in place, holding eye contact with the girl for almost a full minute, before blushing and turning away.

She continued staring at him. She was a radiant being, no more than fifteen, Ingalls recalled. Her eyes, widely spaced on a high-cheeked symmetrical face, compelled one to look back and forth at each. And when he did so, he found she conveyed both a sadness and hope.

She had a comely, slim figure, and her legs were straight and well formed, unlike most of the older aborigine women and men in the region who spent so much of their time with their legs folded under them. She seemed demure and modest, just like all the other native women who had not been sullied by forced prostitution or slavery.

Ingalls had watched the shy courtship quickly unfold in the camp that night.

She spoke Chinook jargon and a few words of English.

"Take me with you. Take me," were the first words she said to Pickett, and she articulated it in a way that Ingalls understood to go far beyond a plea for an elopement. She spoke with the urgency of a young girl who saw the dissolution of her surroundings and feared that disintegration; a girl who saw hope, bound in a projected passion onto Pickett, in an emissary from a bizarre, new world.

The intensity of the plea overpowered the lonely Pickett, Ingalls observed.

After that, the shyness quickly turned into a steamy, constantly charged storm. Pickett couldn't have enough of her.

Within a week, he asked her tyee father, MaNuitu 'sta, for permission to bring her as his wife to the fort in Bellingham.

Ingalls was surprised at Pickett's decision, but, thinking back to those events, Ingalls knew the previous year
had been his friend Pickett's happiest. Until Morning
Mist died.

◇◇◇◇◇

Pickett glanced over at Ingalls and realized his friend had
been observing him for quite a while. When their eyes
met, Ingalls nodded at him and gave him a kind smile.
Pickett knew the look and nodded back, reassured his
friend understood him.

Thinking back over all the events they had experienced together over the past fifteen years, he knew that
Ingalls, more than anyone else, would forgive him for
taking the liberty of searching again for meaning on the
painful events of the past twelve months. He ran them
through his mind for the thousandth time as the boat
neared the Bellingham harbor and the home he had built
for Morning Mist.

It would never be the same, he knew. It would never
be the same.

CHAPTER SIX

⟨⟨⟨⟩⟩⟩

Anah

*The Hudson's Bay Company is offering rewards of up to 25
pounds sterling to citizens or natives for reliable information
leading to the apprehension of the Haida aborigine, Anah
Nawitka Haloshem, a.k.a. "Black Wind"*

—*1857 Circular posted in Victoria, Esquimalt, and throughout
Vancouver Island*

T hree years after the raid into northern California,
another epidemic raced through the Haida and
Kwakiutl clans, felling half the people in the area,
from Queen Charlotte northward up the inland coast two
hundred miles. This time, the disease was smallpox, the

plague planted purposefully by a conspiracy of whites and local natives who would never take the blame for it.

In one circumstance, several large chests containing trading goods, but also carrying diseased wool blankets, were set adrift in three small boats close to the inlet of the Nass River where Anah's clan was wintering. One skiff floated north across the strait into Tlingit territory, and another was discovered by a Haida Raven Clan woman gathering goose barnacles and seaweed.

She dragged the Trojan horse two miles upriver into the camp.

Within a week, the first victims fell ill. Because the telltale pustules didn't present right away, several women attended the vomiting, febrile, disease-stricken first victims and, thus exposed, carried the pox infection throughout the thirty long house lodges.

Five of Anah's wives died, and thirteen of his children perished in two months.

Following gossip from trappers of the epidemic's devastation and betting the Haida clan would be incapacitated, the Hudson's Bay Company sent out another expedition in March, this time a force of 256 soldiers and a small complement of Metîs mixed-breed bounty hunters on three fast ships to capture Anah and destroy his clan. Tlingit allies, hearing gossip about the assault from natives in Esquimalt, British Columbia, where the Royal Navy berthed, again alerted the Haida of the approach a few days before the ships arrived.

But Anah couldn't move this time. Because so many in the tribe were too ill to evacuate, Anah sent out three war canoes to confront and then turn and flee from the approaching ships to try to divert them from the village.

The *Eurydice,* a twelve-gun, sixth-rate ship of the line, peeled off in pursuit, but the other two larger ships, the *Constance* and the *Thetis,* dropped anchor at the mouth of the broad inlet. They set their cannons broadside to the mouth of the river to prevent any ocean escape and sent 220 of the red and green uniformed marines ashore.

Correctly anticipating the most probable landing site, Anah had prepared an enfilading ambush, a tactic he had learned watching British field maneuvers. When the marines in the first boat landed and moved onto the crest of the beach, thirty of his Haida shot a devastating volley into the heavily laden troopers, cutting all twenty of them down.

The troop in the second boat did not have a chance to land and was hit by a volley from a different direction. Caught by the surf sideways, the boat overturned, spilling its wounded and dead onto the beach. The lieutenant in the third boat ordered the rowers to retreat out of distance of the Haida muskets and then signaled back to the *Thetis.*

As the wounded Brits lay dying in the surf, the *Thetis* and then the *Constance* opened up and began shelling the woods that sheltered the Haida. Trees exploded above their heads, ripping them with wood and metal shards.

Anah's warriors retreated in confusion. In the bombardment by the combined twenty-two cannons from the two ships, forty men and women from the clan were wounded or killed outright.

Within a half hour, British marines disembarked the remaining 180 marines and took the beach.

Anah, watching them land three field cannons, decided to move his warriors beyond reach. He left the wounded to the mercy of the Brits.

They gave none.

The Brits, guided by Antoine Bill, passed through a huge, fresh burial site of smallpox victims. They saw several unburied rotting corpses in the surrounding brambles, and finally found an undefended village with over 260 ill men, women, and children infirmed in several of the smoke-filled long houses.

The Royal Marine captain of the company, Jeremy Brighton, Esq., set out a perimeter guard and ordered the marines to scuttle Anah's huge cedar long boats and spike his cannons.

Then they set fire to the village. Fearing the spread of disease and rationalizing their actions as retribution for their losses, the Brits stationed themselves at the single exit to every burning long house and shot down anyone attempting to escape, including women and children.

None survived.

The village and all its contents, including food supplies, were burned to the ground.

The official report filed by Brighton spoke of a "significant encounter," detailing the twelve dead and twenty wounded marines who had been ambushed on the beach. He spoke of thirty Indians killed in the bombardment and numerous victims of an obvious plague "that has most certainly decimated this Haida clan's ability to wage war in the future."

His report said nothing about the torching of the long houses or the murder of those attempting to escape or of the victims trapped inside.

From a hiding place on the beach, Anah watched and heard the wailing in the aftermath of the terrible massacre of his infirmed tribe. He made his way north to find the escaped healthy survivors and the warriors in the three canoes he knew would have outrun the *Eurydice*.

When he reached the rendezvous position, he learned that his last wife and his two oldest sons had been slaughtered in the bombardment.

Anah's howling rage frightened his followers, all of whom were grieving over their own losses.

In the following days, he mulled over the events and dreamed darkly, carried away by a spirit that circled the ashes of his winter village.

Anah's raiding clan had been reduced fourfold. Expecting further incursions of settlers and British soldiers, he knew he would need to move far out of reach, rebuild quickly, and set out to build re-build alliances with the Tlingit and Skidegates.

Because rumors had spread that the Brits had something to do with the pestilence that killed so many, within six months he was able to construct a formidable enough alliance of angry clans that he was able to start up his profitable slaving enterprise again. Empowered with the proceeds from that, he began planning the revenge he wanted for the killing of his sons and the rest of his people.

It was one of Anah's long boats that Isaac and Sam observed from the spit.

CHAPTER SEVEN

◇◇◇◇

Isaac

God does not explain His ways to those of us left behind.

—*Isaac Evers' Diary, October 8th, 1857*

At first, he thought that the merciful Jesus had sent the dense fog to cover them from the Northerners, but as it established itself and crept under his summer wool, he realized it would also hide movements of a flanking attack if they had been seen earlier.

So, Isaac began to think it more likely to be Beelzebub's trick. The fog would also prevent them from escaping because breakers near the shore would capsize their canoe and drown them if they didn't manage to head into them straight, and they couldn't see, as thick as it was.

Sam and Isaac agreed to wait it out, risking discovery and a brutal fight with the killers.

Isaac fretted that decision. His powder was getting wet, and the thin knives he kept were for skinning and filleting, not for fighting.

Sam, a slight but sturdy survivor of rival clan wars and pestilence, would be of no help if it came to a fight. Isaac knew Sam would run before he would make a stand, throwing his weapons and belongings behind him, squealing in Chinook all the way.

Isaac wouldn't run. He had seen what the worst of these aborigines did to captives. In the Palouse, he had witnessed vengeful acts and random callous cruelty by the natives—gutted men impaled, butt to tongue on long spikes; girls and women bound, raped, and sodomized repeatedly for days until they had begged to be killed; their babies dashed against the rocks.

And he had seen random acts of retribution by military leaders assigned to the region, covered up in the official reports—sporadic escalating viciousness, so that at any one moment the helpless and innocent were more likely to be the victims than those who started the violence in the first place.

By comparison, all told, Isaac believed the aborigines were much more apt to let their anger rampage than were the bluecoats or the militia, usually because so many of the native young men were engaged in the confrontations. But, in trekking with his company across the Snake River, he had come upon the corpses of hapless travelers, emasculated and skinned men and barely living survivors who told them the ones who seemed to enjoy giving it out most were the tribal *women*. While the men were gambling over their plunder, older squaws, in particular, poked, prodded, and flayed. He could never imagine a white woman doing that.

Isaac thought of the civility Emmy had brought with her to the homestead he had claimed, and how everyone on Whidbey and the military with whom she dealt in Port Townsend seemed to go out of their way to stay in favor with her.

It wasn't that she was not turn-heads pretty in an unpretentious way. She was. It was that she held her own and then some against *any* man. It was equanimity, present with every step she took and every word she spoke, that lent itself to every situation. He could never imagine someone like Emmy becoming so vicious.

⟨XXXX⟩

Isaac awoke, surprised he had drifted off on this thought when he most needed to be vigilant. He damned his weakness. Then he looked over for Sam and saw that his companion had moved away from his spot.

Gone.

The fog had lifted Sam away — likely he had hidden himself in the canoe — while Isaac had recklessly daydreamed.

Isaac wasn't sure how much time had passed, had forgotten to wind his pocket watch, initially just fearing that the winding sound itself would alert the marauders, then just forgot about it. The watch had stopped at 2:30 a.m., and there was no sign of sunrise yet.

The water had receded, so he felt higher up from its edge, but he couldn't tell how far. They had covered the canoe, turned it upside down as best they could with driftwood, digging it down into the sand so the visible line of its prow would be broken to a casual glance, camouflaged to look like drift logs. Still, he knew how sharp the raiders' eyes were and prayed the surf and chop in the morning would be sufficiently disruptive to their vision so that, when the Northerners moved out, they wouldn't be able to fix well on the little stretch of beach where he and Sam had hidden the canoe.

Isaac had pulled his tan oilcloth over his shoulders in the darkness and knew he had to take it off and slip behind the camouflaged boat before sunrise. Otherwise, he would surely be seen.

The drizzle started up again, masking sounds of the surf even more than the fog had when it moved in. Isaac had covered the edge of the barrel with his thumb all night to prevent condensation from creeping down into it and dampening the powder.

He kept his cartridge box close to his chest. He might get one, maybe two, poorly aimed shots off at an incoming boat if he was quick, but nothing more. And if they were attacked from land side, it would be one shot then a slashing knife fight, if he were fortunate.

He would have to provoke his attackers enough that they'd want to kill him outright. Or turn his rifle back upon himself, disappointing them with his last shot.

He had thought about that way of ending it many times, when he had taken his company with Wright to the Palouse country to help the army hunt down Kamiakin, the aboriginal Walla Walla tribe's tyee. So had the other men, the volunteers he had brought with him, he knew.

The soldiers, mostly Irish, never seemed to talk about that way of ending it. Kept to themselves, mostly. But the volunteers all talked about it, constantly it seemed, pulling closer and scaring themselves to sleep under the stars, weapons held ready like he held his now. They had talked about where to stick the knife if the rifle didn't go off.

They all had been spooked by what they had found on the river's edge across from the Pendleton crossing, the remains of a small wagon train of Missouri homesteaders. Just the men, propped up in poses like mannequins he had seen in San Francisco. Naked. Fingers and noses and genitals gone, cut off and eaten by the crows, or lying next to the bodies, drying to a leathery brown gristle in the heat of the July sun.

Because it was the best crossing spot on that part of the Columbia River, someone had left that scene as a fresh warning. When, following one of several trails from that scene, they had finally confronted a large group of aborigines in the Walla Walla territory, Isaac was surprised at how easily discouraged the savages seemed to become after a few volleys from the soldiers and his militia.

And when they discharged the eight-pounder howitzer they had pulled behind them for days, the Indians just turned and ran in every direction. Then it was a matter of hunting them down, where they were hidden in the gullies, and dispatching them one by one.

Isaac and his men never found any of the kidnapped women or children, and it made him wonder whether they had punished those responsible for the river crossing massacre or whether the white women had been abandoned or killed by this sorry lot. It didn't matter after what he had seen at the river. In his opinion, the region had to be cleared for those higher on the ladder God had created.

◇◇◇◇

Isaac had drifted again. The cold had numbed him asleep briefly earlier, and because he had been too frightened to undo his breeches to pee, he just suffered through it, offering up the pain as a small sacrifice to right things a bit with God, if this were to be his last day.

But he fell asleep again and then awoke, realizing he had just let go while he lay there, pissing away any grace he had accumulated. He wondered if the Lord would forgive him for this weakness. His last moment would be disgraced, but only he and God would know, and perhaps that was the way it should be, humbled in spirit by his body after all.

God would forgive this little mistake, Isaac knew. It was the bigger sins he had visited on lesser beings that needed rectification somehow. He had taken no pleasure in the Wright expedition's most violent actions, had tried to justify it by what he had seen on the river bank, but he had looked the other way when the pathetic beings had wept over their children.

He had not spoken a word to those men in his command who had descended briefly into the same savagery they were there to put an end to, once and for all. Their vicious solution, the cruelest form of eradicating an enemy, was as bad as the problem it was supposed to correct, just more disciplined in its process than the way the savages went about it.

He sighed thinking about those sins and that awakened him to where he was. He could see his hands now, and then he became aware of something faintly moving in from the water line, a sound over the slight lapping of the gentle surf against the rocky shore.

It was moving in from the right.

He pulled back the hammer on his pinfire—slowly, slowly pulling it to avoid its click on the catch; quieting his breath; tightening his eardrums; peering into the fog thinning itself with the new light.

The beach had expanded with a low tide in the night, and he could just make out traces of footsteps in the sand, heading away from his position. Sam's! Had his companion left him?

It came closer now, *two* distinct sounds from different positions on the water that he could not yet see. Couldn't be Sam, he knew! It would take two shots. Impossible.

Isaac flexed his right thigh to reassure himself that his knife was still there, hadn't fallen out in the night, a quick pull for him in a desperate, last struggle.

His heart was racing, pushing his pulse into his neck, roaring in his ears, loud enough, he was certain, to give away his position.

Gulls started squawking at something in the distance off to the right somewhere in the fog. And then, another movement to the left, closer now, within a few yards of his position.

He slowly swung his muzzle to the left, expecting the marauder would appear at him in a rush, or perhaps, alternatively, would just be standing there waiting for the fog to draw back and reveal Isaac's hiding place. And that moment would be the bastard's last because Isaac would not hesitate to strike him dead.

And then the sound from the right again. More distinct, cautious, water dripping off something.

Then the sun cracked through the thinning mist, and Isaac saw two brown eyes, then four. A mother and her fawn watching him on the beach.

They turned and walked away, leaving hoof prints in a parallel track to those left by Sam. The gulls made a fuss again in the distance, and he could estimate how far away they were now. And then the sun came over the tallest tree on the shore and the rocks gleamed, and Isaac could see the water line below.

More wildlife sounds now—a sea lion calling for companionship and the water lapping below—reminding him he was still alive.

When enough light raked the beach, Isaac slowly placed the hammer back down and moved cautiously to hide behind the canoe. He hoped he would find Sam there, but he did not. The supplies were intact, and his powder was dry enough.

He pulled a piece of salted pork and a rind of cheese and ate them quickly. Although he couldn't see much behind him because of the brambles, he could watch the beach, and as the fog melted away as quietly as it had arrived, he could see for several hundred yards.

He remembered to wind his watch so at least he would know how much time had passed. Likely it was at least six. After an hour, he quickly moved back to his position by the crest of the spit to look at the beach to the south, which was now visible in the distance. The long boat was gone. The cabins had burned to the ground, and he could see there was detritus on the beach below.

Isaac waited for another hour, scanning the horizon up and down the waterline and into the tree line, watching for any movement. He saw from the footprints that Sam had moved off into the woods at the south end of the small beach. There was a hill beyond, and if Sam had survived his flight, he was likely watching the beach below from a safe perch.

Isaac put himself in Sam's mind and tried to understand why he would have run.

He hadn't expected much from Sam, so it didn't surprise him when Sam met those low expectations. But he decided he would kill him if he ever again showed up on Whidbey.

By ten o'clock, Isaac thought it safe enough to move down the beach to where the long boat had berthed. He kept his musket cocked and untied his side knife in its sheath.

When he reached the smoking remains of the three cabins, he found broken furniture, a few overturned boxes and chests, smashed crockery, and mail-order catalogs from Chicago, all awash in the advancing tide.

Two dogs lay clubbed-dead on the beach. Between the rock foundations of the second and third cabins, he found a path into the woods.

He thought of Whidbey and Emmy and Sarah and Jacob, and knew he needed to head back southwest to the island in case the marauders had moved in that direction. He was comforted that his brother Winfield and the Crocketts were close by and his home was on the opposite side of the most direct northward waterway route for the raiders' long boat.

But it was unusual for the Northerners to appear in single boats, he knew. There likely would be others or a larger group of boats somewhere in the vicinity.

He thought about getting into his skiff and departing, but he had to know what was in the woods, and if there were victims, to bury them, or at least give them a prayer that they likely hadn't had time for themselves. So he walked carefully down the path, his breathing quick and shallow.

In a clearing, he found five men, two with bullets in their chests and bellies and three bludgeoned, their heads caved in.

All were stripped naked and mutilated. And all were Negroes, likely freed or escaped slaves from the South. No women or children, except for one small boy, about seven or eight, who was cradled in one man's arms.

Isaac thought of his Jacob. Would his son run to him as this boy likely had during his final moments? What would his own thoughts be as he tried to defend his boy, his family? How many of the Indians would he take down with him before he succumbed?

These poor Negro folk likely had not been armed, or at least not armed enough to leave evidence of fighting back, although the Indians seldom left their own dead at the scene of the fight.

He had heard that the Indians were even more vicious against Negroes, more likely to rob them when they attempted to settle. Perhaps it was because they were easy victims, who hadn't learned to defend themselves very well. Or perhaps it was because they tended to live isolated from a supportive community, like the one he had established in Whidbey, where folks came together to help one another in times of need.

He pulled the bodies together in one group, a gruesome task, reminding him of some of the things he had done in eastern Washington. The woods were wet from the constant drizzle and the fires he had seen the day before all but burned out, so a funeral pyre would be useless.

He began piling rocks and wood debris over the bodies to delay the depredation for a while and keep the birds away at least.

That took several hours, but it was only decent. And then he set out.

As he pushed his way back across the sound in the late afternoon, he thought about the irony of the massacre, that the victims had likely escaped somehow from a life of slavery only to find death and new captivity here in the Northwest from new oppressors. He wondered whether, if left alone, they might have made a go of it in this fertile land.

He was grateful for what God had given him and his family, grateful and relieved the weather had remained calm, allowing for a safe crossing—a good blessing in a dire situation. He would need to stop to rest at intervals over the nine hours it likely would take for him to cross against the tide and a mild southerly.

Caught, as he was, between hope and fear, he would need to watch for any activity that might indicate a ship that could carry him. Or a Northerner long boat that could catch up with him.

He would return with a militia detail to bury the settlers. When it was safe. But knowing somewhere out there was a long boat, likely with some new slaves, and more like it, moving down into the Puget Straits, he had to get home.

"Dear Jesus, Lord, give me the strength to endure this next travail. Let me see my porch and find my bed. Watch over the children and Emmy. I will do Thy will, but give me, Lord, this one last day."

He said that same prayer over and over again as he paddled slowly across the sound.

CHAPTER EIGHT

◇◇◇◇

Emmy

We shucked fourteen bushels of winter corn, cut four more cords
of Alder. Easier chopping than cedar. Received correspondence
from Cmdr. G. Pickett, inquiring re: provisions. Isersons
visiting from Port Townsend in a few weeks. Bracing myself
for that. Heard rumors that long boats seen off Camano. No
word from Isaac. Worried. It is raining for the 6th straight day.
No let up.

—*Emmy Evers' Diary, October 5ᵗʰ, 1857*

H er duties filled the full day and much of the evening before it was too dark to do much else than
sleep, bone tired, on a hard but sufficient mattress.
The big feather bed her father had sent them as a wed-
ding gift never made it around the Horn. The clipper ship

had been given up for lost. Other small amenities, sent by her family to them across the Rockies on the Oregon passage, were abandoned with many other things by Isaac's brother, Winfield, in a horrible trek that nearly killed everyone in his party.

For that decision, she couldn't criticize Winfield, an amiable but emotionally labile redheaded young man, because he had arrived with himself intact, in the company of Isaac's father, Benjamin, Isaac's feeble-minded, lame, older sister, Corinne; the Crocketts; the Mastersons; and five other families, all with little remaining in the way of possessions but determined to make their passage worth it.

The new settlers all had settled in quickly, making vigorous pursuit rebuilding their lives on Whidbey on, and in the near vicinity of the fertile plateau Isaac had surveyed and claimed in '50. It was a splendid homestead, flat, with the richest soil they had ever seen and easy access to the beach.

Isaac had built an unadorned but ample house with a porch, cedar roof shingles and siding cut at the Bellingham mill. When the family had moved up from Olympia, the children had a bedroom upstairs next to theirs, and the kitchen, next to the small parlor, was large enough to accommodate six people for dinner.

Emmy was patient. She was also young enough that she understood Providence would provide for material comforts in due time, if she kept to her duties, loved her children, and obeyed her husband, although Isaac had made that very difficult many times.

Loving her children was the easiest thing God had given her to do in this life. Each day was new with them, and that was how they each embraced it as well, especially Sarah, who Emmy had decided was much like herself, having a natural curiosity for the big and the small. As little more than a toddler, Sarah would sit for long stretches studying the ant piles near the woodshed. And Emmy had observed her walking around and around the deck of the British steam cutter during a visit to Port Townsend, touching every knob and dial in the engine room, following the straps and levers. Only after she had found questions she could not answer by deduction, did she render questions to the engineer, who delighted in the young girl's precocious intelligence.

Emmy wasn't sure who Jacob resembled in disposition, except that his temper fits sometimes reminded her of Isaac's brother, Winfield.

Jacob was direct and always ran ahead. He needed to be watched and pulled back. More than once Isaac had to correct him and apologize for his son's interruptions into adult conversations. But she also mused that at least on one occasion, the person with whom Isaac had been speaking turned to Jacob and thanked him for his passionate observation.

Jacob would become a fine young man someday, if he survived. And someday, soon she expected, a delivery of books and a good slate board would arrive in Bellingham, and she could start teaching her children what they must learn if they were to prosper in this new land.

Until then, she drilled them about rudimentary arithmetic and tested them daily on English grammar. On

Saturday mornings, she used Dr. Roget's book to help Sarah expand her vocabulary, and employed every appropriate opportunity to teach both children, but especially Jacob, about proper manners.

◇◇◇◇

Shortly after Isaac departed that week on yet another official trip, she received a letter directed to her from the Bellingham military commander, Captain Pickett, who inquired whether she could provide fresh beef for his forty-man garrison. He announced he would visit that week and, if she was amenable, wanted to inspect the cattle before consummating the order. He also wished to introduce himself and pay his respects.

The order would be smaller by a third than the one they had negotiated last year with the Port Townsend fort commander, who had ordered four hundred pounds of prime beef each week. She had always been surprised that the small garrison in Port Townsend could consume so much meat. But as she reread the letter, she suddenly realized he had been receiving his fort's allotment from the commander at Port Townsend, who was reselling it, likely at a significant markup, with some of the proceeds going into his own pocket.

Captain Pickett had either discovered the little scam, or unwittingly found the supplier, but in either case was trying to reduce his cost.

By his florid language, she realized he was an educated man, and from his looped and gentle script, she could tell he was a sensitive one.

He chose sad, ornate phrases. One sentence she reread several times in his official communication was, "I beg your indulgence, madam, lest I create an importune imposition on loyal hardworking settlers like yourselves, most certainly beset by the arduous work and sometimes desperate difficulties of surviving in this hostile land."

He signed the letter, "Your most obedient servant, Captain George E. Pickett, Commandant, United States Army."

Thus bemused, she wrote back to him that she would be most pleased to sell him the beef and, without revealing that she surmised he was being swindled by his fellow officer in Port Townsend, offered a price five cents less per pound than what she was delivering to the cheat. She and Isaac could afford the few dollars a week that this was likely to cost them, if, as she suspected, Port Townsend subsequently cut back its order. And it made her smile at the propriety of such mischief.

CHAPTER NINE

✕✕✕✕

Pickett

We are exploring the region south of Bellingham Bay and bargaining with local suppliers in the area to better provision our troops for the upcoming winter.

—1857 memo by Captain George E. Pickett to Lt. Colonel Rufus Ingalls, Quartermaster General, Oregon Territory

H e had heard she was comely, a looker, by the description of one of the grain merchants with whom his supply sergeant was bartering.

The merchant, a dour, unctuous, pot-bellied man with a pock-marked face poorly covered by a gray-yellow stubble, also noted that Emmy Evers ran her husband's business with a tightness that surprised anyone who casually might be taken in by her soft countenance. In his experience, the merchant said, if one tried to push past her civil and gentle demeanor, one found something quite durable, a "spirited filly," not easily swept aside by casual assumptions.

Most men in the region believed she was the perfect complement to her mate, Isaac Evers, a hardworking and honest dreamer who, until he had brought her to Whidbey, had little to show for all his ambitions. After she married 'Ol' Isaac', the merchant said, things began to fall in their right place, and the entire Whidbey area started to prosper.

George Pickett was intrigued by this banter, and as he listened to it, he thought about what another good mate would bring to the unique loneliness he felt here, so different from what he had experienced in the parched Southwest, where he had buried his first wife.

The perpetual gray skies of this area, the inescapable drizzle during the winter months, overwhelmed every bit of disciplined fortitude he had at his personal command.

He dreaded the oncoming winter and the gnawing boredom that drove everyone in the garrison to fits of mischief and frequent day-long drinking bouts with contraband whiskey obtained from local mill workers who helped load ships in the harbor. The last year had been particularly bleak, and he reprimanded himself for the example he set for his men.

He had remorse for the punishment some of them endured because he believed, with some certainty, that he had contributed to their transgressions.

He had built a home away from the post so he could find privacy and indulge himself without betraying the trust he was expected to build, but the whiskey did not cure the boredom.

Now, with cold winds sweeping in from the Bellingham bay into the meager community, the locals were shuttering up the windows and themselves inside, bracing for another bitter winter. He kept himself busy, mostly by writing lengthy reports to General Harney about local hostiles and the likelihood of their renewing attacks on settler communities.

Despite this, and over the next few months, curiosity turned to an obsessed daydream, and he found his thoughts tugged to an image of Emmy Evers, constructed from what he heard from the merchant.

Did she resemble Morning Mist or Sally Vinge, his first wife?

Was Emmy Evers' reputed steely constitution discernible from a distance?

How deep was the soft shell that supposedly lay on the surface?

He decided to make an excursion south.

Accompanied by his sergeant and armed appropriately for the hostile environs, he rode fifty miles along the coast, encountering both black bear and a small group of young aggressive Lummis.

The bear turned and ran away at the sight of the mounted twosome, but Pickett had to draw his saber and then finally fire a warning shot to get the natives to clear off.

Remembering a bad experience with the Apache in Texas, when a similar encounter had been followed by a nighttime attack that had nearly been disastrous, he and his sergeant traveled ten miles beyond the site of the confrontation to provide safe distance between themselves and the Lummi youth. He would have given himself even greater berth if he were in the Southwest or the Lummi were mounted, but these northwestern natives were likely more curious than truly dangerous, he reasoned.

Further south, in a natural safe harbor, he secured western waterway passage on a small logging boat to bypass the deep and treacherous channel they called Deception Pass that separated Whidbey Island from the mainland. One day later, they landed on the flat, sloped western landing on Whidbey that Isaac and Emmy Evers had created for their flourishing businesses.

Pickett didn't know what he was looking for on this trip, wondered whether Emmy would be demur and slight like his first and second wives, or hardened like most of the white women whom he had encountered in the Northwest.

How did a reputed Northwest beauty compare to the women he had met over the years: the refined, wealthy ones in Virginia; the more adventuresome in Illinois and Ohio; and the aggressive, worldly-wise women in New York? He tried putting that thought away and justified his trip with the notion of official and responsible discharge of business duty for the United States Army.

CHAPTER TEN

◇◇◇◇

Emmy and Pickett

*Rain stopped for half a day. Getting cold now. New bull
broke the pen fence again. Took two hours to herd him back in.
Finished mending the fence by sunset. Sent offer to Bellingham
Cmdr for beef supply. Isaac gone for over almost a week now.*

—*Emmy Evers' Diary, October 6th, 1857*

S he was surprised when Pickett arrived, as it turned
out by coincidence the very next day after she had
sent off a response to his letter.

When her neighbor's son, Stephen Crockett, arrived
at her door announcing the landing of the two soldiers,
Emmy ran upstairs, quickly washed off the morning labor's

perspiration, pulled her hair into a tighter braided bun, and furtively glanced at her outline in the bedroom's vanity mirror. As she did so, she wondered at her motivations, deciding that such attention to personal detail was really in the best interest of her employing a disarming presence for negotiating an enduring contract with a reliable client.

Driving her buckboard to meet Captain Pickett, she determined to take measure of him against his ornate script.

"Captain Pickett, this is quite a surprise. I received your letter last week and just yesterday sent a response to your query. I expect you and my offer passed each other out in the straits. I believe you will be pleased with our proposal," she said, noticing with a bit of embarrassment that she was speaking much more rapidly than she usually did.

Pickett was dressed carefully with obvious attention to detail, and she noted that he spoke with a soft and gentle cadence, less florid than his written word, but with a refined, precise selection of words nevertheless.

"Madame," he said, with a doffed-hat bow, "I am most pleased to hear that, and I humbly beg your pardon for not waiting to receive a response. This was the most convenient time for me to go on this excursion. The weather will get inhospitably mean in a short time."

Hearing this gently voiced excuse, Emmy wondered if he also spoke this way to the men he commanded and watched the quiet exchanges between the captain and his sergeant, who seemed to respect his officer's orders. Pickett carried himself with a dignified solemnity that was unassuming at the same time.

Emmy read a sadness that lay beneath his ornately designed ensemble. In contrast to the enlisted man, who

looked as if he had slept for a fortnight in his dirty clothing, Pickett's uniform was proper, clean, and tailored with
attention to detail, from his boots to the nonmilitary-is-
sue cape that covered his shoulders. The difference told
her that Pickett gave an almost dandy-like attention to his
own appearance but obviously was less concerned how the
men he commanded represented him or his office.

When she extended her hand to receive his, she felt
hard yet small and carefully manicured fingers. His nails
were clean and trimmed. She inhaled discreetly to sense
whether Pickett used any cologne, but could discern none.

Ordering the sergeant to drive the buckboard, Pickett
accompanied her back to the house on his beautiful gray
mare, and it was apparent to her that he understood how
to cut a dashing figure by his canter and carry. Indeed, as
they proceeded up the incline from the beach and onto the
homestead, he kept slightly ahead to her right in a privileged, very visible position, so he could not be ignored.

He dismounted and quickly moved to the buckboard
to help her down, and then, as the sergeant *hiyawed* the
horses off to the barn in the back, waited before advancing
further, almost shyly, until she had mounted the steps and
beckoned him into the house.

"Come along, Captain," she said.

Sarah and Jacob, ever observant, were waiting on the
porch stoop and watched Pickett enter after their mother.
Following after him into the small, modest parlor, they
stood expectantly until he noticed their presence, at
which point Sarah stepped forward and asked to take his
coat and cap.

Pickett obliged and, seeing wide-eyed Jacob, winked at him, then unbuckled his field saber and handed it over to the boy.

Jacob, duly impressed with this privilege, hefted the sword, three-quarters his own height, with a solemnity that made Pickett smile.

The children quickly returned from their task, hovering, until Emmy motioned for them to go upstairs to their rooms.

"Sarah, Jacob. Captain Pickett and your mother have some important business." She turned to Pickett with an apologetic smile.

As Sarah was about to turn away, Jacob stepped forward. "Do you ever fight the Indians, Captain? My father has. In the war east of the mountains. He's a colonel in the volunteers."

Pickett knew about Isaac's participation in the fight against Kamiakin. All the military in the region had been grateful for volunteerism after the Elliott Bay attack in the south of the Puget Sound, but the eager participation of untrained militia had caused its share of problems as well.

After a similar attack on Bellingham a few months later, Pickett repeatedly had to intervene to rescue innocent natives from lynching by angry settlers. There were decent citizens and ones who simply made a mess, he thought to himself, and wondered into which category Isaac Evers fit.

He squatted before Jacob, bringing his eyes level with the boy's, then glanced up at Emmy and Sarah.

"Well, I heard that your father is a brave man, son. We try to avoid picking fights with the aborigines. I just try to keep order up in the North Sound."

Emmy gave Sarah a look, and with that, Sarah took Jacob's hand and pulled him away. "That's enough, little brother."

Sarah turned and watched Pickett carefully as she guided her brother up the staircase.

◇◇◇◇

Pickett remained standing until his hostess sat down on the small parlor's one soft-cushioned chair and then, after she motioned for him to be seated, placed himself opposite her on the divan, discreetly observing her motions and mannerisms.

It was evident to him that she was with child, although early enough in her condition that her posture and gait were not yet tentative. Emmy had finely cut lines and a smoothly curved back; sturdy but not overly broad shoulders; and strong, well-proportioned hands with long fingers, similar to the velvet- and lace-covered ones on the beauties he remembered from the cotillion ball celebrations in Virginia.

He thought of his two wives. Sally, his first wife, born of a wealthy family and well bred, had smaller hands than Morning Mist, but both women had a brown hardness to their touch, developed from the toil necessary to get along in their harsh environs. Emmy Evers had the same type of calluses as the other women, but somehow she had preserved the gentility of motion from her well-born origin.

Her handshake was strong, firm and what he sensed was an unforced confidence.

Her face was finely featured with high cheekbones and bright, fiercely honest brown eyes that were fixed on his own in a way that discomfited him.

Some women's eyes, he reflected, betrayed an angry self-pity and others a naïvety that made for contempt or tempted seduction. There was none of this in Emmy's deep brown eyes. Rather, he found them hard to observe because of what her eyes pulled up to his own surface, overwhelming him in an instant.

He knew from the moment he met her that she would never let him get away with a lie.

◇◇◇◇

"So, Captain Pickett, it is apparent from the soft cadence of your speech that you are a Southerner, but not from the Deep South. I would guess the beautiful state of Virginia. Am I correct?"

Seeing a flash of appreciative affirmation in his eyes and sensing in him the melancholia she had witnessed in others during this fall season of quick-darkening skies that followed on mellow Octobers, she nodded over to the parlor window and the slate-colored seascape below.

"What does a Southern gentleman think of this sad green and gray?"

He followed her wistful glance and nodded.

"Astute, madame," he smiled. "I would say that, to one who rode for a few but, at the same time, too many years in the Southwest and on the baked Mexican deserts, the color green has always provided a welcome contrast for me. The perpetual gray skies of the winters here, however, make one almost forget the definition of verdant and what a full palette of colors can do for one's disposition." After a pause, he continued, "I miss my home very much at times, particularly during this change of seasons."

"I understand, sir. I understand."

That commiseration established a bond between them, and for a few moments, neither spoke. Their eyes moved again to the window.

Then, for a short while they exchanged in a simple, formal banter, with short forays into each other's perspective on a variety of subjects. They discussed each other's vision of what constituted propriety, God's purposes, and, as well, the destiny of their young country.

Because of his mannerisms, more than by the words he chose on the topic of political debate raging back East, she was not surprised when Pickett professed a deep disdain for slavery. She had found that, unlike other soldiers she had met, he worried for the welfare of the aboriginal inhabitants of the region.

She heard him use the word "unwitting" repeatedly in his description of the unfortunate peoples' response to their rapidly changing living conditions. He was particularly vehement about his condemnation of how the Brits behaved in Vancouver, which he believed was greedy, despicable, and deceptive. She sensed that he held back criticism of his own federal government, as likely he must.

"My husband, Isaac, believes the same as you do, Captain. While he is as eager as many to see our nation's boundaries expand, he believes we are part of a grand plan that must ultimately also include a fair outcome for *all* its creatures, whatever the original station in which they have been placed. That said, we have had difficult challenges, and he believes it is our burden to change all of that for the better, perhaps through faith and hard work. Perhaps through miracles."

As she said this, she thought about how Isaac's brutal encounters in eastern Washington had profoundly changed him from a young man with a cornucopia of enthusiastic, albeit undisciplined, applications of energy into a pensive, sober, and phlegmatic adult who increasingly found it difficult to finish the various projects he had started.

It no longer amused her to manage him as she often admitted to herself ultimately had become her responsibility.

Isaac, over the past year, had developed a fear of death, she realized, that now outweighed his sense of opportunity. In the early years of their marriage, she simply had listened to his list of ambitious projects and added an ordered, practical prioritization to them so that a good number of them actually were completed.

But Isaac was stalled now. He seldom spoke of enterprise or the future.

Pickett responded, "As I believe I conveyed to your son, Jacob, my hopes are to keep confrontations minimized between all the inhabitants of this region. Although conduct as a warrior has been my calling, my experience has taught me that peace is always better, madame. And perversely, perhaps, it seems that assuring peace sometimes requires a stern, if reserved, intervention."

Emmy considered this and understood that Pickett, at least by the words he carefully chose, had armed himself for those necessities, and that, as a disciplined soldier, he likely had found a comfortable balance between self-preservation and duty.

She wondered if poor Isaac, with all that he had seen, had it in him to fight in the same manner anymore. She wondered whether martial training amplified the appetite or, alternatively, resigned a man to the cruelties of armed conflict.

In Pickett, she sensed the latter.

After a long pause, glancing again outside at a brooding sky, Emmy suggested to Pickett that they inspect the cattle as a prelude to a formal proposal on price. Then, because of the impropriety of offering him lodging in her home while Isaac was away, she told him about the plain but comfortable rooms a mile away that Ben and Missy Crockett generously provided for a modest fee to wayfarers.

Pickett thanked her for that suggestion.

"After we inspect the cattle, I will introduce you to the Crocketts, and after you have had a chance to rest, may I invite you and your sergeant to have a meal with Jacob, Sarah and me?" she said.

Pickett immediately accepted her kind offer.

That evening, Emmy proved that her skills as a cook were as formidable as were her abilities as the manager of the family business.

While she served them a dessert of apples crisped with cinnamon and caramelized sugar, Emmy negotiated an arrangement: twenty-five cents per on-the-hoof pound, by which their farm would supply the Bellingham outpost with all its beef in the future.

Pickett seemed surprised that she offered him terms that were much more favorable than what he was paying to the supplier in Port Townsend, not realizing that the intermediary he used usually purchased the same Evers beef. Emmy knew, however, and again smiled to herself at the justice of this new arrangement.

After the meal, they shook hands on the deal, and Emmy realized, by that gentle clasp, that she had won his trust in similar manner to how she had won over every other man with whom she had business dealings.

At the same time, she felt sad that he was so naïve and earnest a person that he could be so easily swindled by his military peers. He was likely a very brave and noble man, but one with many gaps in his character that needed a complement to make him whole. That gave her pause and reconsideration, seeing that Pickett, like so many lonely men in this rough land, might need the help of angels after all.

CHAPTER ELEVEN

◇◇◇◇

Isaac

*Our family and the island's faithful flock is again spared
the sorrows.*

—*Isaac Evers' Diary, October 10th, 1857*

Isaac arrived home two mornings after Pickett had
departed, several days sooner than Emmy expected.
Rather than rowing another four miles, he had
beached his canoe on the northeastern shore, far from the
docks he had built, and left the contents with the Negro
who lived near the landing.

After he rounded the area by horseback, alerting the
neighbors that trouble was in the waters again, Emmy,

seeing that he was exhausted and pale, helped him lie down. He slept for ten hours, barely moving during his respite. His brother, Winfield, Tom Iserson, and the Crocketts shared watch over the straits that week. He had Emmy, who knew how to shoot and did it as well as any man, take her turn.

As a result of the predation Isaac had witnessed, the island families moved into a watch status. Two years before, the fifteen Whidbey families in five different parts of the island had worked out a simple plan so that, should a Northerner raiding party attack any one of the local cluster of cabins, those under siege would fire shots and ring the warning bell kept in each cabin. The homes on Emmy and Isaac's plateau were close enough that a relay of shots would send the alarm quickly to all settlers who could be in harm's way.

In a watch, all families, including children during the daylight, participated taking turns observing the straits, watching the water for signs of long boats.

Three weeks into the vigil, as the fall light started to fade more quickly on the broad fertile plain, Ben Crockett spied six long boats in the middle of the strait. They were heading north. He was certain he saw captives in each boat.

In the preceding decade, before the smallpox had devastated the Northerners' ranks, the sight of six boats heading northward, presumably back to their homes on the Queen Charlotte Islands and northern British Columbia, would have provided little comfort to white settlers and local tribes, because it was reasonable to assume there might have been others lingering in the area.

But the straits had been relatively quiet for some time now with fewer sightings, so it was widely assumed that increased patrolling by British gunboats was acting as a sufficient deterrent.

No reports from any neighbors had come in the recent weeks of any other large groups of marauders. Winter was coming on quickly. It was believed that the Northerners seldom raided during the cold season. So, Isaac and the islanders relaxed a bit.

Eight days later, Isaac left the guarding of the homestead in care of his brother Winfield, and took a small contingent of volunteers back across the sound to bury the Negro settlers.

It was a depressing and grim journey, but Isaac reasoned it was the only decent thing to do, commenting to the few who protested that he hoped someone would do the same for him and his family if, God forbid, they ever were taken in the same way.

Emmy, who was not pleased with his departure again, understood the decency of such a mission, but threw herself into all of the unfinished business at hand.

Not far away from the site of the slayings, Isaac's party found Sam's body, twisted in an outstretched contortion at the base of ravine. Apparently he had fallen off an embankment, likely in the fog the morning he fled, breaking his neck, dying, Isaac hoped, with swift mercy.

Over the large grave they had scraped in the clearing behind the cabins, Isaac prayed for forgiveness from the Lord who had spared him but had taken these sad, frightened lambs.

He regretted his curses against Sam. He put himself in Sam's situation on that horrible day, tried thinking in the same way as Sam must have thought. The quiet, competent fellow had never been malicious or lazy, and Isaac forgave him for his cowardice.

Remembering his own terrible fear on that day, Isaac wondered whether God had heard the curses he uttered against the poor man, hope God had not answered those curses at the same time as He was granting him his own deliverance, and thought about God's strange way of showing mercy to him in that exchange. He told himself that his own selfishness had to have had some purpose - perhaps a counterweight in some a strange form of Providential balancing perhaps - with a purpose that he might not ever understand.

He would accept that, forgiving himself as he did so. It was the will of Providence after all.

CHAPTER TWELVE

<><><><>

Anah

A half day before Ben Crockett saw the long boats on the strait, two other Northerner boats, commanded by Little Raven, split off to find water and look for more to plunder.

Anah with his six long boats continued north, carrying fourteen captives, to the mouth of the Campbell River on Vancouver Island. There he quickly sold the captives, all young healthy women, to a trapper who served as an intermediary to a prostitution slaver.

The trapper, Rene Marté, and his companion, a huge, one-eyed Negro known as Cull, had developed a number of similar business arrangements, including smuggling stolen contraband goods to the Tlingit and Haida. Their prearranged contract allowed Anah to obtain powder and winter supplies as well as the alcohol he would use to barter and stoke the rising anger of numerous tribal allies he hoped to recruit.

Anah understood the power of alcohol and guarded it as carefully as a weapon, distributing it just before an assault. But he also always carried a small flask for himself into his initial parlays because that seemed to make things easier.

In Port Gamble, near a new sawmill enterprise that had imported forty Irish men and women to work it, Little Raven's raiders found an encampment of local natives, mostly Salish and Chimakum, who had converged on the small mill community. The Indian groups had come in gradually over the summer to see the mill, many out of curiosity, some for trading, and others for handouts.

By August, over four hundred natives surrounded the mill. The mill foreman had sent repeated requests to the forts at Port Townsend, Bellingham, and as far south as Olympia to see if some soldiers could be dispatched to break up the encampment and avoid what the foreman perceived as an inevitable calamity.

The foreman had reason to be concerned, for he had heard several rumors that the coastal Salish, rich in some parts of the Puget Sound and numerous in diverse, small bands throughout the Olympic peninsula, were being recruited by the powerful tyee known as Leschi and by other tribes to join in another attack on the Elliott Bay community and the white settlements further south. But thus far, the Salish had resisted.

Still, incursions by settlers throughout the region were disturbing to the Salish because of the audacity of the whites and the arrogant contempt they all seemed to display at every official encounter. It was rumored that Leschi, in particular, was angry about a land and reservation treaty that had been consummated at Medicine Creek a few years earlier, which, Leschi protested, he had never signed.

To further aggravate the hostilities, it was widely known that Stevens, the Washington territorial governor, had declared a war of extermination the previous year against the regional aboriginal tribes, thereby giving justification to both sides for senseless violence. As the white settlers increased in numbers, the disputes also increased, resulting in numerous deaths, reported and unseen.

A few Jesuit and Oblate missionaries had established a presence and had converted a good number of the clans in the preceding fifteen years, but most of the Salish had resisted that, as well. Thus, they hadn't been exposed to the Christian concepts that likely prevented conflict from erupting in areas where the missionaries had built churches.

When Little Raven's raiding party found the encampment surrounding the mill, it was already in a state of agitation, with arguments erupting between families over a variety of issues and old grudges as well as a few new ones, including the presence of the mill that many argued would soon attract more white settlers.

That was fine for some, who anticipated the advantages of trade. But others argued that their freedom would be taken from them, as had happened to those living in the eastern part of the sound and in Vancouver. The whites were experts at that, they knew.

The arguments were loud and hot.

Little Raven, despite an infirmity that year from a stroke that had left him with a clumsy left arm, still had his keen sense of strategy and immediately perceived opportunity in the making. Although the Northerners were likely not known by these Salish, he ordered the Haida and Skidegate in the long boats to remove their face paint, don clothing stolen from various raids against the settlers, and leave their long boats hidden in an attempt to conceal their identities as they moved through the Salish encampment.

They settled into a secluded area on the long beach near a stream, to rest and quietly observe.

Because so many clans and tribes were present, tribal languages and dialects spoken in the area were diverse, and, thus, many resorted to the Chinook trade jargon to communicate with one another. Observing this as an advantage, Little Raven, adorned with telltale double labrets on his lower lip and prominently tattooed, kept himself covered. He forbade his warriors to speak in their native Makah and had the least conspicuous of his Haida warriors be the spokesperson, conversing exclusively in Chinook when any interaction was necessary.

Thus, the Northerners' presence in the camp went unnoticed for several days. On the fifth day, however, a Makah woman, slaved to a Salish tyee, passed on the outskirts of the Northerners' encampment to retrieve fresh water. There she encountered a young Haida man bathing in the stream.

At first, she was aroused by the warrior's well-proportioned, naked physique and, while observing from a thicket upstream, found herself flushing and faint. But after a few minutes, the young warrior turned to the front, and she recognized the significance of his tattoos. As a little girl, she had witnessed a terrifying raid by Haida against her Tatoosh clan.

He was a killer.

Each one of his tattoos told a story, and the way he bathed himself, watching with narcissistic pride as the water fell over his young, muscular body, instantly reminded her of a vicious experience imposed by similar arrogant men, likely from his clan, who had left her family decimated and enslaved.

She hurried back to her own encampment and passed this information to the tyee of her small group, TsasiTa Na, also known as "Trader Johnny."

Johnny, well known to white settlers in the area, was a shrewd and enterprising man and, always looking for profit, decided to keep news of the Northerners from the other Salish. Instead, he sold it to the mill foreman.

When the already frightened foreman heard the news, without waiting for full details, he immediately sent off a native messenger with a hastily scribbled letter to Port Townsend, where it so happened the steamer gunboat *U.S. Massachusetts* was docked, provisioning itself for a redeployment the next week to San Francisco.

Arriving two days later, the message was misinterpreted by the commandant of the naval ship, who ordered an immediate departure to rescue the mill from what he perceived as an imminent attack by "several hundred Northerner Indians."

By the time the *Massachusetts* arrived the next day, the native encampment was in turmoil over other issues. That morning, several shots had been fired in anger by Salish men who had squabbled during a bone-dice throw, and two men were wounded.

The mill workers, hovering nervously in their houses, heard angry shouts and yelling. Thoroughly terrified now, the mill foreman ordered all the employees to crowd themselves into a block house he had constructed for defensive purposes.

When the *Massachusetts* finally steamed into the Port Gamble bay at three o'clock in the afternoon, the foreman signaled from the block house that the camp was now under siege and had been fired upon.

The captain of the gunboat decided that the best way to break up the attack was to fire warning shots into the encampment woods nearby. Two fell short, killing several men, women, and children.

The Salish natives fled in several directions, but Little Raven's Haida, seeing their opportunity evaporate, gathered their equipment and ran up the beach to where they had hidden their canoes, hastily pushing themselves into the high, late afternoon surf.

Because theirs was the only activity on the northernmost beach, it was easily observed from the *Massachusetts*. The commandant of the steamer, Captain Henry S. Melton, finally seeing an opportunity to destroy Northerner long boats within firing range, turned his starboard guns on the two canoes.

He ordered canister and grapeshot rather than shells, anticipating that the scattered discharge would provide better hits than shells from the eighteen-pounders.

Both of the fleeing cedar long boats were riddled badly in the cannonade but moved out of range of the

Massachusetts, which by then had turned its attention back to the Indians on shore.

When the mess was complete, thirty-eight Salish and Chimakum on shore had been killed or wounded by the fusillades.

In the canoes, Little Raven was wounded in his back and belly by canister shrapnel and suffered a slow, agonizing trip back north. By the time they reached the Campbell River, he was dead, along with six other Skidegate and Haida.

And on the day of the Port Gamble massacre, Anah dreamed of his sisters again. This time they were blowing into the nostrils of Little Raven telling him to come back to the house because it was cold outside. But Little Raven refused to get up at their beckoning.

It was pouring down in a warm fall rain when the canoes arrived in their rendezvous place. Anah saw the drained, white body of Little Raven and, overcome by his angry grief, tore away his shirt, then ran into the woods and stayed there, naked for several days.

In lulls between cloudbursts, the Haida, preparing a makeshift funeral ceremony for Little Raven and the other warriors, could hear Anah in the distance, howling in a way that none had ever heard before. When he finally returned, he was covered with dried blood and the stigmata of self-flagellation and mutilation, fresh knife cuts along his legs and arms. He had pierced himself with branches through his ribs and chest. And he had a look on his face that never left him thereafter, a terrifying black mask of a stare, signaling to all an absence of any hope of mercy.

In the ceremonies, he vowed in front of the other lead men that he would have the head of a big white tyee to act as a footstool for Little Raven in the next life.

CHAPTER THIRTEEN

✕✕✕✕

Isaac

ATTACK THWARTED!
Heroic Naval action prevents another outrage
Northerners routed in bloody engagement
— *The Colonist - October 16th, 1857*

We are host to friends and prospective settlers.
God's blessings shared.
—*Isaac Evers' Diary, October 16th, 1857*

N ews of the Port Gamble conflict reached Whidbey a few days later with descriptions of destruction of Northerner canoes and warriors.

The commandant of the *Massachusetts* reported a great victory and predicted that the bloody beating he had administered would finally end Northerner aggression, so demoralized were the survivors of the cannonade.

Official reports to General Harney stated that the Indians around the mill, "mostly Northerners, had been given ample and repeated opportunity to disburse but had refused to do so," forcing Captain Melton to open fire.

The captain did not mention that long boats had escaped and he minimized the number of casualties that the natives had suffered. The ship's marines had placed several of the wounded Salish, unable to flee into the forests, into irons, and the captain made a big show of transporting them out of the region and depositing them on a small island southeast of Victoria, presumably to perish. Without interpreters, he never realized that none of his captives were Northerners.

When the Whidbey settlers heard the initial reports about the events in Port Gamble, most assumed the raiding would stop, at least for the rest of the year, because the weather would soon preclude canoe travel on most of the sound.

Their reassurance was based further on common knowledge that the Northerners had always avoided direct confrontation with better-armed foes, and the presence of a fast steamer gunboat like the *Massachusetts*, independent of the wind, surpassed the ability of the raiders to move quickly in any weather.

If the gunboat patrolled the sound, as they had assumed it would henceforth, the Indians would desist. They did not know that the *Massachusetts* was bound for

San Francisco in one week. They also did not fully appreciate how important revenge for wrongdoing was to the
Haida and all other tribes.

Isaac returned from his burial detail to a settlement
much relaxed from the week before. The Whidbey families had seen no other long boats. The regional newspaper,
The Colonist, had reported that a large contingent of northern marauders had been clapped in irons and taken away.

Hearing the stories related to the Port Gamble battle,
Isaac smiled at heaven, which had surely sent an answer
to his repeated requests to General Harney, Governor
Stevens, and the numerous legislative contacts he had
in Olympia.

Isaac had good reason for his requests. For the past
two years, since the uncoordinated attack by several tribes
on the Elliott Bay community, most of the naval patrolling
had been done with small, slow-sailing gunships that con-
centrated on the south sound, where numerous tribes still
were considered hostile.

The thirty-four-gun *Decatur* sloop-of-war that had
saved the Elliott Bay Settlement during the attack had
long since departed the Northwest waters. The United
States Navy did not have enough ships deployed on its
long West Coast to patrol all the waters it now owned, and
General Harney, without ever creating any formal agreement, had decided he would leave the major responsibility
for containing the most hostile of the aborigine tribes to
the British navy, which by contrast, had established a formidable presence in Victoria.

Yet the Brits seldom ventured into southern Puget
Sound ports. The sporadic violence that every settler

anticipated as a risk of pioneering could not be predicted, and thus, it was almost impossible to halt. And so, the Port Gamble events and the reassurances that had come from them did, indeed, seem like a godsend.

But Providence had not established a real balance.

Four weeks later, in mid-November, immediately after a three-day deluge, with high winds that toppled men and trees alike, two Indian visitors, an elderly man and woman, landed on Isaac and Emmy's western-facing beach, just south of the small community on the plateau.

Dressed in pioneer garb, each wearing long pants and red calico long-sleeved shirts, they bore no visible markings on their faces or hands. Speaking in Chinook, they found a local Salish native, Jim Thomas, who occasionally worked for Emmy. They queried him about where they might find the local physician, Dr. Joseph Edwards.

Edwards, trained and apprenticed in Philadelphia, had settled on Whidbey three years before and had established a widespread reputation for compassionate homeopathic care. He delivered his potions and repaired broken bones with enough success that some even sought his opinion on other, nonmedical matters, travelling from as far as Elliott Bay and Bellingham on occasion for his consultation.

He, like Isaac, had developed a good amount of influence on legislative processes in Olympia, and both men had more than once been mentioned as possible gubernatorial candidates to displace Stevens, the mercurially tempered politician who had commissioned war in eastern Washington against several tribes and had infuriated even friendly native populations with his inflammatory rhetoric.

But Edwards was not at home that day, having departed in the morning for the south of the island to sit up with a young woman confined in the last stages of a first and very difficult pregnancy.

Normally, Edwards would have relegated the delivery to a competent island woman, Jenny Searing, who had a good amount of midwife and wet nurse experience. But this baby was malpositioned in its mother's belly and just wasn't descending as it should, so Edwards was going to try to rotate it for a head-first presentation to minimize the risk of delivering a breechling or stillborn infant.

Jim Thomas explained to the old couple that he had seen the doctor depart, carrying medical equipment with him on his Morgan filly.

They seemed disappointed with his answer, and when he asked what they needed, the couple responded with a question about whether any other big tyees like Edwards lived in the area.

Pointing toward Isaac and Emmy's home, Thomas told them that a very important tyee lived in the house on the bluff, then went about his fish net mending.

The couple departed back down the beach.

The wind from the western strait always blows easterly in the early evening on the prairie plateau. On that evening, it kicked up earlier than usual and then settled down by seven.

Isaac was in the woodshed when the Indian couple appeared at his picket fence. His big old Labrador, Rowdy, began barking loudly, bringing Emmy to the door.

Because of the dog, the couple did not advance farther than the fence and asked Emmy if they could borrow a hammer and some nails so they could repair their canoe down on the beach. They seemed surprised when Isaac came around the house to see who was talking.

The old man, sturdily built with a hard and pock-marked face, turned his attention to Isaac. Both visitors looked at Isaac carefully from foot to head, as if measuring him, Emmy noticed.

The old woman, weather-beaten and almost toothless, repeated her request to Emmy, adding that she wanted to buy some sugar or molasses and coffee.

Emmy sensed a nervous, stilted manner in their speech and heard a dry sticking hesitancy in the man's enuncia-tion of the Chinook trading jargon.

Isaac paused, glancing over at Emmy, then told the couple they did not have a hammer or nails nor did they have any food supplies to spare.

The couple turned and left quietly without a word.

Rowdy finally stopped barking when they were out of sight down the pathway to the beach.

Isaac thought no more about it. Natives and wayfarers occasionally stopped, and none had ever created problems.

Emmy thought the couple was odd but turned her attention to the dinner she was preparing.

A few hours later, the guests arrived, including Tom Iserson, his wife Rebah, Major Robert Campbell, and his wife Thomasina. The company ate two full helpings of Emmy's roast beef; shucked and cob corn; a fine spiced, late summer squash compote; warm bread with freshly churned butter; and the clove-spiked pear pies from a rec-ipe Emmy had brought with her from her grandmother in Boston.

The major introduced some decent English port imported through San Francisco, and all partook, offering a pagan libation to the change of seasons, followed by a brief prayer of thanks to God for sparing Isaac from harm on his recent journey.

They talked about many things, including the dispute with the Brits that was heating up over the ownership of San Juan Island to the north, and the perennial congressional strife over the Negro slavery question.
Campbell and his wife, originally from Alabama, expressed strong sentiment for allowing new states to determine their own rulings on that matter. Iserson, always the "wiggling Whig-turned-Republican," as Rebah liked to refer to him, believed new states should be accepted into the union only if they agreed to be free from the evil curse of slavery.

Despite entrenched positions on the matter, and Tom Iserson's somewhat irritating, sanctimonious pontifications, the discussion remained civil and quiet. The two sides held onto their positions, and the discussion ended as each agreed on the other's right to disagree.

By half past ten, the Campbells begged their leave, noting they had early morning chores, including completing repairs on a roof that had started to leak in the past week. The Isersons lived too far away to trek up island in the dark, so they excused themselves to the guest bedroom in the back.

◇◇◇◇

Getting into bed that night, watching Emmy pull her brush through her hair, Isaac thought about all the things he had witnessed during the past several weeks and how rapidly events changed in this world, teeter-tottering, it seemed, from pain to fortune, and how much that had benefited him and his family. If he could persist, surviving the challenges that Providence had in store, he would keep moving upward, he knew, being righteous in the presence of the Lord on his judgment day. He just had to endure the sufferings because God would balance it all.

That was the plan and the pathway.

And it was working.

Only a short while ago, he had been a penniless gold miner looking for opportunity in uncharted territory. Then, using the surveying skills he had learned in Ohio, he'd mapped out the inland lake east of Elliott Bay and later, on Whidbey, had acquired the best piece of land in the Puget Sound region.

Certainly he'd had his pain, losing his first wife, Rebecca, to a tumor that had grown in her breast and had just eaten her away in less than a year. He couldn't watch her in those last few weeks—the seepage and smell of rot, seeing her suffering, weeping out of her mind until she just didn't recognize him or anyone else, blind and wasted.

But he had found Emmy not long after and moved her up from Olympia where she had been stranded by the carelessness of her late husband, who had allowed himself to get whipsawed by a falling tree near the big mill he had constructed in Tumwater.

Isaac, visiting Olympia as a north Puget Sound representative, had seen her at the funeral and, from that first moment, knew he had to have her.

For a very young woman of twenty-one, she carried herself with repose and dignity, and she was absolutely stately in black.

From a discreet inquiry, he learned that she was a well-born Boston Irish, who had rounded the Horn with her new husband, an ambitious, wealthy, and extravagant dreamer, twenty-five years her senior. The gossip was that they had shown little affection for each other, and some thought she was lonely out here in the cold, wet green, despite the wealth his venture had brought. She would head home after this, taking her infant child back to a wealthy civilization.

So, Isaac did what he had learned worked for him when he needed something badly. He took a gamble, sending a card to her the following week, asking to speak with her.

Emmy came to the door at the cedar-clad home by the mill she now had to dispose of, expecting another solicitation for purchase of its fallow equipment.

Instead, Isaac, hat in hand, offered her a large bouquet of white roses and told her, "My name is Isaac. I live up north on Whidbey Island where I have staked out the prettiest, most fertile land in this entire Northwest. I am a strong, prosperous man. Please. Please do not return to Boston. Stay here. With me."

That was the hardest and most insane thing he had ever done in his life. But it was the best thing he had ever done as well, because she took the roses.

Watching Emmy's quiet movements, he tried to remember the fragrance of those roses as he closed his eyes, knowing he was drifting off now and, because he was so very tired, he would sleep well for the first time in many nights.

◇◇◇◇◇

About two o'clock in the morning, Isaac awakened from a dream that left him in a cold sweat.

In the dream, he was running down a long beach after a woman. It was Emmy. She had turned and looked at him in horror.

"Wait, Emmy. Can't you see it's me? Wait!"

Then she got that look only she could have. Fierce. Resolute. That was all he could remember as the scene faded away.

It was then that he heard Rowdy barking, behind the late October night wind that had started up again. Sometimes Rowdy would holler at raccoons or deer wandering up from the beach. But this time it was persistent and anxious in a way that frightened Isaac fully awake.

He reached over for his shotgun and remembered he had lent it to Tom Iserson for his watch last week and Tom had brought it back with a broken hammer.

So, stuffing his nightshirt into his pants, he picked up a large walking stick and felt for the bedroom door.

Emmy was awake then, asking after him.

"Isaac?"

"Rowdy is making a lot of noise," he said, descending the stairs to the front door.

He looked out the window onto the porch.

"Visitors," he said.

He lit a lantern, picked up a knife from the kitchen table, then opened the door and stepped out onto the porch.

CHAPTER FOURTEEN

⟨⟨⟨⟩⟩⟩

Anah

Jim Thomas was almost finished mending his fish net when the old Indian man and woman came down the path from Isaac's house. They walked fast and passed him without words or thanks, pushed their small cedar canoe into the light surf, and turned it about, heading north.

They were out of sight within a few minutes, and Jim thought nothing more of it as he gathered up his thread and netting. Only a few days were left to get into the water before the cold November swells would be too big to fight.

Three miles from the beach, out of sight of the small settlement, the Indian couple turned shoreward and found a quiet cove, not dissimilar from the one Isaac had settled.

There they met up with a medium-sized war canoe, ten warriors, and Anah.

The old man and woman beached the canoe, stripped off their long pants and shirts, and reclaimed their jerkins and furs.

Anah and the warriors intently watched the old man—Klixuatan, the clan's shaman—who seemed in no hurry to impart news. Then the old woman, his remaining wife, started to chant, and Klixuatan began a song and did a small five-step dance.

They were singing to the raven god for a new special strength, and then all the warriors knew they had found the big tyee. A few minutes later, the sun dipped below the Olympic Mountains, casting a red hue onto the water.

Anah knew the omen was good. Blood on the water.

Over the next five hours, they chanted quietly to a clan song led by Klixuatan, "Moon bird running quick, bringing back the day and all our children. Water giving moon a second life."

When the half-moon showed itself, Anah and four of the warriors stripped naked and painted themselves with bear grease and red ochre from head to their ankles. They pulled the ornaments from their labrets, whet their knives on beach stones, rechecked their powder, and then pushed off southward in the larger canoe.

The cold would keep them alert.

They did not sing any of their clan songs en route, instead, each warrior had his own private song that he hummed to himself, synchronized by Klixuatan, who tapped the side of the canoe with each dip of his oar.

Anah had moved into a trance during this part of the journey, and while he paddled, the ugly events of the past year rushed past him. Forging the coalition with other tribes had proven more difficult than he had anticipated, partly because so many of them also had been devastated by the smallpox scourge, but also because, under his leadership, his own clan's predatory actions over the past ten years had diminished the number of aboriginal tribes willing to deal with him. In the grand wake of events, with incoming settlers, aggressive actions of the British and U.S. governments, inventions and addicting conveniences that had to be assimilated, and new diseases that had to be endured, aboriginal groups were suffering severely throughout the entire Northwest. Some groups assimilated, many were extinguished altogether.

Anah also felt alone as he never had when he was younger.

Over the previous twelve months, with the loss of so many companions and then Little Raven, his past and the map it provided had been torn away from him. With the deaths of so many of his children, it was as if his horizon had disintegrated, as well.

He thought of this as he beat his syncopated rhythm against the side of the canoe. He knew that each warrior in the canoe carried the same burden. He would regain all of the hope for future bounty that rightfully belonged to them and snatch happiness back from the white intruders who had stolen it so viciously.

He would cleanse away the shame.

Anah had never been afraid of Death because it was always around him from the time he was a small child.

Instead, he played with it as if it were a curious friend that hid behind every living thing and showed itself when he called it forth, when Anah cut into the flesh hard and deep enough.

Over the years, he had killed enough men, women, and children to know well the measure of another human's proximity to death.

And, as he came to understand that his special friendship with Death made him an exception to all other men — accepting that he had been given a privilege that had to be revered and honored, he had attempted to visit Death several times on his own, off away from where there was movement or noise, deep in the forest, away from the interference of other spirits. Knowing he could only really speak with Death if he offered himself, he beckoned to it with his own blood and starvation. It always ended with him alone again, the conversation incomplete.

But each time he understood more. On a few traumatic occasions, he had been impulsively driven there, as when he had received Little Raven's wrecked body and when he beheld the charred bodies of his children in the smoking remains of his burned-out village.

In his grief, he had run as fast as he could into the forest hoping to catch Death, knowing that in so doing, he might look one more time at the spirits of his loved ones. But he was never fast enough.

As a complement to his companionship with Death, in a lesson he learned on many journeys with Little Raven, he always had the comfort of others like him who understood. The ferocity of their every action was a language that endured and resonated universally with all creatures.

All who followed him understood this. By their clan's actions, they defined and marked out their close proximity to Death and their status as its favorite companion. His actions in a fight, and those of the few who were privileged to learn from him, were direct, immediate, and instinctively centered on an opponent's most vulnerable weakness.

He knew his foes would invariably expose it by their protective actions. And then Anah would immediately counter with vicious decisiveness. Anyone who hesitated to think, aim, or react was simply swept away. The deliberating actions of the whites, in particular, were cumbersome compared to his own instinctive tactics, so none of his lumbering opponents ever survived. Such was the ability of Anah, who lived with Death as an ally.

They reached Isaac and Emmy's beach as the moon reached its zenith, darting in and out from a cobweb of blue-black clouds. They pulled the canoe far up the beach because the tide was coming in and left Klixuatan to guard it and protect their passage away from this tyee's magic. Each man draped himself with an otter skin nooksack and, carrying their rifles, clubs, and knives, moved up the beach to the pathway that Klixuatan had indicated led the way to the Isaac and Emmy's home. It took ten minutes to traverse the pathway onto the plateau.

The Evers' home was first, prominently perched looking over the entire plain from a short, cresting, north-facing hillock. In the moonlight, intermittently revealing the harvest stubble of the manicured land, several cabins were visible in the distance, but no lantern light or fires.

As they drew closer, a dog began to bark from behind a white picket fence. Closer still, and then a light came on inside the house, and a tall, powerfully built man came out onto the porch.

Anah knew it was the tyee he had come to kill.

CHAPTER FIFTEEN

⟨⟨⟨⟩⟩⟩

Isaac and Anah

When they saw each other at that moment, eyes locked in the pale moonlight, each man knew the world had stopped around them to watch a death dance. No sound, no movement, just the focus of equals carried quietly over several heartbeats.

Anah knew in that instant, because of an aura of vibrant life surrounding his opponent and this homestead, that he was now closer to Death than he ever had been before. It would come rushing forward eagerly, he knew, and take one or both of them.

⟨⟨⟨⟩⟩⟩

Isaac knew he was staring into the face of his own personal exterminating angel, and from that realization, he thought of protecting his family. Before he could call out a warning, the tall, naked savage moved first, leaping over the picket fence, clubbing Rowdy aside, then bounding up the steps to the long porch, aiming with his ball club for a finishing blow to Isaac's left temple.

Isaac, watching his attacker's fierce eyes, saw the blow coming and ducked away.

From a stooped position, he thrust his heavy walking stick's butt with an upward blow into the man's sternum, knocking him off balance. As the attacker staggered back, Isaac followed with a roundhouse swipe with his knife that caught the man's left pectoral chest, cutting deeply into the muscle. But not deeply enough, Isaac knew.

He saw that the pain from the laceration seemed to energize his assailant. Isaac saw him spin away and reclaim his balance, then move forward onto the deck.

His attacker swung again, but lower now, at Isaac's neck.

Isaac ducked again, but this time the attacker's heavy ball club, razor-sharp spikes jutting from three sides, struck him with a bone crushing thud on his left temple.

The blow carried him over the rail onto the yard below. He hit the wet sod, wrenching his neck and left shoulder, but quickly pulled himself back up, still holding the heavy walking stick.

As he righted himself, preparing for the man's next blow, two younger warriors he hadn't seen simultaneously discharged their muskets at him.

One musket ball struck Isaac in the chest, fracturing his clavicle, and the second blew off the thumb of his left hand.

Isaac was thrown back, but kept his feet. Holding his bloodied hand to his punctured head, he stumbled toward the ocean-facing side of the house.

As soon as the bullets hit, despite a numbing confusion and a searing pain that pushed deeply into the back of his head and down into his neck, Isaac knew he would not survive this fight. That one thought defined the rest of his existence.

In his confusion, he had lost his sense of direction, but somehow stumbled to the side of the house where there was no door.

As the big aborigine and the four others rushed at him, Isaac struggled to hold up the heavy walking stick to ward them off and detain them a few moments longer. But he knew he had done his duty. His family might escape from the other side of the house.

◇◇◇◇

Anah was upon the white tyee and this time used his knife in a jabbing movement to the tyee's neck, cutting directly and deeply into the wound made by the musket shot.

The knife severed first the jugular vein and then the carotid artery.

Anah's foe collapsed and fell forward, his hand still holding his head, eyes rolling up at his heaven.

Anah took a handful of the white tee's long, blond hair and pulled his head back, then cut his throat in one swift motion, at the same time motioning to his companions to break into the house.

As they turned to the house, Anah cut again deeply into the tyee's neck and, in five quick, practiced motions, severed his head from his neck.

The tyee's heart, still beating rapidly, emptied itself in less than thirty seconds.

Anah had seen this before, although not with such a big tyee. In his triumph, he lifted the tyee's head up and turned its face toward him.

In the cold moonlight, he saw the tyee's head open its eyes briefly and close slowly with a look that startled Anah so much that he gasped and dropped it onto the ground, knowing he had been cursed in a way that would haunt him forever.

CHAPTER SIXTEEN

✕✕✕✕

Emmy

M oments after finally crawling under the covers that night, Emmy fell into a deep sleep. She had been sick all day, starting in the morning with dry heaves. She knew it was the pregnancy souring her stomach.

The bleeding had stopped a few days before, and Doctor Edwards suggested she might just keep this one, if only she would rest and hold food and water down. The nausea made it difficult for her to prepare food for dinner because she couldn't stand even the smallest tastes to sample her work and couldn't concentrate on the recipes.

After dinner, she had not participated much in the lively conversation and had excused herself to clean up the kitchen.

She hated the political discussions and, in particular, had a difficult time tolerating the pontifications of Tom Iserson, who never would let anyone forget he had studied at a prestigious seminary in the Midwest for two years before moving west to prospect for gold and, although he wasn't ordained by any church, had converted aborigines to his personal interpretation of Christian redemption.

Emmy had put the children to bed shortly after dinner and, because the participants in the parlor were very loud during their impassioned conversation, she was not surprised when she checked on Jacob and Sarah. Both were awake.

They had been listening to the adults in the parlor debate about whether Governor Stevens's call for extermination of the aboriginal natives was evil and impractical or just plain stupid and provocative.

"Is it true what Major Campbell said tonight — that Isaac might be nominated to run against Governor Stevens? Uncle Winfield said the same thing yesterday," Sarah asked Emmy.

"I'm certain a nomination is the least of your father's concerns," Emmy responded, smiling and hiding her concern about the implications of such a development. He would have to travel all the more.

"Now go to sleep you two little eavesdroppers," Emmy said, kissing Sarah and Jacob goodnight.

By the time she had returned to the parlor, Major Campbell had opened up a bottle of English port and poured six small glasses.

Despite her nausea, Emmy accepted the offer and sipped it politely as the conversation turned from politics to news about the gold strike on the Fraser River near Vancouver, and finally to gossip about the large Catholic family that had moved onto the southern part of the island.

Shortly after the clock struck ten, the Campbells begged their leave, and only a few minutes later, Rebah and Tom announced they would retire as well. It was just as well because entertaining the Isersons without the genteel cushion of the Campbells would be a chore, and she was already exhausted.

When Rowdy started barking a few hours later, Emmy was in the deepest part of her sleep, settled in a place that was comfortable and familiar.

But it wasn't in the Northwest. In her dream, she was visiting her family in Boston, and her father and sister were at the parlor table waiting for her to come in from the garden with Isaac, Sarah, and Jacob. She had arrived first, and Kathleen, her older sister, had that impatient, bothered expression on her face that she had always used to keep her and her younger cousins in a state of perceived inadequacy.

Kathleen was looking past Emmy at the kitchen door, and Emmy turned to look for her little family to enter. But she could only hear the children, bickering over some silly thing.

She waited for Isaac to correct the children and then formally present himself to her family. What was taking him so long, and why was he not attending to the children?

As the dog's barking grew more frantic and insistent, she incorporated that nuisance into her unfinished dream.

She saw that Rowdy had cornered a raccoon in the big Italian plum tree that grew outside her parents' brownstone window. He was jumping up at the treed angry creature and snapping and grabbing at the big plum, stripping pieces of bark from its trunk, as if that would somehow dislodge the hissing coon from its perch.

She heard Isaac then, and she hoped he would shoo the pesky little bandit away quickly so she could reassure her family that she was married to a reliable man.

But Isaac made so much noise fumbling around in the dark that she suddenly felt the hard bed and remembered she was not in Boston at all.

She felt anger at Isaac for his inconsiderate clumsiness, waking her from the first good sleep she had had in a week. She was about to murmur a chastisement, but as she turned to him, she realized his movements conveyed anxiety.

It was enough to rouse her.

Still hoping to return to the colors of the dream, she pulled herself out of bed and pulled a blanket around herself, following Isaac to the stairs.

As she stepped into the hallway, she stubbed her right great toe badly on the doorstop, peeling her toenail back.

That wakened her fully, anger spilling out with a curse at Isaac who had already reached the bottom of the staircase and was fumbling with the lantern.

He did not respond to her and seemed to ignore her pain and anger. When she saw him pick up a kitchen knife, trepidation replaced the pain.

"Isaac?" she called down to him.

The expression on his face as he looked up briefly told her he was determined, but frightened. As he opened the door and stepped out onto the porch, she immediately thought of Jacob and Sarah and rushed to their room.

Jacob was already awake and looking outside the window when she entered. As she walked in, he gasped; she heard Rowdy yelp in pain, then silence followed by a loud jostling on the porch below.

Jacob cried out, "Northerners!"

Emmy was now fully functional. "Run! RUN!" she heard herself scream so loudly that Sarah awoke immediately and, without questions or protest, headed for the stairs.

The cry awakened the Isersons, and Tom emerged from the bedroom downstairs naked, wearing only his socks, with Rebah following.

"RUN, children, run!" Emmy cried again.

Iserson, hearing the fighting outside, ran to the back window and, his face contorted by his uncontrolled panic, pushed up the sash and jumped out, leaving his screaming wife and everyone else behind.

"Tom, Tom! Wait for me! Wait!" wailed Rebah, then moaning and rocking from one foot to the other, as she watched her husband disappearing into the darkness.

Emmy grabbed and shook her, interrupting the terrified woman's palsy.

"Rebah! Move, Damnit!"

The first gunshot shook the house.

Pushing Rebah out through the open window, Emmy heard horrible, vicious screams from the porch outside and knew Isaac was fighting for his life—and for theirs.

CHAPTER SEVENTEEN

◇◇◇◇

Jacob

Jacob, Sarah, Rebah and then, Emmy crawled out the window after Tom Iserson, who by this time had leaped the backyard fence and disappeared into the brambles up the hill and into the woods.

The moon cut through the clouds for just a few moments, giving Jacob his bearings as his mother ushered him and sister through the blackberry thorns in a different direction, toward the small road that led up to the Crocketts' home a mile away.

Jacob could hear the marauders now in the house, crashing through the kitchen and overturning furniture, but he kept running as those sounds faded away, running, knowing that just behind him on that same path Death would be pursuing him silently and relentlessly.

He could not see his mother or sister now — it was so dark, and Rebah kept bawling for Tom someplace off to his left by the big woods.

Jacob heard his mother holler out in the darkness, "Run, kids. Get to the Crocketts. Run!" but he couldn't tell where her voice was coming from.

He was old enough to reach that destination without directions, if he could find the pathway beyond the blackberries that crossed the cattle pasture. And then he stumbled onto the path.

As he struggled to stand back up, he heard careful footsteps behind him.

Mother?

The last thing he remembered about that night was the strong hands that covered his mouth.

CHAPTER EIGHTEEN

◇◇◇◇

Emmy

After she called out, Emmy hesitated for a moment, telling herself that if there were pursuers, she would jump in to protect her children. As she reached the pasture, she saw no one on the path, but heard grunting noises that made her remember the young stud bull that was supposed to be penned up in the barn — big, stupid, unpredictable animal that protected that field, studding and crapping. Tonight it was an ironic bit of fear to add to the terror.

The field was uneven, and each step tore at her wretched toe as she continued running toward what she hoped was the Crockett home.

Where were the kids? Where were the kids?

Then she heard Sarah screaming up ahead. They must have reached the Crockett's.

Emmy ran past several squawking geese and knew she was there too, past the small brown fence and up the stairs.

Sarah was pounding frantically on the big oak door. When Sarah heard the footsteps behind her, she gasped, but then released her held breath when she saw it was her mother.

They pounded on the door together, louder now, hollering out for Crockett to awaken.

Emmy turned, looking for Jacob, Rebah, and Tom.

"Hold on! Who the hell is it?" Ben called from inside.

When he opened the door, he had a big knife in his hand, and Missy Crockett stood behind him with a twenty-gauge shotgun pointed at them.

"My God, it's Emmy and Sarah!"

He pulled them into the house, peering past them into the darkness.

Sarah cried out, "Northerners! Father was fighting them, and we had to run."

"My God!" Crockett blurted out, looking down at Emmy. "Em, you're wounded!"

Emmy thought he was talking about her foot and then looked down to where he was staring. Her nightgown was covered with blood from the waist down and was dripping all over the rough-hewn floor.

Missy looked at Emmy's white face, handed the shotgun to Crockett, and said, "Ain't a wound, Ben."

CHAPTER NINETEEN

◇◇◇◇

Emmy

The bell rang louder now. It had a name finally: "Nagger," she wanted to call it.

Emmy had slept hard, and it took hours, it seemed, to wake fully again.

When she came about, the room was still, but she could hear voices quietly talking.

Moving in the bed, she caught her wretched toe again, and the dull pain brought her back to herself. She felt a bandage covering it, dulling its sting.

She wondered if she were dead because the morning nausea that had bothered her for the past several weeks was gone, now replaced with a weakness that went all the way down into her bones, pushing her right through to the floorboards.

The whispers continued, heated now, it seemed, but too muffled to understand.

Was it Northerners?

Did they just come to pay respects and negotiate a deal for the cattle?

Where was Isaac and her children?

This mattress was softer than hers, and she knew from the embroidered, quilted cover that she had to be in Missy Crockett's home, maybe her bed, even.

She was embarrassed not to be in her own bed and felt like an intruder, like someone who, just to get a moment's rest, might have slipped through the window in the night.

She needed to get out of there.

Where was Isaac, and why weren't the children up running about and fussing as they always did?

She was wearing a different, clean nightgown, but she was wet hot. She threw the quilt off and pulled at the gown. The bell clanged outside again, longer now.

The bell clanged again, insistently. Nagger!

She called out to the voices, which stopped abruptly.

She sensed someone outside the door. After a few moments, Missy Crockett pushed it open and entered with Joseph Edwards. Both wore concerned and sad expressions that cut right to her chest.

Missy immediately sat down at the bedside, took Emmy's hand, and smoothed her damp hair. She was holding back tears, Emmy could tell.

Joseph Edwards had a gruff, clumsy way of saying things for a doctor, but she always knew he meant well. He knelt down at eye level with Emmy and reached over to touch the top of her hand hesitantly.

"Emmy, it is so good to see you awake. I was beginning to worry that the combination of the ether and sedatives I used might have been too much." Then he touched her forehead. Turning to Missy, he said, "She's burning up. Get some rubbing alcohol and water and wet her down."

He paused, seeing Emmy struggling to understand. "Dear, you lost the baby. And now you've got an infection that's going to put you to the worst test you've ever had."

What was he saying? She tried to form words but her mind seemed full of cotton, then slowly, around the edges, the terror returned. Everything was coming at her at once and she wasn't even sure where she was. The baby?

As she stammered out "the baby?" Edwards interrupted her. "You have to preserve your strength and rest. Please drink this down," he said, lifting a cup of apple juice to her mouth.

Emmy then remembered she had been pregnant, and the misery pounded her down harder than when she had lost the first baby two years ago.

Somewhere from another room she heard a man's baritone laugh.

Isaac?

Edwards paused, watching her closely, "Isaac and Jacob are fine. Now rest."

But she hadn't asked Edwards about Jacob, she thought, as the drift from the laudanum overcame her, she heard a crow cawing and the flutter of wings outside the window, and she was in a field by herself, counting and losing count.

CHAPTER TWENTY

Joseph Edwards

A practitioner familiar enough with the benefits of ether surgery, Dr. Joseph Edwards had put Emmy under when her miscarriage was inevitable and she needed help clearing out the clots that followed the small stillborn fetus.

With the bleeding stopped, he was now worried about the morbid fever that followed bloody miscarriages like this. Sometimes the woman survived, but so much depended on her residual strength. Frail ones passed in a swift night, shaking and melting away in front of the bereaved. But Emmy could beat this; he knew because of the temper of her mettle.

He had been called on the morning of the awful attack, after Ben Crockett, Winfield Evers, and a few men from the east side of the island had ventured out together to be certain the marauders had cleared. When they went to the Evers' homestead, they had found Isaac's headless remains.

Edwards had gone to the Evers home before attending to Emmy because it was on the way to Ben Crockett's house. But just for a few minutes, because he hated violent death scenes. The men had brought the broken carcass into the ransacked house to keep the crows away.

He had seen decapitations before. Felt it was such a robbery of a body's dignity.

On Elliott Bay where Edwards had first started practicing, before Evers convinced him to move to Whidbey, there had been several decapitations after a twenty-five-dollar reward had been posted for the head of the Indian who had raped and killed one of the Elliott Bay settlers.

Eighteen heads, all likely taken as retribution for miscellaneous grudges, had been brought in before the settlers realized the bounty had been a mistake. He had seen some of the heads returned to the families of the deceased. The headless bodies always seemed so much smaller and foolish looking.

This desecration was no different than others he had seen—thumb missing, a big hole blown out of Isaac's back from a heavy slug, likely a .54 caliber.

The body wouldn't have survived that wound anyway, so the missing head seemed irrelevant, except that it wasn't.

When the burial took place on a body rotted away from a cancer or simply dwindled into a frail carcass, he always imagined the full person in good health, no matter what.

But this was so hard to put to rest.

By the time he got to the Crockett's twenty minutes later, Emmy had collapsed, and Ben had carried her unconscious, upstairs.

She was bleeding heavily and had already passed the fetus, which Missy Crockett, a devout Catholic, had wrapped in new linen and placed next to a votive candle, lit she said, so the baby's tiny soul could find its way to Purgatory.

Edwards inspected the fetus and saw that the small placenta had not pulled away intact from the uterus, which meant that Emmy would continue bleeding and die unless he could evacuate the fragments along with any large clots left.

He took a bottle of opiate from his bag and told Missy to mix a half bottle into a pitcher of water and then to arouse Emmy enough so that she drank a full tumbler.

After Emmy ingested the mixture, he soaked a handkerchief wrapped around a large cotton ball with ether and held it over her mouth and nose.

She didn't struggle much. When she was limp, he began searching for the remainder of the placenta.

He had lied to Emmy about her husband and son because she needed to sleep through this infection. The searchers hadn't found Jacob, and now they were walking through the underbrush in the west evergreen woods near the Evers house to see if he turned up or was dead.

A day after the attack, Tom Iserson had emerged from the woods and came walking up to the Crockett's cabin, naked except for his right stocking, babbling biblical verses and profane curses.

It took a full two days to find his wife, Rebah, cowering under a fallen tree, crazed, bawling her eyes out, broken down. The men had to talk to her for an hour before she would come out. But Jacob was nowhere to be found.

Edwards, watching Emmy struggle with a fever that most likely would consume her, decided it would be best to order the burial of what remained of Isaac Evers. He would keep Emmy heavily sedated and deal out the terrible news when she was strong enough to receive it. His lie would not matter if she passed on, and he would be spared the pain of telling her the truth.

Edwards officiated over Isaac's burial the next day, Sunday, November 15th. Islanders had come from Whidbey's four corners, arriving with gifts and condolences for Sarah and Emmy.

By the time the ceremony started shortly before noon, a near freezing rain blew its bitter bite across the fertile homestead that Isaac and Emmy had so successfully developed. Winfield and Ben brought the cedar plank casket up from the Evers home, then all the men who had been standing by waiting moved over to help lift it off the carriage and lower it into the drenched grave.

Corrine Evers, Isaac's lame sister, and Missy Crockett, placed a large wreath of rosemary onto the casket as it passed by.

After the men pulled the ropes out from the grave, as the cold rain started pounding the earth and water pooled around the edges of the coffin, they picked up shovels and covered it. When the last shovelful had been placed, Edwards stepped forward to speak:

"We all knew Colonel Isaac Joseph Evers. He was a handsome, hardworking, visionary man. He helped all of us settle in this rough land. He and his wife, Emmy, created a homestead that is the envy of everyone here. It is a tragedy that his great effort and love have ended in this way. God has a purpose. Dear Lord Jesus and God Almighty, watch over Isaac in his journey and take care of his family, in your wisdom and mercy. Amen."

That was all. No one else spoke.

The cold rain was fitting to the horror of the past several days, and the neighbors and friends had already said to each other what needed to be said. Those who knew Edwards expected no more words.

Sarah left with Corrine across the plateau to stay with Isaac's brother and wife.

◇◇◇◇

After the mourners had departed in their carriages, Jim Thomas stepped out of the cedar pine thicket north of the gravesite. He carried a small bundle to Isaac Evers' grave and pulled back the loosely packed dirt near the grave's marker. He unwrapped the woven bundle and placed its contents into the hole. It was a head, roughly carved out of cedar, its eyes painted in with blackberry juice.

As he covered it up, he sang a little song in Salish: "Go into the dark place with these eyes open. With these eyes open."

CHAPTER TWENTY-ONE

◇◇◇◇

Emmy

Was it Isaac?

She heard him first before she saw him, and as she got closer, walking through the Madrona saplings through a fading light, he made a raspy sound that reminded her of his sighs when he had expressed his most desperate doubts about his life.

Each step toward him made him seem to move farther and faster away. When she pushed aside a low-hanging deodar branch, she was in a dark clearing about fifty feet at its widest.

She saw his back moving out and away, deeper into the woods. He was weeping, she could hear.

As she crossed the pine needle floor to follow, she heard a cry from a long way off to her right: "Mama!"

Was that Jacob?

When she turned to locate the sound, she saw a black-red shadow emerging from the clearing not far behind her, close enough that she could hear it panting and smell its fetid exhalation.

She stopped, hoping it would pass by her while she held herself motionless. But it stopped too, and she could see it was watching her from its cover.

Then the cry again. Her eyes moved in the direction of the sound, and she forgot for a moment that she was being stalked.

When she looked again, the shadow was gone.

Had it swept by? Where did Isaac go? Why was he crying and running away?

Where was Jacob?

Sarah, go get your brother, she struggled to say, but the words wouldn't come out.

She woke for a moment and found herself in the still of a dark room. It wasn't hers, and then she remembered she was in Missy Crockett's home.

She was dripping wet; her nightgown was soaked. She pushed the light cover off and lay there exhausted, looking up at the pine wood ceiling, its rough textures becoming clearer as her eyes accommodated to the early morning light. It felt like a big coffin.

Why was she here?

Where was her family?

She tried to get up from the bed, pushing herself up by the elbows, but the room faded away again.

She was on the shore looking out at a gray chop, peering into the northern horizon, up past the huge snow-
capped Olympic mountain range to the west.

What was she looking at? She knew it was out there,
whatever it was that had brought her down here, facing the
chill and cut. She knew she had been watching for it for a
long time, and yet, she understood that she had just gotten
down to the shore a few moments ago.

She saw it coming toward her place, getting bigger
against the dull whitecaps, and as cold as she was already
from the icy-angry gusts, a chill drove deeper straight
through to her backbone.

She stepped back across the beach, unable to pull her
gaze away, and then stumbled back onto a barnacle-en-
crusted rock, cutting the heels of both her hands.

It landed on the shore a few feet away from her and
began chopping with its large beak, a massive black crow
that floated halfway into the water.

It hovered over her for a moment, dripping salt
water and saliva, and then swept past her up the track to
her home.

She pushed herself up, tried to cry out: "Run, kids,
run!" but nothing came forth. Ran up the path but could
not get her footing and kept falling backward, backward
again and again, back onto the stones below.

Where was Isaac?

She clawed her way up the pathway, one agonizing pull
after another, and when she got to the top, she saw that her
home was gone. It had never been there.

She wiped the sand off the cuts with one quick swipe
and ran back down to the beach. The specter had receded

and was moving away along the coast, back north. It was carrying something on its back and in its beak, and she knew they belonged to her.

◇◇◇◇◇

On the third day after Isaac's burial, Emmy's fever broke. She slept heavily for two more days, intermittently waking, alternating between delirium and mute silence. Missy Crockett, Corrine Evers, and an Indian woman named Princess Susan attended to her, bathing her and changing her linen.

Missy and Corrine brought Sarah in with them as often as possible. She was old enough to see someone struggling with a horrible illness, and the women had agreed that Sarah's constitution was much like her mother's, so she would only grow stronger with witnessing something as difficult as this, whether Emmy lived or died.

Edwards instructed Missy to gradually start reducing the laudanum. He had seen many women die during postpartum fevers and, believing that Emmy had a chance to survive, had kept the women working the poultices, mustard plasters, and cooling baths, watching and logging every change in her movement, color, and excretions. Emmy had lost enough blood in the miscarriage that Edwards did not believe additional blood-letting was wise or necessary, and he had been pleased that the discharges from her private areas had never changed to the sulfurous smell that usually preceded a terminal change.

So, he let her rest.

The next day Emmy woke for a few minutes while being bathed and brightened when Sarah came into her view.

◇◇◇◇◇

Emmy was on the plain overlooking the pastures and farmland. She wore the breeches she used when working the cattle in the pens below. A cooling breeze swept up her legs and pushed orange-red maple and yellow aspen leaves swirling about her knees.

Across the plain and into the sunset, a tall man walked toward the western beach landing and disappeared over the cliff. She was now there at the embankment's edge overlooking the shore where she had previously seen the raven specter.

The man was Isaac. But it wasn't him. And then he was gone.

She looked northward again.

◇◇◇◇◇

Emmy awoke the next day, and after eating a few bites of her first solid food since the night of the attack, she asked Missy to take her outside.

Doctor Edwards and Ben carried her to the porch and set her on a chair prepared with blankets and a comforter. It was a warm late autumn afternoon. She could hear the cattle braying in the distance and saw a big eight-point buck walk down across the plain and back up into the woods that bordered her fields.

Corrine and Missy fussed and talked about doing a press of cider from the apples. She saw Sarah crossing the pasture with Winfield.

Edwards was watching her. He pulled her lower eyelids down, looked at the creases on her palm, felt her pulse, and stepped back, hesitating.

Emmy looked up at him and at Missy.

He stepped forward: "Emmy, Isaac's gone. Jacob's been taken."

"I know," she said.

Three days later, Emmy was strong enough to walk about, and the next day she asked to be taken to the gravesite.

Edwards and Crockett lifted her off the buckboard, and Missy accompanied her and Sarah halfway, then stepped back when Emmy waved her away.

Emmy stood there for half an hour, holding Sarah tightly and peering south across the hillside resting place onto the magnificent gently rolling homestead below. She knew that Isaac had died protecting her and her children. All the suffering and success from hard work and vision, the discipline to fashion chance and opportunity into a measurable and sustainable fortune, the heritable hope for her family—all of it had been destroyed in one night by cruel acts she still did not understand.

Who were these people?

What was God saying to her by this event?

Why did Isaac fight instead of run?

Did he know he was going to die?

Was it a sacrifice?

And why hadn't she helped him?

Why had she been so cross with him for awakening her and fumbling around in the dark?

Why had she run and abandoned him?

Her thoughts circled back again to Jacob. Why hadn't she kept Jacob by her side? Where was he? Was he hurt? Did he know about his father's death? Did he know she and

Sarah were alive? Was he hungry? Was he cold? Was there someone in that savage crowd who would care for him?

She wept. And for the first time since she had surmised from her dreams the dimensions of her personal tragedy, she felt a release that cleaned out a muddy confusion about what she could have done to protect her family. She looked west, out toward the strait, remembered the dreams about herself on the shore, then pulled Sarah closer.

It rained for five straight days and nights.

One week later, word came from Port Townsend that a British provisions ship had sighted two long boats heading north near the Campbell River. They had veered course and closed on the ship.

The crew braced for an assault, but the long boats kept out of range of the ship's small cannon and ran parallel to the ship's course.

The captain reported that through his telescope he glassed ten men in each boat and a small white boy in the second canoe.

In the first long boat, a tall warrior, left arm in sling, stood facing them.

In his right hand, he defiantly held up a severed head.

CHAPTER TWENTY-TWO

◇◇◇◇◇

Jacob

The two long boats moved north, keeping close to the eastern shore of the sound. When they passed the first cluster of Lummi fishing houses south of Bellingham, they moved in closer, and Anah had his warriors push their way into the shallow harbor, which berthed a few lumber ships and small fishing ketches. Several Lummi canoes lined the shore beside racks of dried salmon and halibut.

It was six a.m., and the water moved slowly with a mild outgoing tide.

As soon as the Haida rowers got within hailing distance of the fishing village a mile away from the larger lumber vessels, they began chanting and beating their oars against the sides of their canoes. They fired two shots that rumbled across the still water, breaking the morning's peace.

Curious Lummi natives and white settlers emerged half awake from their shacks. The Haida began hollering and jeering.

Anah, in the lead boat, held up Isaac's bloodless head and screamed, "Tyee. Tyee."

The long boats then paddled out of the harbor moving northward. They repeated this at every village they encountered along their trek toward the rendezvous point near the mouth of the Campbell River.

◇◇◇◇◇

Jacob had fought his captors as soon as he regained consciousness on the first night and, despite being a small child, had doubled over two of the warriors with swift kicks to their groins.

One of them, the younger of the two, pulled a knife, but Jacob saw the other Northerner, holding a bleeding wound to his chest, waive off the younger and give orders to the others in the encampment.

Thereafter, Jacob was kept bound and slept during the journey north, drugged with a mixture of alcohol and herbs by Klixuatan's wife.

On the sixth night of the trek, he awoke to the old woman's quiet, rough voice singing a song he did not understand. As his eyes became accustomed to the darkness in the smoky tent, he heard the patter of rain hitting the lean-to's sealskin covering and found himself next to another boy, a frail-looking towhead, possibly a year older than Jacob's six years.

The boy, also bound at feet and wrists, was coughing and shivering. "I'm sooo cold," the boy said.

Jacob looked about but could not make out much. He could see the flicker and shadow of a fire outside the tent, and he could smell meat roasting. He was hungry.

"Please help me. I'm so cold," the boy beside him said again.

Jacob didn't feel cold. He looked at the skins covering the boy and realized that he had more coverings on him than Jacob had himself and wondered how the boy could possibly be feeling cold.

The boy started coughing again, and his teeth began chattering.

Jacob wanted to say something but drifted off to sleep. When he awoke, it was starting to get light outside. The chanting had stopped. The boy next to him was breathing intermittently now with a wet, raspy gurgling choking with every inhalation. Finally, it quieted down and then stopped altogether.

Jacob slept. When he woke up again, he was alone. Where had the boy gone?

He came awake again with a bitter taste in his mouth and realized he had been fed. It reminded him of berries and salmon, but it was rancid and stuck in the back of his throat. He felt like throwing up.

Now he was in the back of the long boat, facing forward for the first time, and could feel the rain and wind kicking up as the men rowing the boat quietly pushed steadily ahead.

Where were his mother and father? Where was he being taken? He looked at the markings on the inside of the canoe. They matched the tattoos he had seen covering the body of the old woman, now faded and sagging into an ugly indistinct story, that of beasts fighting and devouring each other, crows crowing, whales with big eyes and rounded teeth, animals with angry blank stares in the middle of a fierce battle.

The old woman, wrapped in several skins and a wool blanket, sat next to him. She stared forward, singing to herself in a simple and repetitive chant. It was the same hoary voice he had heard when he was sleeping in the tent next to the boy who was coughing.

Jacob dozed off again but awoke with a start as he heard hollering.

The men were excited and talking loudly, pointing off to his left. He tried to sit up and saw several killer whale fins crest out of the water ten yards away. Dozens more crested on the other side of the boat. Some of the whales were small, while others were big enough to capsize the large canoes. But they just moved on.

After a while, the men calmed down, and the silent paddling continued. It rained for what seemed like a terribly long time, and then it stopped.

In another hour, the sun came out, and the clouds seemed to spread apart showing off the land to his right, and after another few hours, the boats moved into a small cove and beached.

He slept in the boat.

The next morning, he awoke to shouting as utensils and camp supplies were being thrown into the long boat. The early sunlight had just spread over the cove, and he saw the warriors looking past him out at the harbor.

Jacob turned and saw a small ship flying a British flag resting at the south end of the bay.

They shoved off and moved to the right of the harbor, heading north. He saw puffs of smoke from the ship, heard deep popping sounds, and then saw large splashes approximately one hundred yards short of the lead boat.

The men in the canoes started jeering. He saw a warrior in the lead boat climb to the front and hold up a long pole. On top of the pole was a head.

"Boston Tyee. Boston Tyee. Boston Tyee!" they all started hollering.

The ship spread its sails and made way, and for a short while, it seemed to be gaining on the rowers. But the wind failed, and the ship fell back and began to recede from view. Soon it disappeared around the bend of the coast.

Jacob watched for signs of the ship but did not see it again.

Two days later, the long boats reached a rendezvous point where Jacob saw nine other long boats beached along the shore. As they came closer, the men in the boat began to chant loudly, and the camp on the beach came alive.

He heard them shout, "Tyee!"

The old woman nudged Jacob, looking to the front of the long canoe, and he saw the warrior in the lead boat mount the trophy on the pole again. Jacob, groggy from the cold, the drugs, and hunger, thought it looked like his father's head.

Breathing fast, a dull, nauseating pain deep in his gut, Jacob looked down the pole from the waxen head and saw the man who held it up, staring at him intently.

Anah.

CHAPTER TWENTY-THREE

◇◇◇◇

Sarah

She looked in the mirror and, for the first time, saw a face that was older. In the past, she hadn't spent much time grooming or preening, so a mirror was simply a place to look for tidiness. But over the past four weeks, with the burial of her stepfather, Isaac, and helping her aunt and Missy care for her mother, it seemed that her self-awareness had diminished so much that when she saw her face again for a moment, it was really a stranger looking back at her.

Something else was different, too: she had two white hairs, one on each side of her head! How could that be? She was only eleven.

She fingered them along their entire length, feeling if they were different in other ways.

She pulled them out.

Sarah was relieved when her mother regained her strength and was able to move about. Emmy had recovered quickly. As much as her Aunt Cora and Missy Crockett fretted, Sarah knew her mother would recover because she had never let anyone or anything best her. Sarah could never imagine her mother dying. Emmy had too much living to do.

In many ways, Sarah had always sensed that her stepfather was vulnerable and would die long before Emmy. When he had been away in eastern Washington, Sarah had prepared herself for hearing that he had died in some massacre or by drowning or from snakebite.

He always put himself out a little too far and didn't look out for himself as much as she thought someone should. Long before he died, she had imagined herself at the graveside with the mourners, all saying sad praises for his departed soul. And she would cry and have to wait to see him again in heaven.

She had practiced crying for that event, and it felt sad the first time and less so the second time she did it.

She knew about death, of course. She had seen animals slaughtered, remembered when that farmhand was trampled, and had seen Jimmy Falcon's washed-out body pulled from the sound when he and his brother had capsized their boat two years ago while fishing too early in the season.

She understood the grief that relatives showed, and that was why she had practiced doing the same for the time when her father would die—so she could do it right and with some dignity. And when it happened, when Cora told her that Isaac was dead and Jacob had been stolen and her mother might die too, she had taken it in and knew the practice had been useful.

She hadn't expected Jacob to be hurt, and she knew her mother would survive, but she had practiced weeping for Isaac, so she got through it and all the people told her that she was a brave girl.

But she was just doing what she had practiced.

How would she find Jacob? Would they hurt him or slave him or turn him into a savage or feed him to wolves? What would he be like if she got him back? Would he be different?

Would he have grown white hairs, too?

CHAPTER TWENTY-FOUR

✕✕✕✕

Emmy and Pickett

Three days after she heard about the sighting of the long boats near Vancouver Island's Campbell River, Emmy received an army change-order requisition in beef shipments. Beef was to be shipped to San Juan Island rather than to Bellingham.

From the transport agent, she learned that Captain George Pickett was under orders to move most of his command to San Juan to establish a fortification in anticipation of a dispute with the British over control of the region. She also learned that Pickett would stop for a fortnight in Port Townsend to complete filling his supplies and await reinforcements from Oregon.

She decided she had to act quickly before a distracting engagement between the Americans and the British ensued and she could not get assistance in retrieving Jacob. Accompanied by Sarah and Isaac's brother, Winfield, Emmy booked a short passage to Port Townsend and requested a meeting with Pickett and the commanding officer of the fort.

◇◇◇◇

Winter was early, and when Emmy and her party arrived, snow had already covered the pine and cedar forest around the fort.

Pickett was surprised by Emmy's visit and made himself immediately available, meeting Emmy and Winfield in the temporary office he had been given for his stay. He had only heard about the attack on Whidbey the week before and had struggled with a letter to Emmy, uncertain over the proper response.

He had written three versions, each proper but incomplete and empty of the feelings that confused him all the more in the face of this tragedy.

When Emmy arrived, he was still debating whether to send the last version, which offered to visit her at some point in the future to express his condolences in person. Would she accept that offer?

Pickett looked at Winfield, a bantam redhead with a tense, angry posture, and immediately dismissed him as a weak, unworthy, and annoying distraction. But when he saw Emmy, he noticed that her mourning black reinforced the power of her eyes, and he felt immediately overwhelmed by her again.

He tried to remember the terms of the arrangement he had made with her and recalled that it had been a hopeless negotiation for him from the start. He didn't remember a whit of it, so taken with her as he had been, and when he had inspected the Evers cattle with her, he had bumbled his way through the transaction, peeking at her in a way that made him feel like a schoolchild.

So, here she was again. And her earnest expression made him turn away, to hide the blushing he felt.

When he regained his composure, he looked up and saw Winfield glaring impatiently at him.

"Captain Pickett, thank you for receiving us," Winfield began. "I have been told you know about what has happened to our family. We need your help. I want you to dispatch a contingent of soldiers, perhaps an expedition, to hunt down the brutal savages who kidnapped my nephew and killed my brother in the prime of his life, a man who contributed greatly to the safety and prosperity of so many in this region."

Pickett listened but did not respond. Despite his habit of maintaining his imperturbability during heated discussions, he feared that his expression likely conveyed annoyance at Winfield's irksome insistence. As he listened, he watched Emmy, hoping she wouldn't notice his momentary loss of disciplined behavior. What would *she* need? What could he possibly do to help *her*?

Winfield, reading Pickett's resistant expression, went on, tears welling up in his eyes, "Surely the military has some leeway in matters like this. This was not a common infraction or a random act of violence. This was a vicious attack—and this was my brother. He was a heroic man, and society is in debt to him and his memory. This was cold-blooded murder. It was an insult to the order that you are here to preserve, Captain. They decapitated him! We had to bury him in that condition. We have heard they have been parading his head all up the coast for the past two weeks. And who knows what has become of my nephew. We have modest means and do not have the wherewithal to establish rescue and retribution. But you do."

Pickett calmly measured his response, "Mr. Evers, I am, of course, very sad about the tragic events that have befallen your family. I share your concern about the safety of our citizens. Unfortunately, I am under orders to quickly establish fortifications on San Juan and will be unable to provide any of our resources. Perhaps in the spring we can discuss this again."

Winfield persisted. "You do not understand, Captain. This act, if it is allowed to go unpunished, will be seen as weakness on our part to citizens and heathens alike. That will, in turn, certainly provoke additional violence. The military has a chance to do something heroic and greatly symbolic. Acting now will convey a stern message to all the aborigines and reassure all loyal whites."

Pickett simply shook his head and smiled. "You have my answer, Mr. Evers."

Winfield could not contain himself. He stood up, his fists balled before him. "Captain, were I but a single man without family obligations, I would venture forth myself and take on these heathens. I would bring them to justice. This is a sad disappointment, and I shall bring this matter directly to Governor Stevens for help, to overturn your decision here."

He turned, pushed open the door, and walked out, slamming the door behind him and storming past Sarah who stood outside in the hallway, leaving Emmy and Pickett in the room.

◇◇◇◇

Emmy looked at Pickett, who seemed to be chagrinned, perhaps embarrassed for her as well as for himself. She maintained her composure, however.

"Captain, Winfield is highly educated and likes to show that off, but he also has always been a tempestuous man who seldom thinks before he speaks, although that was better than most of the exchanges I have witnessed over the years."

She forced a small smile, cracking past a stern sadness. She paused, then continued, "This is no small request, I understand. My son is missing, and we believe we still may have the opportunity for rescue. We have been informed that this event was likely the work of a well-known renegade band of Haida. They winter up north, on the mainland across the strait from the Queen Charlotte Islands. I am told there are neutral trading camps up there too, with the Bella Bella and Tsimshian. We could send emissaries offering a bounty. I have a small amount of gold I have gathered that would likely be more than enough to establish a fair trade for my son. If it were possible to retrieve the rest of Isaac's remains, his head, I would bring that back, too, so it could be put to rest . . . where it belongs. But Jacob—he is only five."

She saw that Pickett listened to her carefully measured but passionate request. He sighed deeply, and a sadness seemed to come over him that told Emmy the answer. He stood and moved over to Emmy before he spoke.

"Mrs. Evers—Emmy—I am so very sorry. There is no way that I can help you at this moment. We are told by reliable sources that the British plan to send several companies of marines to fortify their claim on San Juan Island over an incident that recently occurred. I have to get there first and hold that ground. I have no choice in this matter. I cannot spare a single man."

Emmy studied him for several moments and then stood. He was telling her the truth.

"Thank you, Captain. I am disappointed, but I understand." After a pause, she said, "I shall book a passage and will go to Fort Simpson and to the Tsimshian winter camps myself then. Without the help of this government. As you know, I am capable, and I negotiate quite well."

Emmy turned, but as she started to leave, she saw Pickett's stunned expression at the directness of her pronouncement.

"I am not afraid," she said.

She found Sarah sitting outside the door, took her hand, and made her way to their quarters.

As she did so, Emmy shuddered, and an intense anger swept over her. She knew the captain was duty bound and had accepted that before she had even asked for his improbable assistance; still, she had had to make an attempt lest the dutiful but insane course she planned be criticized. She had rehearsed the request as well as the response upon being denied assistance.

She would not play upon Pickett's emotions as she knew some might. She had wanted to say to him, "Jacob is my little boy," but she prevented herself from making that final wrenching appeal. She knew she would keep that phrase to herself and she would be repeating it over and over again privately as she had for the past several weeks. It would guide her and drive her.

And now she had many things to do.

◇◇◇◇

That evening Pickett couldn't sleep. He thought about Emmy making her way far north into the aborigine winter encampments and the grim likelihood of her finding nothing but suffering and disappointment at best and, at worst, savage and brutal treatment and a painful death. He had failed to extend anything that might bring her some hope or intervene to dissuade her from this madness.

He thought of himself making the same effort. Wondered if he would ever have the temerity to overcome the inertia of doing so, letting go of the security that even the rudimentary civilization of this region provided.

Could he, would he, ever take on such an arduous task for anyone he loved? Of course he could, he thought. But in his entire life, he could not think of one instance in which he had done so—put himself in harm's way for someone he had loved. He had risked his life for glory, certainly, and for orders, but he had no recollection of tempestuous acts for the love of woman or child.

Did that make him bad, practical, or just selfish?

He wondered what it was about love that could compel someone to such actions. He had conceived a child, a boy, with Morning Mist. He was fond of the child but felt no pride or devotion to him. He wondered if that feeling would have been different had the boy not been a half-breed.

He thought about whether he had ever understood or accepted the weakness of his feelings, instead of containing them as dangerous out-of-control calamities waiting to uncoil themselves, snakes in a box with its latch broken. He had seen men withered and besot in a drunken, shrunken state in the aftermath of what they called love.

He had detested it when he let himself go like that, had fought and always defeated that weakness, and thus wondered whether he had ever really been truly in love in the way that seemed to drive so many. He had been in sadness, certainly.

He recalled that he had been head over heels enraptured by Morning Mist and had wept when she had died. But was that what they called love? Or was it rather an infatuation followed by the profound loneliness that comes with deprivation and self-pity?

Had he ever been so compelled by his feelings for her, or for his first wife, that he allowed himself to defy logic or counter reasonable orders? If being enraptured was the same as being in love, he did not know how far he could trust those wondrous, terrifying feelings—of letting go.

He felt so much comfort in the presence of order, determined by a rational set of calculations, grounded in a mathematical precision that pushed aside emotion. He thought love was the antithesis of order and the settling peace that accompanied it.

But Emmy's determination drew him to think of her, and he could not put that out of his mind as he slept restlessly.

What did she need? Did he, by oath of his station and office, have a responsibility to her as a citizen, one that superseded his responsibility to follow his orders?

Did he, drawn as he was to her by his admiration for her qualities and equanimity, need to preserve her for his own peace of mind or, for that matter, some future opportunity?

Did he, from his notions of chivalrous behavior, have a sacred duty to protect her as a vulnerable woman? Could he extend his best efforts so that she might not suffer in her insane quest? How could she, the very epitome of order and control, framed in a wondrous sturdy and symmetrical visage, risk herself so?

By morning he still had not answered his many questions and self-doubts, but he took it upon himself to seek out Emmy with what he had concluded.

When he found her in the trading post that afternoon having a calm yet intense discussion with the provision merchant, he was again struck by her dignified demeanor and beauty.

He waited for her to finish her bargaining and then stepped forward, doffing his hat and extending a flourished but gentle bow. "Madame Evers. May I speak with you a moment?"

Emmy turned to him and, with a glance, dismissed the storekeeper.

She nodded to Pickett and stepped to the corner near the dry goods section, then turned back to face him, waiting.

"I know you will not be dissuaded, Emmy. I respect that. One part of me wants to defy my own orders and go there with you myself. But I cannot do such a thing. You know that. Another part of me wishes to extend a protecting wing over you. But I believe I know you would not accept that from me, or anyone. I have little to give to you other than a recommendation for a guide and this."

He handed her an ornately carved and inlaid box. "Please take it with you. It has proven to be reliable."

Emmy opened the box. Inside was Pickett's pepper-box pistol, a Belgian-made six-barrel Mariette, and a note with an aborigine's name on the envelope. She looked at Pickett and nodded. "Thank you, Captain. Best of luck to you also."

Pickett watched her leave and carried to bed with him that night the image of her fierce resolve pushing her forward into dark winds. He did not believe in prayer, but he would pray for her, nonetheless.

CHAPTER TWENTY-FIVE

<><><>

Emmy

In the port, Emmy booked a passage the next day on the *Pietrevos*, a Russian trading ship bound for Japan but scheduled to stop in Fort Simpson to drop off supplies and pick up whatever furs were still being harvested in the region.

The large, clumsy vessel had ample room for extra passengers. Its captain, Vladimir Varienko, a swarthy, tub-bellied lout with a greedy, incisor-dominant, salivating smile that immediately made her feel unsafe and uncomfortable, was more than willing to accommodate her.

She had purchased supplies and chests of trading goods to buy her way into the Tsimshian tribe's winter camp, which served as a neutral trading place used by all the neighboring tribes to exchange supplies. She also carried with her a small box of gold coins minted in Phila-delphia, a small diamond, and several semiprecious stones that would be part of the final exchange with the North-erners, should she be given the opportunity.

Knowing that Winfield had angry, vengeful designs that likely would thwart any chance for a trade, she asked him to take Sarah back to Whidbey and plan on joining her in a few weeks. She reassured him she would find assis-tance from the Brits and meet him in Esquimalt with Jacob.

Sarah protested vigorously and pleaded with Emmy to allow her to accompany her on the recovery of her brother.

But Emmy knew the real danger of this quest. She told Sarah that their best chance to find Jacob was if she went prepared to travel beyond Fort Simpson, quickly moving upriver for the winter encampment, if necessary.

Sarah did not seem convinced and sobbed angrily for a while, then suddenly quieted down and spoke no more of the matter.

The ship moved out on the next early morning tide and, despite a strong headwind and tumultuous high seas, reached Fort Simpson three days later, on the evening of January 4th.

Confined to her cabin, Emmy had tried to write in a journal, but mostly slept when she was not sick. She hated sailing, and this short trip brought back the horrid mem-ories of sailing around the Horn, so terrible a journey that she vowed never to return to Boston unless she could go by land.

She thought of Pickett and wondered how he would fare in the future, sensed that his confidence diminished in her presence, and wondered whether he was like that with all women.

By his calm handling of the brief confrontation between him and Winfield, she knew that the killer in Pickett could dispatch most men easily. But she wondered about his deference to women, realized his chivalry was genuine, and that it made him exceptionally vulnerable.

She thought of Isaac.

As painful as it was to bring his memory forward, she forced herself to do so. He always had been so willful— predictably running down foolish paths so often but with a fervor that usually won him allies, outworking most and out-wishing everyone else.

In the last few years, she had hated seeing that part of him broken down, the stubbornness persisting so that it was read by others as a weak and brainless perpetuation of his vision. She knew he had never been a prudent man and that his proclivity to put himself directly in the path of danger — usually for the excuse of enterprise, but more likely just because it justified itself — probably had caused his death, as well as contributed to her miscarriage and Jacob's kidnapping.

He had left without saying good-bye and without asking for her help. She was finishing his business again at great expense, and it made her angry.

It was snowing hard now, covering the decks with an inch of frozen blanket, and once the ship had been secured in the inner harbor, it settled quietly into its anchorage, sleeping finally after a long journey.

Emmy looked out from her cabin window onto a moonlit scene that resembled a Christmas painting of a seaside village, much like the ones she had seen in an art exhibit as a child in Boston.

She would be ferried ashore the next morning, and she fretted for the wait she had to endure. Perhaps Jacob had been sighted. Perhaps the British authorities had news or already had even intervened in some way.

She had heard that such a thing had happened before, across the strait on the Haida Queen Charlotte Islands two years before, when a British surveying expedition had made an exchange with one of the Haida clans for two Vancouver children who had been snatched earlier in the year.

Perhaps Jacob was in Fort Simpson already!

She looked at the small town and said a prayer to St. Jude, whom she was told the Catholics considered the patron saint of the impossible.

Two hours later, she was awakened by a loud knock at her door. It was the first mate.

"Come. Captain has something belongs to you."

Emmy followed the mate up to the snow-covered main deck and then aft to the captain's quarters.

Varienko, dull-eyed, obviously awakened from a drunken sleep, and wearing a filthy smock coat and shoe-less, was slouched against the doorway of his cabin, wait-ing for her.

As she came closer, he leered at her, eyeing her up and down in a way that made her reach up and pull her robe tightly across her neck. Then he pushed open his door.

Sarah, covered with soot, pale and anxious, was sitting next to his cabin stove, shivering.

Varienko belched.

"Eet appear da lyetel gyurl want to companyou, Mee-zus Hyevers."

With a terse apology and an offer to reimburse him for the extra passenger, Emmy turned to take Sarah back to her cabin, and as she did so, she noticed Varienko followed both of them with a strange, sly, perusal.

Emmy was furious. She pulled Sarah across the deck and down to her cabin in the aft hold.

"How could you do something like this after I told you how dangerous this could be? How could you?"

Sarah, shivering and exhausted, stared numbly ahead.

Emmy stopped talking, poured water into the small basin on her bed, and proceeded to vigorously start scrubbing Sarah's face of the soot from the coal bin in which she had hidden.

But if embarrassment and anger had overcome Emmy, her fury with Sarah's actions was short lived. In her cabin an hour later, while grooming Sarah's hair from the knots and grime, she heard another knock at her door.

It was Varienko.

He held a bottle and two pewter goblets, and his britches and underpants were off, fully exposing him. He pushed his way into the room.

"Meezus nyeets a dryenk with captain." Then he grabbed both Sarah's and Emmy's wrists and fell forward onto Emmy.

In the screaming, angry struggle that ensued, Sarah wrested herself away. Without a pause, she quickly picked up the flagon he had dropped and struck him with it squarely across his right temple with such force that the bottle broke into several pieces.

He collapsed to the side of Emmy and did not get back up.

Stunned, Emmy pushed herself up and looked at Varienko. Had Sarah killed him?

When Varienko groaned a half-minute later, she sighed in relief, then recovered her wits.

She and Sarah dragged Varienko out to the deck, bolted their door, pulled out the pepperbox, and held each other closely all night, listening to the commotion out-side an hour later as the crew discovered their inebriated, bloodied, and snow-covered captain on the deck.

The next morning, the first mate ferried them across the harbor and deposited them with their belongings onto the wharf. He did not make eye contact with either of them during the entire passage and left them without a word.

Emmy did not register a complaint, fearing retribu-tion. The *Pietrevos*, with its cargo loaded hastily by a crew on double time, was gone by the evening's tide.

Emmy learned quickly that the only lodging available was at a small tavern inn, the Red Pelican, on the west wall of the fort. She had sent word to the fort's commander to query assistance but was told that he and most of his staff were south in Victoria participating in an official recep-tion for Douglas, the territorial governor.

Undeterred, she presented herself to Captain Simon Whitefall, the acting commander, who received her after making her wait for a full day.

Entering his sparse office, she noted that unlike the other soldiers she saw in the fort, he wore neither jacket nor wig. He hadn't bothered to shave for a few days she saw, and, sitting across the table from him, thought she smelled alcohol on his breath. A faded print of Queen Victoria's image was pinned to the wall behind him. She handed him the letter she had received from the Fort's commander, Colonel Pardeen, and repeated the questions she had conveyed upon her arrival at the fort.

"Well, I'm very sorry to disappoint you Madame," Whitefall said, as he inspected the letter.

"In answer to your first question...no, no captives, adult or children have been reported in the past month."

Whitefall showing no sympathy at Emmy's disappointment, continued. "In response to your second question... yes, we know about the Tsimshian Potlatch scheduled up the Skeena River beginning in a few weeks...Ksi Amawaal, the tyee up there, is a well-known neutral, an enterprising fellow, who conducts such events...and this Potlatch is reported to be a significant given that it is a celebration for his son's marriage to a Bella Bella. Might actually reduce tensions a bit in the area for awhile," he smiled wearily.

"And yes, it is likely there will be many slaves bought and sold up there."

Seeing Emmy's interest increase with this response, Whitefall went on. "In response to what you haven't asked yet...the answer is a resounding no...we don't send troops to accompany citizens, especially those that are not subjects of her majesty, into the wilds on 'recovery expeditions,' as you referred to it."

Undeterred, Emmy leaned forward, "Captain, I can compensate the crown quite well for its efforts and expense."

Whitefall handed his commanding officer's letter back to Emmy.

"Madame, I am so sorry you were misguided by my commanding officer's ambiguous response to your recent query. Unfortunately, he is not here now... detained with all of the senior officers in Esquimalt."

He smiled to himself at some secret.

"Confidential business I cannot discuss, I'm afraid. I have only one company to keep the peace up here, in any case."

Emmy persisted, trying another tack. "Captain, I have been told that the *Northerners* likely will be trading slaves at this potlatch."

The mention of the Northerners turned Whitefall, but he recovered, countering, "If the Northerners truly *were* to be sighted up here, of course it would be our obligation to make every effort to bring them to justice, Madame. But I do not have the authority to put my troops or the good people depending on this fort at risk based on rumors."

He stood, walked past her, and opened the door.

"I'm sorry for your losses and the disappointment my response provokes, Madame. But that's life, is it not? You can wait for Colonel Pardeen to return, if you like. But I doubt he will countermand this decision."

He smiled confidently, certain he had made his point. "Please make your passage way back home safely."

Emmy stood, embarrassed by his dismissal.

She addressed Whitefall's mention of "confidential matters."

"Captain, the rumors betray your government's intentions to occupy San Juan Island, which is American territory. You may meet your match, knowing the resolve of your counterpart, Captain Pickett."

She looked at the image of Victoria on the wall.

"That said, I say to you as I said to him, and with all due respect to you ... and to your queen, I will find a way to get to the Tsimshian potlatch. With or without the military's help. Thank you in advance for not interfering with what I intend to accomplish. It's my son, not yours."

Emmy turned and departed, leaving the Brit captain with the same stunned expression she provoked from Pickett.

Returning to the inn, she re-read Pickett's letter of introduction to a potential guide, a native named MaNu-itu'sta. As hesitant as she was to invoke the help of an unknown aborigine, she gave the letter to the innkeeper to be forwarded.

◇◇◇◇

The Red Pelican was a simple establishment, with rudimentary accommodations on the landing above the dining area.

The tavern filled with a rowdy lot by the early evening, and the noise from the customers usually continued well into the night. Emmy and Sarah took most of their meals in their tiny quarters, awaiting the return of the commander in the following week.

Emmy had asked the innkeeper, Edward Edween, a mousy, nosey, but proper enough cockney Brit, to query locals for any news of Northerner raiding parties and captives.

The next day she told Edween to spread the word that a reward would be given for good information leading to Jacob's return. She also conveyed an interest in hiring able men should she need assistance to travel to the Tsimshian winter camp upriver.

On the fourth evening, Edween notified Emmy he had heard some rumors that might be of interest. He suggested she speak directly with the source, a trapper named Rene Marté, who occasionally passed through the region and had come into town to meet the *Pietrevos* with some trading items.

Initially encouraged, Emmy noticed that Edween seemed hesitant.

"You have concerns, Mr. Edween?"

The innkeeper nodded, "Yes, ma'am, I do. These are rough men, and there are stories that Marté hangs with all sorts. And doesn't confine his trade to furs. No, ma'am. That's all I know for sure, but I believe it."

He said that Marté had heard about Emmy's quest and sent word that he would visit the Pelican that evening.

Emmy and Sarah took dinner in the tavern main room that night and, as the pub filled with village locals—a filthy, surly lot—waited for the appearance of Marté.

She noted that Sarah was fascinated with the characters and struck up a conversation with a black robe named Tomas DeSetre, S.J., who had just come from working with the Haida on the Queen Charlottes.

The priest, a Frenchman from Nance with a soft voice and sad, weary eyes, spoke of the great skill and elegant craftsmanship of the Haida people and did not believe any of the aborigines with whom he had lived could ever be responsible for heinous crimes.

"Still, they can be childlike and, as such, quite vengeful in perceived wrongs," he noted.

He gave Emmy and Sarah a blessing and told them he believed that God would watch over them, even in the most extreme of circumstances.

"And may God and the Virgin keep you free from sin, especially near the moment of your death," he said.

Emmy was not pleased with this.

"Father DeSetre, I don't need blessings for which I haven't asked."

Embarrassed, DeSetre apologized quietly and turned back to his meal.

Sarah also introduced herself to a man at another table, a ragtag also dressed in a black robe, who introduced himself as Marano Levi, a converted Jew preaching for the Jesus he had found in his world travels.

He told her he had lived in the region for three years and was convinced that the Haida were one of the lost tribes of Israel. He said he had found several passages in a well-worked Spanish Bible to recite as proof.

He seemed simple and harmless enough to Emmy.

She observed DeSetre watching Levi.

She wondered if the disdain she saw on the Jesuit's face was from frustration at the imitation he perceived, or pity for the man's soul, given that, irrespective of his baptism, he was not Catholic and therefore was likely to spend a good portion of eternity in purgatory.

Levi paid no attention to the priest and ate his small meal with the fervor of a starving man, picking and eating crumbs of bread from his beard. Then he departed immediately into the darkness of the cold night.

She wondered where he slept.

Marté, a small ferret of a man with pock-marked cheeks and a sharp nose that seemed fit for cutting, finally arrived, accompanied by a very tall, cachectic Negro cyclops who called himself Cull.

Marté spoke quickly to Edween, watching the door and stairway during the conversation as if expecting an unpleasant interruption.

Cull, however, immediately picked out Emmy and Sarah from the crowd and kept his one eye fixed on them from a perch he found by the serving bar.

After the quick exchange, Marté made his way over to Emmy and Sarah and sat down without an introduction, his back to the wall, watching the door and stairway, swinging his gaze between each entry point and then back to them.

He looked over both of them as if they were prizes.

◇◇◇◇◇

Sensing a predator, Sarah moved closer to her mother as Marté spoke, yet she was fascinated at the same time with Cull, wondering how he had lost his left eye.

The large rubbery scars that ran across his left brow and into his cheek had to be related to the empty socket, she surmised. She wondered if the meanness on that deformed face had preceded the painful injury, and if so, whether the anguish she perceived in him could ever be relieved.

She wondered if the man had sinned to deserve the injury.

◇◇◇◇◇

Marté addressed Emmy with darting glances while looking at Sarah.

"Madame is interested in a lost boy? Perhaps one that
has been taken from her soon ago? She is interested in
l'échange? So I am told by Edween over there."

Emmy flushed but did not respond. She leaned forward as he spoke.

Sarah, losing interest in Cull, leaned forward also.

By their attention, Marté immediately knew he had
the advantage.

"It is possible to help the bereaved mother. She will
barter, should a possibility exist? Yes?"

He quickly looked at the few wayfarers who still were
in the tavern and then again at the door, then at Cull and
back to Emmy.

"And . . . where is the father?"

He read their faces. Smiled again.

"Condolences. I lost my family in the same way when
I was small like this one," he said, pointing with his chin
at Sarah.

Sarah reached for her mother's hand on the table.

Marté saw this and changed his expression, softening
for a moment.

"I see this is still very painful subject. You will need
some time, yes?"

Then he looked over Emmy and her daughter again
and smiled, showing his canines as he did so.

◇◇◇◇◇

Emmy wondered what he envisioned for them, and observing the way he looked them over, saw a smile that could

not hide the anger in his eyes. She sensed something painful in this little man's past, some horrible unknown thing that made him perceive himself as a victim, rationalize taking perverted pleasures at the expense of others. An opportunistic predator.

She firmed up, seeing he was also surveying her wherewithal and resources. She still did not have the comfort of any official connection with the local British authorities or military and had no knowledge of the area beyond what she had learned from Edween.

"Yes. We have a quest. And yes, I need more time. I am waiting for Colonel Pardeen to return from Vancouver."

She saw Marté's expression change, a slight narrowing of his eyes and another quick look to the door.

"I am told the madame wishes to be guided upriver," he said, glancing at Cull. "It is hard travel now. But we know this country well. The Tsimshian will be in a place called Three Spirits until the spring. You know they will host a potlatch, for the marriage of the tyee Ksi Amawaal's son. It will be very big. We will go because some of the gifts will become trade items for sale."

He watched for Emmy's reaction. Reading none, he went on, attempting to lure her in.

"Many tribes will come. Many stories." His eyes narrowed into two slits. "There may be things of interest for you there, I am feeling . . . the madame may come with us, yes?"

Emmy listened and confirmed in his expression a deep danger. She had enough information.

"I will wait for the colonel."

Marté smiled and rose, sensing she was attempting to throw him off her intentions.

"Madame may lose her one chance. The potlatch is in a fortnight. The river may be frozen, and it is a good long journey even in the summer."

He looked over Emmy and then at Sarah, then smiled again at some private thought.

"*Bonsoir*, madame." He left.

As he and Cull departed, Emmy saw DeSetre in the corner watching her.

He shook his head and continued reading his missal.

CHAPTER TWENTY-SIX

◇◇◇◇◇

MaNuitu'sta

I t took five days for the message to reach him, but he departed immediately to meet Emmy and Sarah. MaNuitu'sta, also known simply as "Patient River," was a tyee of the Nuxalk Bella Coola Valley clan, who, like many of the tribes along the coast, had been subjected to a swindle attempt by the Brit territorial government.

Unlike most of the other leaders, however, he had not signed the treaty, and thus, he had retained his stature among tribes in the region.

But it did not matter, because the whites had come anyway, swarming in from the depleted gold fields in San Francisco to make another attempt at riches in gold and coal. The resulting land disputes and differences mediated by the territorial government invariably resulted in judgments in favor of the settlers.

Even then, MaNuitu'sta had always counseled that a careful, quiet negotiation with any enemy, either the British or other tribes, brought his people better results than did angry confrontation.

That moderation came as a result of learning about others and noting that a gentler approach, mastering the paths but staying out of the way of raging, intemperate actions, always seemed to win in the long life of a survivor.

The Brits were here to stay, he reasoned, so it was smarter to preserve relationships and keep enemies at an observable distance rather than provoke and then justify hostile maneuvers. Early in his life, after observing the communication abilities of some of the pioneer black-robe missionaries, he realized the value of assimilating languages and became conversant with all the dialects along the coast.

He learned English, as well as some Russian and Spanish, and applied them to protect and enrich his clan.

Of all the tyees who had participated in the signing ceremonies, he alone had realized the discrepancies between what was being read aloud and what Antoine Bill, the Brit's hired Metís interpreter, had conveyed to the assembled tyees.

He already had a suspicion of Antoine Bill because of the Suquamish's guidance of a large contingent of bounty hunters out of Vancouver two years before that had resulted in wanton killing during a brutal takeover of Nisqually lands by coal-mining settlers. But not really knowing the details of that business, MaNuitu'sta had suspended judgment.

Antoine Bill's dishonest actions during the signing ceremonies had confirmed his concerns, and he withdrew from the agreement, after unsuccessfully attempting to convince other tyees about the British deception.

The Brit gifts of blankets and copper and iron utensils were enough to persuade the other elders to ignore him, with some reasoning out loud that they could always take back what they had given. A few hollered him down, embarrassing him. So he simply withdrew from the discussions.

Despite that, however, he watched the ceremony, learning from it just how foolish his compatriots were.

Remaining in that encampment resulted in another event, when his youngest daughter became entranced with an American soldier, Captain George Pickett. MaNuitu 'sta had allowed his third daughter, Morning Mist, to be courted by the American, whom they all called "Pickett George."

He had carefully observed Pickett and concluded, by his polite and respectful demeanor, that he was not like the others. He also knew that Morning Mist would never be dissuaded, as stubborn as she tended to be, so he simply consented.

He also presciently understood how rapidly the ways were changing, and also that Morning Mist likely would fare better in a community of whites protected by a white tyee.

Pickett George had proven to be reliable and fair, and he regularly sent supplies up to MaNuitu'sta's clan. He also had travelled up north to personally deliver to MaNu-itu'sta the news of Morning Mist's death.

Thus, when a message arrived with Pickett's markings asking the Bella Coola to help a woman stranger, MaNui-tu'sta did not hesitate. He was old now and needed warmth in this time of his life, so he brought one of his sons, Napen 'tjo, his youngest and brightest, to act as a guide if that became necessary.

His people, the Nuxalk Bella Coola, being more of an inland clan, had worked the rivers to the interior of the region as their transportation pathways and, because they were superb hunters and trappers, were intimately famil-iar with the lands as far north as the Stikene River. As a result, they became indispensable companions for many of the trappers who supplied the Hudson's Bay Company with furs.

Over the years, they had escaped much of the inter-necine predation that beset peoples who lived on coastal shores. Yet, they, too, knew about Anah and other terrors from the north.

Although the Russians and many other northern raid-ing tribes, decimated by a series of diseases, had not waged war for over a decade, Anah had kept the fear of sudden invasions fresh enough.

MaNuit'sta was well known and was held in high regard throughout the region by whites as well as aborigines.

But he was not allowed to enter the fort.

So, Emmy, escorted by Edween and two soldiers dis-patched by the officer of the day, travelled out to meet him on a clear, flat river beach a few hundred yards beyond the front gate.

"Why did they make him wait outside the fort?" Emmy asked Edween, while walking towards the old tyee.

"Well, 'es a heathen, after all," said the innkeeper, who did not notice Emmy and Sarah's reaction to that statement. "But 'e came as soon as he received yer message, e' did. Long trek for the old man in this weather, but I'm thinkin' it was because his daughter was the wife of Pickett George, who wrote the note I delivered for you, Mu'm."

Emmy, irritated realizing that Edween must have opened the letter she had asked him to deliver, responded

"Pickett George? You mean Captain George Pickett?"

"That's what the Bella Coola call 'im."

"His wife?"

"Yes'm. Before she up and died, she did."

Emmy did not say anything more as they neared the waiting chieftain.

As he waited, watching the white party approach, MaNuitu 'sta wondered what would compel Pickett George to make such a request. He had not asked for favors in the past. However, when he saw this Emmy, he understood—it was in her posture and in the intensity of her eyes, a way of looking that reminded him of Morning Mist—that Pickett George likely loved her and wanted to see her protected. That, he knew immediately, he could not guarantee, because from Pickett George's letter, he learned she was asking to go into the dark mouth of death.

He watched the party approach, and when Emmy was ten yards away and had lifted her right hand, he extended his in the French manner and gently touched the top of her fingers, sensing, as he intended, that Emmy immediately felt a calming reassurance.

He saw the young girl with her watching him and his son, Napen 'tjo, closely. She was a younger version of Emmy and had the same demeanor, although less reserved, but seemed just as determined as her mother.

"Pickett George is a good friend, so I came," he said to Emmy.

"Thank you," Emmy said. Then after a pause, continued, "The captain told me I could rely on your help and that of the Bella Coola. You have heard of the tragedy that has befallen my family?"

The sadness in his eyes told her he had heard and that he had empathy for her plight.

"I need to get upriver before it freezes over, up to the Tsimshian trading winter camp, where I am told there will be a big potlatch. I believe there may be a chance to find my son there before he is traded or given as a gift. That is what I am told," said Emmy.

MaNuitu 'sta nodded and then sighed. He knew about the potlatch because word of it had spread all throughout the Tsimshian and Bella Coola regions. It would be a big event because Ksi Amawaal was very wealthy and had much pride. It might go on for ten days. He expected that several different peoples of the Qualicum, Bella Bella, Bella Coola and possibly even the Kwakiutl had been sent Tsimshian message sticks and would find their way there as a welcome break from the winter's tedium.

The gossip from the ceremonies and feasts was as important as the gifts that would be given out to guests by the wealthy tyee Ksi Amawaal. He understood that many slaves likely would be present, and many would be exchanged.

Were she to be so foolish as to make this journey, Emmy's appearance would need to be brief, if at all. He knew that Ksi Amawaal, a shrewd and careful negotiator who had grown fat on trading with the Bostons and Brits, would extend a mantle of protection to her while she was in his winter camp.

But the presence of an unattached white woman, no matter how well protected, would disquiet the festivities and put all the peoples into a state of curiosity and agitation. And if any of the Northerners were to show up in the neutral encampment, he could not predict their actions.

He tried to dissuade Emmy.

She persisted.

"I will find a way to get there," she said finally.

He knew he had no choice in the matter.

"Napen 'tjo, my son, will guide you."

He saw Emmy look at the young man with some concern.

"He is a good young man and has travelled with me."

He had his own concerns, but not because he doubted his son's abilities.

"In return, I will ask a favor from you" he said to Emmy. " . . . that you teach him to read from this book."

It was an English primer.

CHAPTER TWENTY-SEVEN

◇◇◇◇

Napen 'tjo

His sisters and playmates called him Jojo, and he preferred that.

He was born during the confused loud moments immediately after a fierce thunderstorm had torn the roof off their long house. In the discomfited hollering of all the clan members who were trying to secure shelter during the downpour, his cries stood out, and, because they sounded like shrill laughter, his brothers and mother also called him "Blue Jay."

Although his mischievous and sometimes loud antics seemed to confirm that handle, he was intelligent and sensitive, and as he grew, he learned to adapt to situations with a discerning alacrity, repressing his innate impulse to play and jest. For he had witnessed grief.

Early on he discerned the pain that came to his family and village from the bloody disputes that sometimes erupted between clans and peoples, and, observing his father's calmer demeanor, he came to appreciate quieter solutions to disagreement rather than carrying out vendettas.

Like his father, Jojo also had a keen ear for languages and could converse in many coastal dialects. But he had never learned to read the written words of any of the white languages, and thus, as competent as he knew he was in the world, he felt incomplete and disadvantaged.

It was his request — that he be taught to read — that MaNuitu 'sta had conveyed to Emmy. As dangerous as he knew the journey with Emmy was likely to be, it was a fair exchange. By the time the journey was over, he intended to be able to read aloud the entire primary school book to his father and family.

By carrying and reading such little books, which he had been told contained the wisdom of many men, Jojo was convinced he could do anything, even sail a mighty Brit ship to the lands beyond his tribal shores.

As a little boy, Jojo had learned to imitate by watching and listening closely. When elders spoke in important gatherings, he always found a way to bring himself within hearing distance of the conversation, and afterwards he delighted his sisters and brothers by repeating phrases by the various leaders with an exacting nuance and inflection.

As he grew older, he learned what the words meant and understood the significance of phrases, he found ways to repeat sentences out of context, frequently with hilarious applications. Thus his playmates always sought him out and begged to hear his running, imaginary dialogues between disparately motivated participants such as naïve British missionaries attempting to convert oversexed Kwakiutl squaws, or between starving hapless French trappers negotiating for dog meat with Tsimshian, who always were fat from the success of their fall hunting.

Because he was always discreet with his humor, this banter was tolerated by the adults. And when he was twelve, in his father's absence, after he successfully translated a negotiation between Russian fur traders and his tribe, the tribe's elders truly came to appreciate his gifts.

Over time, he was given more tasks. His confidence grew, as did his curiosity and enthusiasm for newness.

Jojo wanted to see the world because, he knew, it was a wonder of delight.

They were to set out in the early morning of January 20th, three days after Emmy received word that the colonel and the rest of his senior officers would not return to Fort Simpson for yet another fortnight.

Jojo agreed with MaNuitu 'sta that the potlatch could likely be over if they waited for Colonel Pardeen to return and again attempt to secure military assistance, so Emmy decided she could delay no longer. Whitefall again refused to offer any contingent to accompany Emmy and vigorously argued for her to stay, assuring her there would be no rescue should she persist in her hard-headedness.

She sent out word to acquire the services of another packer-guide and quickly arranged with Edween to outfit three sturdy canoes, one for provisions and the trading goods and two to transport her small company.

She told Jojo she would bring Sarah, as well, because she knew she could not convince her daughter to stay behind, and Emmy sensed there was as much danger leaving Sarah behind in Fort Simpson as there would be to bring her along. There were very few women at the fort, and none appeared reputable, in her estimate. And René Marté's behavior had frightened her. How many other men were like him up here? She wondered.

Jojo argued vehemently against this, noting that the girl would be a serious encumbrance and an additional temptation for slavers should they encounter them.

But Emmy, thinking of Marté's leer, refused to reconsider.

The evening before they were to depart, Edween brought her three men who came forward to apply for the expedition.

"I'm sorry Ma'm," Edween said apologetically, "...sent out the word a few days ago, just like you asked. Only three souls responded to the job offer, as generous as it was. Yes'm. It's just too cold out there now and no one wants to go up into Tsimshian territory, no matter. They value their hides too much, they do."

Edween looked at Jojo for affirmation. "Not the Tsimshian, exactly. It's well...sometimes these potlatches get a bit carried away, and all."

Emmy did not seem deterred by the innkeeper's comments.

Edween went on. "First one, e's a handy one. Not much woods experience but he says he needs the money. Second one's pretty experienced on expeditions and such. He's my bet. Third one knows the woods pretty well too, and he's known by the natives 'cause he's traveled into their territory. But," he paused, smirking at Jojo, "well, you'll see."

In the near vacant tavern mess hall, Jojo and Edween watched Emmy assess the first man, a huge slovenly lout with a protuberant, hanging belly. He professed he was skilled as a carpenter.

"You, sir, are dismissed," she said quietly to the man, without hesitation after speaking with him for only a few minutes.

The second man said he had some experience as a guide, but Emmy noted that he carried the external characteristics of a chronic alcoholic—a flushed red face, withered limbs, firm protuberant belly, and a constant fine tremor.

"You, sir, are dismissed," Emmy said, again politely but firmly after a few minutes of conversation.

The third volunteer for hire was Marano Levi, the disheveled man she had seen a few nights previously, still wearing a torn black cassock, under a tattered fur coat that had been sewn together with the pelts of different animals.

"You, sir...do you know the Tsimshian people?" She asked. "Can you speak Chinook?"

"*Si, señora*," Levi said, eyeing Jojo and Edween as he responded. "I have baptized a few of the people up there. Yes, I can speak Chinook."

Levi then professed he knew the region well, having travelled it in his quest to spread the Word of the Savior. And he had survived living alone in the wilderness for six years.

"Very well," Emmy said, looking over the man carefully. "Please show me your hands."

Levi stepped forward and, again looking for Jojo and Edween's reaction, put his hands into Emmy's. She looked up into his eyes.

"You, *señor*, are hired. You may leave now." Emmy said.

Levi, stunned by her decision, nodded and backed his way out of the door.

"Mrs. Evers...the woodsman..." said Edween.

"We should wait for more volunteers to show up," Jojo protested.

"You know we don't have time to wait, Jojo," Emmy said emphatically. Turning to the innkeeper, her voice was commanding: "Mr. Edween, that carpenter you provided has no woods experience and would eat all of his rations in the first day, and then likely will start on ours."

Edween, embarrassed by Emmy's conclusion, nodded numbly.

"The second man, your 'woodsman,' Emmy continued, "is an obvious alcoholic. I have no desire to attend to a man's rum fits."

Looking now at both Jojo and Edween, she said firmly, "The third, this Marano Levi, who dresses like a priest, but you say is not ordained, has honest hands and an honest face."

"Mrs. Evers — " Jojo protested again.

"I've made up my mind, Jojo," Emmy said. "Mr. Edween, please inform Mr. Levi that we leave before sun up."

"I'll do me best, Mu'um," the innkeeper said. "Nobody knows where he sleeps."

Overhearing this, Sarah looked out the window. It was snowing again.

Jojo was disturbed by Emmy's decision, despite understanding that Levi was likely the best of a weak lot, and
despite the need for an extra set of hands to help them
paddle the canoes. Jojo believed his own job had just been
made all the more difficult by her stubborn decision. Levi
was known throughout the region and was left alone by all
the tribes, for he was a touched man.

⟨⟨⟨⟨

It was raining lightly the next morning, and the snow from
the previous week had turned into a slushy nuisance that
made their transport of supplies to the canoes on the river
below slow. Some morning light silhouetted them as they
pushed off. That concerned Jojo, who had wanted their
departure to go unobserved.

He knew that gossip might betray the small size of
their party, unaccompanied as it was by any soldiers. And
they had to make time. On a spring or summer day, the
journey would take a week and a half at most, but in the
winter it could take three times as long if the river was
frozen anywhere along its length leading to the tributary
forks that defined Three Spirits.

In his winter travels along the rivers in that long winding valley, Jojo had found ice obstructing canoe passage
only twice, and the plateau where the Tsimshian encamped
during the winter was seldom, if ever, snowbound. But he
knew that if it was, it would be disastrous for their quest,
and not just because of the dangers of the cold.

Survival in a winter shelter would not be a problem,
nor would the winter starvation that killed many travelers
trapped by blizzards. They could forage easily. The deep

rivers forming and emanating from Three Spirits were bountiful with edible life, and the winter cold made it less likely for them to encounter wolves, bear, or cougar, although he had seen plenty during this time of the year in the past.

It was being late for the potlatch that would hurt them.

The first two days bode well for their passage. Jojo was pleased and told Emmy that if they made as much progress, taking them past the big gorges forty miles upstream without encountering snow, they would likely arrive a few days before the potlatch. That would give them the opportunity to meet with Ksi Amawaal and possibly have the shrewd tyee himself do the negotiating on their behalf, without the slavers knowing who was really doing the asking.

While making camp on the third day, Jojo pulled Emmy aside. "If your son is with other slaves . . . if the Northerners show up to do trading and he is with them . . . it is best that you not be seen. Because that will show them the value of your son. They may not know his family is looking for him." He saw Emmy consider her alternatives.

"I may have already betrayed the secrecy you wanted, Jojo," she told him. "I asked the innkeeper to spread the word about this search. For all I know, he might have told listeners that it was being commissioned by a naive white woman carrying a sizeable reward."

Jojo nodded quietly, troubled at this news.

"Will this Tsimshian tyee take advantage of us?" Emmy asked, breaking the silence.

"Ksi Amawaal is honest, but he is also very clever, Mrs. Evers. I have watched him trade with the Brits and with trappers. He is known for always winning."

"Will he help us?"

"He will understand the value your son brings right away. If we ask him to do so, he will take the chests you bring and all the gold you carry, consider its value, and will offer half of it to the Northerners for all their slaves, making them think he wants to give the slaves as gifts to his family and guests during the potlatch."

"I don't really care if he offers all of it to them," Emmy said.

Jojo shook his head. "The slavers may be insulted at the offer because they know the slaves are *very* valuable, but they will not fight with anyone while they are there. Ksi Amawaal will argue loudly for his position, but I have seen him do this with others—it will be a bluff." He laughed.

"It will be his game," Jojo continued, "and he likes to play like this. After he calms the Northerners down, he will make them another offer, and then, to show off his wealth to all the guests and visitors during the potlatch, he will reduce what he asks for the same amount he offered. You will get your son. He will get half the gold. Everyone will see him to be a wealthy and generous tyee, and the slavers will go away thinking they have outsmarted him— but only if they do *not* know he is acting as a trader on your behalf."

He saw Emmy pondering and then brighten a bit over what he predicted would happen.

Then, as if to dampen the brief glimmer of hope he sensed he had given her, with a solemn, sad expression, Jojo said, "But, if they discover us before we reach the Three Spirits, if they know you are there—carrying gold—the

Northerners will come after us, kill me, and take you and your daughter as slaves. If they do not kill you, too."

Jojo watched Emmy's reaction to his words. She was quietly nodding, looking up at the darkening sky, and by that, he saw Emmy understood that this would be much more complicated than she had expected.

CHAPTER TWENTY-EIGHT

<><><><>

Anah

Anah had given Little Raven the footstool he knew he deserved. Word had come from the south that he had indeed delivered the right and vengeful coup by taking the head of a grand tyee. He had also captured the tyee's only son. Still not understanding the ultimate value of this child, he thus held back on what he might have otherwise done to any other white captive.

There were other reasons for Anah's restraint.

Three days after his canoes reached the Campbell, a small three-masted ship flying a Portuguese flag anchored in the tight harbor off the river.

On the shore of the rocky beach, Anah and Klixuatan displayed their ware - thirteen bedraggled female and four male captives, all taken in Northerner raids up and down the Vancouver coast and Puget Sound straits against native and settler encampments over the previous five months.

Four armed Europeans landed in the first boat while the sailors in a second boat kept off shore, far enough out of reach of the Haida, that the trading goods in it would safe. On the beach, the ship's mate, a tall, thin, swarthy man, conducted the Portuguese bartering with the help of an old Tlingit translator.

"Has he ruined all of these, as he did with the batch we purchased two years ago?" the mate asked the translator, while inspecting each of the women, lifting up their skirts as he did so.

"He wants to know if Anah has made any of these ones pregnant," the translator said in Haida to Klixuatan and Anah.

Klixuatan glanced at Anah.

Anah smirked.

The mate didn't wait for an answer but pointed to six of the young women, the prettiest ones, two of whom were white, two black, and two natives, then nodded for his mate to hand a small bag of gold coins over to Klixuatan. He then motioned for the skiff holding off shore to land and unload its goods - a small cannon, several leather bags of grape shot, and a dozen barrels of powder.

Referring the seven women and the four men not chosen, he laughed, "He can keep these ones and try to pedal them at the Tsimshian potlatch at Three Spirits."

Then he noticed Jacob.

Jacob, a collar around his neck, was tethered next to the Haida long boat by a chain.

Walking over to long boat, the mate leered, looking Jacob up and down.

"And what about this little one?" he asked the translator.

Jacob withdrew a step as the mate attempted to touch him on the thigh. When the mate persisted, this time attempting to fondle him, Jacob gasped.

Then suddenly Jacob recovered and rushed the surprised mate.

"Leave me alone!" Jacob screamed, biting the man on the hand, then doubling him over with a kick in the groin.

Klixuatan, laughing as the embarrassed mate picked himself up, pointed to two of the Haida warriors who had bandages on their hands.

"This little wolverine is the son of a powerful white tyee," he said to the translator. "Worth much more than your Portuguese can pay."

"They call him Little Wolverine," the translator told the mate, who was still recovering from the blow. The mate had started to reach for his knife, but withdrew it when he saw Anah's warning expression.

"A fresh one, eh?" the mate said to the translator, when he finally righted himself from the blow. "I'd take the little son of a bitch off their hands. I'd break him good."

"My father will come and kill you!" Jacob yelled.

Anah and Klixuatan exchanged a look, smiling.

"Not for sale," Klixuatan said.

While watching the Portuguese slavers rowing back to the ship with their new possessions, the shaman said to Anah, "You must harness the little wolverine's rage, Anah. It is powerful."

Anah did not disagree. From the time he had defeated Isaac, the big tyee, and looked into his dying eyes, Anah knew he had killed one with a special magic who had bestowed a curse onto him. Fascinated in a way he did not understand, he now knew he needed to watch Jacob to see if he had the same power as had the tyee, his father.

CHAPTER TWENTY-NINE

<><><><>

Anah and Jacob

On the fourth night in safe harbor, Anah brought Isaac's decaying head into the tent where Klix-uatan's wife kept Jacob drugged and bound. He compared the blackening face of the trophy to Jacob's sleeping visage. He returned the next night as well, again bringing the head right next to the boy's face. And it was there—the same sweep of the brow and deep-set eyes, the determined jutting jaw, strangely similar between the gri-macing movements of a child in his drugged dreams and the now exaggerated, stretched features on the trophy.

The smell from the head was becoming putrid, and he would have to skin the face and scalp off soon, then tan it quickly if he were to keep it from rotting. There would be some value to that skin, he thought. Perhaps he could seize some of the tyee's power with it.

In the cold three weeks from the time they landed by the Campbell and then moved farther north to the inland side of the channel, as Klixuatan had advised, Anah observed Jacob as often as he could. There was something about the boy.

Anah could not comprehend what it was, but it was related to the curse, he was certain. And thus while watching, sedentary during the healing of the deep chest wound from the death struggle with the boy's father, Anah began to think of his own early childhood, a period of his life that remained confusing to him.

He had always been ashamed that he had been unable to grow up fast enough to protect his family, and yet, he missed the happier times when he was a child, when the colors were softer. The pervasive, seething anger he felt from the time he lost his sisters had evaporated his childhood, like the way the bitter fog of a sudden cold Southerly immediately smothered a spring's early morning sun.

Early on, before most men, Anah had become an adult, with all his adult appetites at once accelerated and intensified, but with none of the wisdom or temperance necessary that would allow him to live safely with other men.

Despite adherence to a strict warrior's discipline, taught over the years by the harsh lessons of Little Raven, Anah had never learned civil restraint because Little Raven and Klixuatan encouraged him to indulge all his passions, believing that would promote the reinvigoration of their clan.

As Anah watched Jacob, he wondered whether this boy might grow up quickly as he had, driven by a desperate need for survival and vengeance. Was this boy a replica of himself? Was this somehow part of the curse?

On the fifteenth day of Jacob's captivity, he ordered Klixuatan gradually to begin reducing the drugs. He told the shaman to untether Jacob two days later and, with Klixuatan, watched to see if the boy would flee.

He did not.

Still, Anah and Klixuatan continued watching the boy, unsettled, for Anah had observed what Klixuatan had seen. He understood that Jacob had a smoldering fire in him, which the shaman told him was likely ready to burst forth if left uncontained.

In the hours after his capture, the boy had fought so vigorously that Klixuatan had had to strike him repeatedly and then bind him tightly to try to stop him from provoking retribution from others. All of the men now referred to him as "Little Wolverine" because of the painful bites and scratches Jacob had given them.

One warrior's deep bite marks from Jacob had festered, despite the poultices the shaman had applied. Drugging Jacob was the only thing that had worked to keep the boy down.

Klixuatan, for his part, would have killed any other child with such venom. But he knew about the curse the five year old's father had made on Anah. Killing the boy would only make it worse.

They had to contain his spirit.

◇◇◇◇◇

Jacob was watching *them*, also.

As his delirium dispersed and his exhaustion diminished, he began to understand his dilemma. And then, after looking without success for the other boy he had seen in the tent on the journey up the sound, he realized he now was the lone white in the encampment.

He became aware of the difference between those who were enslaved and those who had the freedom to move about freely. But the difference was more than the tethers; it was the depressed countenances and fearful actions that distinguished the captives when they were spoken to by others. And they never fought back when pushed or shoved.

On one of the few times he saw any resistance from one of the slaves—a heavily tattooed young native woman who looked the same age as his Aunt Corrie—he saw her receive a severe beating that left her in a bloodied mess. After the beating, the old crone, Klixuatan's woman, who had been in the boat with him, went to her and helped her up, berating the woman while she administered water and covered her with a blanket.

When the slave pushed Klixuatan's woman away and angrily spit out several bloody teeth at her, he saw the shaman stand and quietly walk over, pull the hapless captive's head back by the hair, and cut her nose off right down to the flat of her face.

After witnessing that, Jacob kept quiet.

And he watched.

In the night, shivering in the tent under a lean-to that looked like it had been present for many seasons, he thought back over the events that had brought him here, a dark passage, and he was alone. With each breath, his ribs hurt from the kicks he had received from one of the men he had bitten. He held himself from coughing to avoid the stabbing pains beneath a deep black bruise on his right side. For two days after that beating, his pee was dark brown.

Despite all that he had seen, Jacob told himself he was not afraid.

At first, he tried not to look at the line of rotting heads impaled on tall poles surrounding the encampment, placed there, he realized, to protect the tribe from enemies and keep its slaves trapped inside. But after a few days, he was able to look up at the totems. And on the fourth day, he forced himself to consider the features of the spiked head closest to his tent.

It was covered with flies and maggots, and much of the skin and deeper flesh had been eaten away, exposing all the teeth on the left side of the face. The hair was a silky black and straight, short enough that it must have been a man's head.

From his tent, he stared at it for a long time.

The next day, he walked up to each of the other heads, ten in all, and studied each of them, each one in a different state of decomposition. All were males, but he could not tell their ages or their races, except for the three that had beards, the heads of white settlers most likely.

The head he thought he had seen when they had first landed—the one that looked like his father's—was not among them. It had to have been a dream. His father was too strong and great a fighter to have succumbed, he tried to reassure himself.

Jacob watched and knew he was being watched by everyone in the camp.

He saw that the big warrior who had the chest bandage had to be their tyee, for when that man spoke or gestured, everyone turned to him, some stooped, and a few cowered.

Jacob felt contempt for them. He wasn't going to be afraid of that man.

And every night he reached into his pocket and felt for the reassurance of the small collection of treasures that had been there the day he was captured. He pulled them out when he was sure he was alone, reexamining them one by one: a piece of sand-polished blue glass from the beach near his home, the beak of a downed eagle he had found one day while walking with Sarah, a lead musket ball his father had given him while molding bullets, and a small ball of multicolored twine with a hundred knots tying the bits and pieces together.

That reoriented him, and with that nightly exercise, he found the courage to resist.

He was not going to be afraid of that man.

He was not going to be afraid of the old woman or the old man either. Or any of them.

He knew he could escape when the right moment came. And if any of them had hurt his father or any of his family—the flush and anger built up and made him breathe so fast that he got dizzy—he would kill them.

"I will kill them," he told himself repeatedly.

◇◇◇◇◇

Four days later, a southern Kwakiutl trading party canoed into the encampment. Little Raven had always been careful to keep raids away from these particular Kwakiutl villages—a prudent decision because more than once the Kwakiutl had given him important information as well as valuable outlets for trade.

After exchanging lead, powder, and sugar, the traders told Anah details about the upcoming off-season Tsimshian potlatch up the Skeena River. Ksi Amawaal, a wealthy and powerful tyee, had extended a generous and broad invitation, sending message sticks to surrounding tribes, the Kwakiutil told him. They also told him that the family of a white tyee from the south was seeking a kidnapped child and was asking questions at the British fort.

Anah wondered whether the child being sought was the white boy in his camp.

Anah knew the danger inherent in making a long trip upriver, but enough trading would occur in that gathering that he could exchange slaves for many things. Still, he would have to be careful to disguise himself as Kwakiutl or Skidegate.

It would be unlikely that he would be recognized, in any case, because, even as far flung as his reputation as "Black Wind" had become, almost all his predation against other tribes had been against coastal, rather than inland villages. And he had seldom left witnesses alive to identify him.

He also understood that enslaved humans were commodities that had never lost their value, and he had many to trade. Even after the Brits and French had stopped directly authorizing any form of slavery by their citizenry, they ignored the practice of slave trading by non-whites in the region, thus condoning its continued use as a currency.

He exchanged three muskets for the message stick bearing the invitation that had been sent to the Kwakiutl.

He would make this trip up into the Tsimshian country, Anah decided. Come spring, when he could again rendezvous with intermediaries like Marté and Cull, who had a convenient connection to ocean-bound buyers like the Portuguese and Russians, a raid into the south Puget Sound waters again would bring him enough women to buy another cannon.

He would make this trip. And he would bring his slaves with him, including the Little Wolverine boy, if he could keep him contained. And he would study the boy to take his power.

CHAPTER THIRTY

◇◇◇◇

Emmy

Emmy was not afraid of the cold. Each winter, passed over the years under the dull and sulking skies of the Oregon territory, had presented to her new problems that she had to bridle quickly. She knew that if she did not prepare properly, the deterioration of everything touched by the withering, relentless rain would deplete her strength and ultimately run her down and over. She had watched others succumb.

But she repeatedly had succeeded in besting the challenges of the elements, had endured because she held to hope and purpose — and that process had hardened her to the perennial coming of the cold, personified in her mind as a wretched and angry misanthropist. And when she reemerged into its presence, when its piercing, aching grasp reintroduced itself to her fingers and nose and cut to her core, she was prepared to defiantly withstand and survive.

And on the cold came that week, seven days into their trek east, first with a flurry of pea-sized hail that started in the early afternoon, followed by a torrent of freezing rain that lasted all night. The rain turned to snow by morning, stuck quickly, and within a few hours was five inches deep.

Emmy listened with considerable anxiety to Jojo's recommendation that they prepare to wait. She did not want to lose time. She needed to find Jacob. She knew he would be there. She turned to Marano Levi.

"Marano, you said the weather is usually milder in the valley of the Three Spirits."

Levi, who had said little during the trip thus far, nodded warily, as he watched for Jojo's reaction to his opinion.

"*Si, señora*. The valley is protected by the mountains that surround it. We could keep traveling."

Jojo scoffed, angrily shaking his head at Levi's recommendation. "That is too dangerous, Missus Evers! If the weather stops us, it will do the same to others who are coming east," Jojo reasoned, staring down Levi as he did so. "We have to stay here at least until the snow stops. If it doesn't get cold again, then we can go on."

Emmy waited for Levi to counter Jojo's recommendation. But Levi said no more.

Emmy nodded, grimly accepting Jojo's argument, looking at the gray horizon, hoping for a change in the weather.

But the snow continued for another day, and then a cold hard freeze set in. Ice began to form on the river below their camp. So they stayed put, going through half of their provisions in the next week.

◇◇◇◇◇

On the second day, Jojo, anticipating a long and boring wait, brought the primer to Emmy for his first lesson.

He opened the book and pointed to the pictures of common objects with their titles on the first few pages. "Raven?" he asked.

Emmy shook her head. "No. Bird," she said, pointing to the word.

"Noburd," Jojo repeated.

Emmy shook her head again.

"Bu-ir-da."

Jojo nodded and repeated, "Buirda."

Emmy smiled and nodded. "Bird!"

Jojo repeated the word with the exact emphatic affirmative intonation. And then Emmy knew that Jojo was a perfect mimic.

Within a few hours, Jojo had mastered five pages of pictures and script.

◇◇◇◇◇

Every night and into the bitter mornings that week, Emmy dreamed.

One night she found herself in bed waiting for someone, a man, to come through her door, and she knew it wasn't Isaac. She waited, felt herself holding her breath, for whomever he was to be bold enough to push his way in. The dream, and the arousal it provoked, continued until she awoke to the first light. She ran outside and buried her face in the snow to calm herself before Sarah awakened.

On two nights, she dreamt she was following a spirit who looked like a version of her first husband, John Tern, Sarah's father, a hard-pressing, driven man, who had changed from charming to angry within a few months after arriving in Olympia.

"Why did you marry the man who was Sarah's father?" Jojo had asked the night before, as they huddled around the small campfire.

The question surprised Emmy. She was quiet for a few minutes, thinking about events that had occurred so very long ago, it seemed.

"He was a big dreamer, Jojo. A story teller. Painted bold pictures about this land. Ambitious, like Isaac, Jacob's father. I believed him. So did my family. I was sixteen when I married him."

She paused again, looking to be certain Sarah was asleep.

"He turned violent after we moved out here. Not so much on me, but on others. I hoped that Sarah's birth would soften him. Didn't."

She stopped talking, listening as two coyotes howled a duet far off in the distance.

Staring out at the dark river running below, Emmy thought about those days. She was fifteen when Tern had come into town to raise money for a speculative enterprise, far from civilization, out in the far Northwest—one that would bring huge fortunes to the down-in-their-luck Boston Brownstone patrimony, most of whom believed in getting something for nothing.

Tern told of an enterprise involving San Francisco provisions in exchange for Northwest gold, furs, and lumber.

He had painted a grand vision, and she had been swept away by the romance of living in a foreign, savage land.

He had fooled Emmy all the way, and yet she stayed with him, even as they became more estranged.

She thought about her mother's advice—to marry someone much older, preferably a man who was beyond roaming eyes. She was twenty-five years younger than him.

In a short time, as Tern's temper worsened, she experienced a growing, despairing loneliness much stronger than the frustrated solitude that had driven her into his arms in the first place.

By her pregnancy with his child, she had faintly hoped for a softening.

It did not come.

And then he was dead — taken by the whiplash of a falling tree on a very muggy morning when, as it turned out, all she could think about was how mistaken she had been to marry that man, and how much more foolish it was to be continuing in that relationship.

But she had felt no guilt. It just was Providence's answer to unasked prayers.

"I don't know why I married him," she told Jojo.

Jojo waited, thinking about her response. He looked at the sturdy white woman, wondering why she married again if she had been so unhappy.

"Why did you marry Jacob's father?

Emmy paused again, then continued, "Because I loved him. That is something I am trying to understand now that he is gone...why it doesn't hurt more. But as we lived through our time together . . . ."

She looked up and saw that Sarah was now awake and listening.

Emmy shook her head. She had said enough of her private thoughts to this young man whom she believed would never understand.

In the pause, the fire crackled as the moist wood it burned steamed and popped.

Emmy turned the inquiry on Jojo.

"Tell me about Captain Pickett. And your sister."

Jojo seemed to blush, Emmy noted as she watched him in the fire's light.

"Morning Mist was beautiful. Like you and your daughter. She was fifteen, like you say you were when you moved away from the Boston-man land. Maybe she wanted to get away, see new things. Like you did."

Emmy saw that Sarah was leaning forward now, as Jojo continued.

"She came home one time with him when she was with child."

Jojo paused, looking out into the darkness. "I never saw her again."

Sarah looked at Jojo, who was now quiet.

"What was she like?" she asked.

"We played when we were young. She knew how to do things, climb a big tree and catch a small bird on the perch, just for a moment, and let it fly again. She taught me to do that. I made her laugh, and she made me want to make her laugh because it was... such a pretty laugh. She loved Pickett George very much."

"Did Pickett George love her?" Sarah asked.

Jojo glanced at Emmy and saw her leaning forward now.

"Yes." He looked away, glancing again at Emmy as he did so.

◇◇◇◇

That night Emmy dreamed of riding on a horse next to George Pickett. They were going someplace important. Inspecting. He wore his field cape and sword and stayed at an even pace with her.

On the fifth night, she listened to Marano Levi talking to himself, walking through the snow in the darkness away from the campfire they shared for dinner.

He was chanting an obscure Catholic office in Latin. When he was out of earshot, Jojo repeated the entire vesper perfectly and then cackled in delight when he received a chastising look from Sarah. The laughter was so disarming that Sarah's disapproval evaporated.

When Levi the chanter returned to camp a short while later, Jojo spoke to him in the exact same tenor, imitating with the perfect nuance of Levi's ramblings in Latin.

Emmy saw a conspiratorial glance pass between Sarah and Jojo, but Levi did not seem to notice, or at least did not pay attention to Jojo's teasing. Levi was likely used to it, she assumed. Then she saw Sarah turn to Levi and, after a brief pause, speak to him with some concern and a tinge of tender affection.

"You know, Marano, you will catch your death out there in this cold. Please have some of this porridge."

Marano continued his chanting for a few more minutes, seeming to ignore the offer, but then closed his missal and quietly sat down next to Sarah.

She put a bowl of hot soup into his hands.

Jojo, now quiet, nodded at Sarah's kindness to Levi.

There was no more talking in the camp that night.

On the ninth day, it began to rain again, melting away the snow and much of the ice. On the tenth, the sun came out and the sky stayed blue all day.

And the next.

So they prepared to strike camp. Emmy and Sarah moved with an anxious urgency. Too much time had been lost.

CHAPTER THIRTY-ONE

<><><>

Marano Levi

Marano Levi was born Ignatio Hortensio Ramonez-Basillon into a family of clever, multitalented Castilian merchants. As a fifth son, however, he was penniless after the death of his father, so he knew at a young age that his opportunities were limited to serving at the beneficence of his oldest brother, an arrogant man who showed little kindness.

Although he had been baptized as Catholic, as had three previous generations before him, the young Ignacio learned by chance, while looking through old ledgers in his grandmother's house, the secret that his family was, in fact, Hebrew, with the surname Levi.

This hidden stigma made him sensitive to the words he heard in church, equally condemnatory of Jews and

Muslims, and by the time he turned fourteen he had developed a painful resentment of his family and its history of capitulation to the deadly ultimatums of the Castilian Catholic clergy.

Increasingly critical of what he perceived as an ignorant cowardice, he left home for the new world, cursed by his family for abandoning his obligation to subservience. As he walked the streets of Castile for the last time, he decided he would adopt the ancient Levi family surname and thereafter call himself "Marano," which was a insulting term reserved by the Castilians for Jews who covertly maintained their heritage, despite the dangerous brand they had been given as Christ-killers.

The curse bestowed on him by his family increased his resolve to never return to the repressed, dark, and angry milieu of that small hilltop home.

He walked all the way to Barcelona, determined to make a new life for himself. After a year of enterprising hard work, he saved enough to buy passage on a trading ship to Veracruz, Mexico. There he applied his energy and bargaining skills, again saving carefully so that he might ultimately purchase his own land to farm north in the rich and fertile American Texas territory.

Before he could save enough to do so, however, he found himself conscripted along with thousands of less industrious but equally hapless men into Santa Anna's new army. He could not buy his way out from the servitude.

Fortunately, because he had learned to cook in Spain and could do many other things well such as repair shoes, tame horses, and cut beautiful carvings from the abundant indigenous mesquite, he caught the attention of one of

Santa Anna's staff orderlies and became a valued member of the generalissimo's officers' camp.

That was a comfortable position, and within a few months, he had been promoted to the rank of corporal. The advantage proved short lived, for a few weeks later the entire army began a long, exhausting forced march to northern Mexico to confront Winfield Scott's American army. Five thousand men perished in that brutal trek across the barren plains of central Mexico, and an exhausted army prepared itself for battle against a smaller but well-equipped and well-fed American force.

◇◇◇◇

In the 1847 battle of Cerro Gordo, as the result of a brilliant tactical exploration by a young captain named Robert E. Lee, Winfield Scott's dragoons flanked Santa Anna, forcing the Mexican hidden artillery to fire prematurely, revealing their positions to Scott's frontal assault forces. Scott thereby successfully flushed Santa Anna's well-ensconced army from a high ground position, and panic turned to bloody pandemonium.

With his defeated army in disarray, Santa Anna narrowly escaped, leaving behind in his haste all his personal effects including his best wooden leg—one which Marano had been entrusted to repair.

Seizing this as his only opportunity to survive a merciless slaughter, Marano stripped off his uniform and, speaking in the wayfarer English he had taught himself while working in a Veracruz cantina, showed the ornately carved prosthesis to a young Illinois lieutenant. Thus, carrying the carving held high before him, Marano was escorted through the American lines to the headquarters of Scott, to whom he surrendered the trophy.

In the confused jubilation of the victorious American camp, Marano was able to make his way out of the territory, safely distancing himself from both armies.

A week later, riding a wild mustang he had lassoed, he crossed the Rio Grande and wisely kept heading north, thus avoiding the Comanche territory he knew many Mexican army refugees would attempt to transverse.

When he reached the Missouri River, he attached himself to a wagon train headed west for California, where gold had been discovered.

His luck changed there again—for while working atop a flag pole during a tempestuous San Francisco spring storm, he was struck by lightning. He remained in a coma for three weeks, cared for by two Irish Catholic Dominican nuns who saw the incident and, finding papers on him that identified him as Marano Levi, apostate Jew, baptized him back into Christianity.

When he awoke, he was mostly deaf and had forgotten all but his name and some of the native Spanish he had known as a child. Thus, at the age of twenty-two, he began his life anew as Marano Levi, Christian convert.

The nuns developed great affection for Marano and watched over him as best they could, providing him with tasks and an allowance that would sustain him. But they worried about his ability to survive on his own, for although he seemed intelligent enough when focused on a task, he was constantly distracted by small fits that left him for several minutes with a trance-like staring affect.

He never was observed in a conniption, but more than once he was robbed of all of his possessions, including his shoes, during the quiet seizure. None of their prayers, poultices, or incantations cured him. During such episodes, he just stopped functioning altogether.

The nuns even tried a concoction provided by a well-regarded Chinese herbalist, who told them it would work only if Marano took the expensive mixture twice a day for several weeks.

He did so but without success; in fact, the fits seemed to increase in frequency.

When their order reassigned them to move from San Francisco, the sisters arranged for Marano to be attached to the service of an aging, frail French Jesuit missionary who needed an assistant for a mission assignment to convert aborigines in the savage Vancouver territory.

Six months later, Marano Levi made his way north with the black robe. The pair travelled together for eighteen months, and during that time, Marano seldom spoke.

He observed carefully, however, and came to understand his master's compulsive devotion to Jesus. The priest awoke every morning before dawn, said his Mass, prayed for an hour afterward, ate a meager breakfast, then proceeded to travel, visiting the camps of tribes friendly enough to receive them and avoiding ones that had reputations.

Marano respected this routine and became devoted to it as well.

At the end of their eighteenth month together on the northwestern shore of Vancouver Island, the priest began coughing. Overcome during the cold night with shaking chills, by morning he could not rise from his pallet. There was no one to send for.

The priest was dead by evening.

At first, Marano continued with his normal tasks: hunting, fishing, and trapping for two mouths to feed as he always had. But by the third day, overwhelmed by the putrefaction in the tent, he buried the priest.

The next morning, after a prolonged seizure that left him disoriented and messed, he found himself preparing for the Mass in the same manner as he had done for the past two years.

When he regained his senses, he changed out of the soiled clothing and donned the priest's cassock. As he emerged from the tent, three aborigines confronted him. They pointed muskets at him and, after gathering up the chalice and makeshift altar, motioned him to their canoe. Their tyee, Tsa ka tien', was dying.

The trip to the chieftain's lodge became another starting place for Marano.

After ministering as best he could to the elderly chief and applying an improvised *Extreme Unction* rite, Marano Levi began a new vocation as a vagrant unordained priest, performing the semblance of a Mass and, for the families that would allow him to do so, baptizing their newborn and anointing with last rites their gravely ill.

In his wanderings through the region over the next three years, he memorized a tattered Spanish Bible and, interpreting passages randomly, became convinced that the aborigines of Vancouver Island were one of the lost tribes of Israel, his *hijos perdidos de los Judíos*. He was inspired by repeated epiphanies, usually occurring right after a prolonged seizure, and understood in a way no one else could that God was all around and in every living twig and hard stone.

He accepted as revelation that his mission was to convert all creatures into a harmonious peace. He was passionate about his beliefs and deeply confused most of the time, speaking in a hodgepodge of English, French, Spanish, and Chinook to whomever would listen.

And because his ceremonies were a spectacle of incantations and improvised motions that infuriated any clergy, Protestant or Catholic, who happened to witness them, word spread.

Within a short time, he was shunned.

The natives left him alone, and Marano Levi became a lonely and depressed shepherd without a flock. It was in that state of mind that he found himself in the camp of Emmy Evers.

CHAPTER THIRTY-TWO

⟨⟨⟨⟩⟩⟩

Emmy, Sarah and Ursa

The snow rapidly melted over the next few days under an unusually warm winter sun.

Jojo ordered the small band to break down camp in preparation for an early morning departure and asked Marano to hunt and fish to replenish their meat supplies.

In the late afternoon light, while Jojo disassembled the supply tent and packed the third canoe, Sarah and Emmy started foraging for dry wood for the night fire.

⟨⟨⟨⟩⟩⟩

They were not alone in the forest.

One hour before, as the late afternoon soft wind changed direction and drifted in from the water and up the hills, it had carried with it the complex smell of a downed animal.

A few miles away, a grizzly had picked up the scent and immediately moved south to the water, pushing with his big shoulders through dense undergrowth of decayed blackberry vines. Other bear and wolves would be on it soon, and the grizzly knew it might have to fight again.

This was an older bull bear that had survived every violent encounter over its many years, always emerging bolder and more confident.

Big by comparison to other grizzly in the region, it needed to feed constantly. Lean from a short hibernation, it had emerged from its den starving the week before, and since then, it had been unable to find much prey.

There were few fish in the stream. The bear knew it had to get to the dead animal first, before other predators. Last fall just before hibernation, the grizzly had been in a fight with an angry wolverine over the carcass of a moose. The disagreeable animal just wouldn't back down and had scraped a gash through the grizzly's right eye before the grizzly had found just the right position and swatted the wolverine with such force that it flew against a big cedar and did not get up again.

The bear gorged itself on the moose and wolverine and then settled down to sleep.

When it emerged from hibernation, it could not see from its right eye, and since then, the fighting was so much more work.

◇◇◇◇◇

Most of the fallen timber was wet, but as Emmy and Sarah moved up a deer trail, they entered a cove with so much canopy cover that it had been protected from the snow that still blanketed much of the area.

While Sarah laid out a drag cloth to tow the wood, Emmy began stacking semidry branches into a neat pile on the cloth.

When she returned to it with a third armful, she saw a tree stump move. But it wasn't a tree at all.

When the massive bear stood up onto its hind legs, it appeared as big as a mountain. Sarah's back was to the bear, and when she looked up, she saw that her mother had stopped still, staring past her.

Sarah did not turn. Both of them could hear the heavy breathing of the grizzly.

Emmy held tightly onto the branches of dry wood she carried. But not tightly enough. A heavy piece slipped, then dropped and deflected off her knee onto the ground.

The huge old silverback, hovering over the decomposing remains of an elk cow, turned to the sound, and as it did so, Emmy saw that its mouth was full of bloody carrion.

The wind was with them, and it was close enough that she could smell the foul dung on its hide and see that one eye was missing.

The bear sniffed the air, sensing for the presence of an intruder. From the way it turned its ears and moved its head, Emmy knew it had not placed them yet.

She motioned to Sarah with her eyes and carefully began stepping backward, looking for a pathway for them to escape unimpeded.

When the grizzly turned its good eye away from her, she dropped her bundle and began running, whispering loudly, "Run, Sarah. To the camp."

The beast turned and saw the movement. Bellowing, it dropped to all fours.

Sarah screamed in a high-pitched shrill that crescendoed over the low roar of the grizzly, which had begun rushing toward the fleeing women.

As it broke through the saplings over the ridge they had crossed, the women saw movement and a flash of light off to the right.

The bear shuddered from the pain of a bullet striking its shoulder. As the bear turned toward the flash, standing fully upright and roaring loudly, Emmy and Sarah continued running in the direction of camp.

When Emmy looked back, she saw Marano Levi fifty feet away from the roaring beast. He was hurriedly reloading his musket for a second shot.

But the bear, wounded and furious, leapt the short distance in four quick, bounding strides and knocked the man to the ground.

It bit into Marano's jaw and head. The dull, crunching sound and screams of the dying man carried loudly through the forest.

Emmy and Sarah cried out in horror. This time the bear caught their scent and turned away from Marano. It charged after them, running parallel toward the river below.

Emmy broke through the trees on the river bank first and saw a canoe beached on its side.

"Get to that boat, Sarah!"

The bear came through the trees sixty yards upstream.

She saw it stand and sniff the air, catching their scent again.

Just as they reached the vessel, it roared and charged up through the shoals toward them.

They put the boat between themselves and the animal. The canoe's gunnels were high enough that the bear could not cross over it and, as the animal started to move around the prow to reach the other side, they both leaped into the boat.

From the opposite side, the bear crawled into the boat as well, and as it did so, its massive weight swung the craft into the water. The canoe started downstream carrying the three of them with it.

As Sarah and Emmy, still screaming, started to jump from the boat, they heard two loud reports and saw the big bear suddenly drop headfirst into the water.

It did not move again, and its weight held the canoe fixed in the shallow part of the stream.

Two men emerged from the woods, each carrying a smoking fifty caliber rifle

It was Marté and Cull.

"Ze girls is playing hide and go seek with the big beast, eh?" Marté said.

Cull, making his way over to the bear with a drawn knife to finish it if necessary, exhaled a deep, coarse bass cackle at Marté's joke.

Moments later, Jojo found them. As he silently approached the canoe, he surveyed the dead grizzly and then Marté and his companion.

Taking in the smug grins of the shooters and with hands on his knives, Jojo stepped between the men and the two women.

Marté smiled. Doffing his filthy fur hat, he bowed deeply toward Emmy as if he were mimicking the formal address to royalty.

"You are most welcome, madam."

Brushing aside his sarcastic display, Emmy wondered to herself what this might cost them.

◇◇◇◇

Jojo, Emmy and Sarah found Marano Levi's broken body and spent the rest of the afternoon burying him in the cold, hard ground. Jojo put the Spanish Bible in the lonely man's grave.

"This was not his lucky book," Jojo said. "But it gave him some comfort in this life. Maybe it will help him find his way in the next one."

CHAPTER THIRTY-THREE

◇◇◇◇

Sarah

S he had wept bitterly as they buried Marano, even more so than when they had put her stepfather into the ground.

Isaac had left with a heroic reputation that would keep him alive for many, and that had comforted her. But Marano was a different kind of hero.

Sarah had developed a fondness for the lonely man that made her feel almost motherly. He had been such a lost soul, she thought, so misunderstood. No one had bothered to try to understand Marano Levi.

In his final act when he shot the beast, he was more focused than she had ever seen him during the short time he had been with them. And the teasing to which Jojo had subjected him sometimes was mean, but it seemed not to affect Marano. She concluded that beset as he was by his seizures, Marano, nevertheless, had found a place of peace in his life. It was a place in his mind where no insults could hurt him.

As they moved upstream, Sarah wondered how men arrived at what they became. Sometimes, she observed, there were signs or marks that gave the life tale away.

On the morning after they had buried Marano, she had come back to the camp and saw the Negro, Cull, working away at butchering the beast. He had stripped away his shirt, and she saw marks all over his back and chest that had to be the raised scars of repeated whippings.

They were old scars and, except for a few on his flanks, had merged together to form an indistinct rubbery mass of flesh. Some of it was dark, and some of it was whiter than her own skin.

And after that, she knew about Cull and suddenly was no longer afraid of him.

But she had never known Marano's story, except for what Jojo had said about him—that he was not a priest and that tribes in the region did not believe in his magic or communion with his God.

That had troubled her. She had doubted Jojo's pronouncement on that even before Marano had saved their lives. Although Marano seldom spoke and had so many funny and strange mannerisms—going off by himself to sleep and almost always eating alone—she knew he was closer to God than any of the priests she had ever seen.

So she understood Cull and sensed that she knew Marano's soul at least, but who was Marté?

She had watched him brazenly even, after her mother had turned away in disgust during their previous encounters with him. She sensed that he delighted in that reaction, the way many men and some women watched for a subtle sign of fear or respect or surprise when they exposed their tattoos or when the soldiers wore their medals or when some of the hired hands who came to the farm showed her notches on their belts.

It meant something to many people to be distinguishable, she had concluded. She understood that. The one time she had experimented with makeup, it had given her a sudden hope that she might be pretty after all.

Her mother had cautioned her about that conceit. Emmy never wore makeup and told Sarah that she likely never would have to do so either to be a comely woman, especially here in the Northwest where there were few females, pretty or plain.

"The power to manage one's relationships resides inside, not outside," Emmy had told her, and if a person worked on that, practiced finding an unflappable balance while keeping one's senses alert, nothing could ever take that away. Certainly no man, no woman, and not the passing of time or inevitability of infirmity.

But Marté was too obvious, Sarah thought.

He was so pathetically transparent in his greed that it would seem almost comical to her, if he were not such a very desperate man. She didn't understand him.

How did he get the way he was? Somewhere, sometime in his life, probably early on, something horrible must have happened to him, she decided.

Instead of scars like the ones Cull had on his back, perhaps they were the ones that grow deep in a person's belly. Marté likely had been defined by the fearful memories of whatever that experience was and had never gotten over it, had never found the courage to go beyond the adaptations he had crafted to survive, so that his cowardice was firmly ensconced into his soul and bearing.

As she watched him, Sarah wondered whether Marté's facial definition and his crouched posture were the result of a carry he had initiated at the same time and whether it had just gotten worse with each passing day—that hunch to his back that made him appear even smaller, that forced smile that only came out on the sides of his mouth, a smirk that betrayed his contempt for others.

She wondered if people instinctively guarded themselves, prejudicially and unfairly and without provocation, against men like Marté with body and extreme facial characteristics—an unfortunate "physiognomy," as her mother had called it. As exaggerated as Marté's features and expressions were, Sarah concluded that most likely the little man repeatedly had been rejected in his life.

She wondered if that distrust by others had compelled Marté into some pathetic pattern of behavior, one in which he would come back over and over for approval from others, just to be pushed away each time—each rejection reaffirming his fears about himself, reinforcing his self-loathing, so that he eventually gave up on himself. Gave up on his soul. Was that what he was about, she wondered?

She would have to study him more.

CHAPTER THIRTY-FOUR

Marté, Cull and Emmy

In the hour preceding total darkness, Cull had skinned and quartered the grizzly.

"Mus bin fi'teen hunded pouns, all tol," he said, stretching the skin onto a makeshift rack.

He held out a long strip of bear backstrap to Emmy and Sarah and leered with a jack-o-lantern grin when Sarah grimaced and then shuddered.

"Sted it eat yo, yo eaten' it," he said, and then put the strip of flesh into his mouth.

Marté smiled at Sarah's reaction.

Jojo knew of Rene Marté. The trapper had established himself in the Nuxalt and the Skeena River area as an opportunistic intermediary between white non-English speaking traders and various coastal tribes, including the

Kwakiutl and, it was rumored, the more predatory of the northern raiders.

Somewhere, in the past few years, Jojo surmised, Marté had picked up Eben Cull as a running companion. Although Jojo had never seen that grim giant before, he had heard of him and knew he was a cold murderer with a reputation that seemed a fitting complement to that of the unctuous Frenchman.

The Brits were without warrant for him and, as thinly garrisoned as they were, had no time to hunt Cull in any case. They simply ignored the rumors.

No citizens would have been bold enough to bring any concerns forward because the frontier had just too many similar denizens, and the consequences of exercising one's citizenship were precarious. Most knew that murderers like Cull and Marté were swift to deliver preemptive violence, and everyone knew about revenge as a prime motivator for those who lived on the periphery.

◇◇◇◇◇

Emmy realized to be in the debt of these men for the rescue from the bear was a horrible conundrum that further complicated her quest. Both she and Jojo knew their lives were in danger, particularly if it was true that Marté and Cull were slavers.

Enslavement was far worse than death, she had decided long ago.

That night she insisted that Jojo sleep in the same tent with the trading goods and with her and Sarah.

But only Sarah slept.

Jojo kept his muskets fully cocked, and Emmy loaded the pepperbox's six barrels and capped the primers on the weapon's nipples.

Emmy hadn't lain this close to any man other than her husbands, and she would have been embarrassed in other circumstances. But she knew there was imminent danger from the new visitors, so she huddled close to Jojo and Sarah all night.

The warmth and their weapons helped, and Emmy nodded off.

In those few minutes, she plunged deeply into a dream and she was back on Whidbey in her own bed and the wind howled outside. She reached over with her foot feeling for Isaac's warmth as she had when they first were married, and he would let her place her cold, small feet on the broad dorsum of his so she could push herself up high enough to kiss him.

But that had stopped when he returned from the Indian war, as had all of the tenderness in their intimate moments. She found herself during that brief dream longing for that. But she couldn't find Isaac, and when she snagged her healing toe on a rent in one of the hides, the pain startled her.

She remembered where she was and stayed awake the rest of the night.

Morning finally came—another clear blue sky, unseasonably warm.

When they emerged from their tent, they saw Cull down by the river packing his canoes. One held several barrels of whiskey among other containers.

Marté was seated directly outside, waiting, smiling slyly at them as he drilled into a huge bear canine that would eventually become part of a necklace. His expression conveyed amusement, either for their precautions or for a projected intimacy between Emmy and Jojo. In either case, his tone barely concealed contempt.

"Madame would like the services of guardians into the gathering?" he asked.

Emmy waited.

Hearing no response, he went on, "I am told there will be many of the peoples of this region at this potlatch. I am told there will be visitors there who very well may have what you seek. I know them. I know them well."

Emmy looked over at Jojo for some direction.

"We will speak directly with Ksi Amawaal," Jojo said. His hand was on his knife. "He is expecting us," he lied.

Marté considered this, sneered dismissively, and rose.

When Emmy did not correct Jojo's assertion, Marté spat onto the ground.

"As you wish." Marté walked down to the canoe and spoke briefly to Cull, then returned.

"You will have no objections if we move upriver to the potlatch with you? It is dangerous in these parts," he said and laughed to himself. "Everyone comes to these potlatches looking for something. And everyone departs with something."

◇◇◇◇

And so, they moved upstream, keeping Marté and Cull visible in front of them but far enough away that a musket shot from them would be difficult.

Jojo and Emmy both paddled, while Sarah sat in the second canoe and kept watch on the other tow-behind.

They were all nervous about their new company.

Emmy had concealed the gold in a small chest under several skins. The rest of the gifts—copper, iron, glass, several beautifully polished and semiprecious stones, fine lace, various small implements such as a large assortment of thimbles, and nails in gross bundles—were individually wrapped in linen or buckskin.

But it wasn't their belongings that concerned them. Marté and Cull were desperate, despicable men, unpredictable and without honor.

Jojo told Emmy that, when they arrived at the Three Spirits Valley sometime next week, they must somehow find their way to Ksi Amawaal before Marté and Cull could mingle into the festivities. The two trappers would certainly expose their presence to the Northerners if they arrived first. Jojo knew he had to immediately invoke Ksi Amawaal's protection for the two white females.

Emmy was exhausted from a sleepless night. While paddling, after seeing that Sarah had fallen asleep in the canoe behind and could not hear, she asked Jojo about Marté and Cull.

"I am told that Marté came from a place they call 'Keybeck,' far east of here," Jojo said. "He arrived in this region twelve years ago, and I remember seeing him when I was a little boy. He traded furs and other things to men on the ships, and my father said he always had information about every deal that went on all around. That's what I remember."

Jojo paddled for a while, then continued, "For a short time, he traveled with old Antoine Bill, a Suquamish Metís who translated for the King George Men. When Antoine Bill finally got himself killed because he lied one too many times, that Marté fella tried doing translation in Chinook. But he wasn't very good at most of the people's words. So I am told he went on to other things.

"As for Cull, I don't know much about that man except that he carries two big knives and eats his meat raw. He is mean like a poked dog. You saw him last night. I know about two gold diggers from a place called LaBama who argued with him one night. They both disappeared a few days later. They never came back for their grubstakes, so many thought he killed them. If so, nobody ever found their bodies. Some say he ate them."

Emmy shuddered.

She felt for the pepperbox in her cloak, hoped the powder was dry. Furious at the inept, rule-bound Brit captain who had refused to send men, she ran her thumb over the hammer, seeking some assurance from the weapon.

She had come to understand the Americans' reasons for declining. They might be facing down the Brits right now. Maybe that's why the Brits hadn't returned to their post at Fort Simpson.

She also thought about the first time she saw Pickett, and it strangely stirred her— but she could not afford to hold on to that thought . . . dismissed it with the feeling that she was stronger than him . . . but knew, insecure as she sensed he was at his core, that he was probably an efficient killer like so many of the military she had met over the years . . . and wished that she could have had George Pickett with them right now.

In the presence of killers, it didn't matter if someone who was on your side was a good person, just that he was calm and competent.

She wished that Isaac had not gotten himself killed. That thought made her angry with him, and then, holding back a shiv-like piercing that went to her chest and caught her breath, she was angry with herself.

Isaac always had been so noble and so foolish—and so taken with her as he was that he always did what he thought she wanted. But he had not understood her, and that had kept her isolated in a way that added a blue dimension to everything she did, all year round, an enveloping wrap that couldn't be broken by comforts or reassurances.

She thought about the conundrum that comes when one has reached the thin boundary between love and hatred, and how impatience bridged the gap between those two very deep emotions. She thought to herself how swiftly a person moved from the blindness of love and admiration to the clouded emotions of contempt and hatred.

She had never crossed over into hatred for Isaac in the way she had with her first husband. She just had grown tired of reassuring Isaac constantly and picking up after his messes, quietly accepting the societal dictum that gave all credit to the male in the relationship.

They had created an unacknowledged partnership, but he had never really given her equality in it. His pride had been too great to acknowledge it, even in private with her, and that, in its finality, was what she resented most in him.

She had accepted that with equanimity but, by the time he had left to fight Indians east of the mountains, she had come to an uneasy conclusion about the fairness of their relationship.

And when she was given the opportunity to manage the estate, she embraced it with a hungry vengeance, and it all prospered as it never had before.

She had been disappointed, she realized, when Isaac had returned. And things were different ever after that.

She thought about cowards like Tom Iserson, who had jumped out of the window that night, naked, leaving everyone behind. Fitting it was, that naked state, for the imbecile he was. Then he had the gall to tell people that he had "held the door to keep the killers at bay" while everyone else escaped.

She felt herself getting hot, and then the cold breeze evaporated the fluster. So many men were cowards like that—pathetic partners to women who had even less backbone. Fortunately, most of those partnerships did not survive for long out here, unprotected by the well-meaning conventions of a civilized society that believed there was a place for everyone.

As she paddled quietly, Emmy thought about this foolish fix she had gotten herself and Sarah into.

She watched Jojo and hoped he was as smart and skillful as he seemed. He was earnest and wise, far beyond his years, and had a keen instinct that allowed him to assess every situation quickly and correctly, yet he also had the manners to allow her to retain a sense of control.

She had learned by watching him and how he approached each decision and crisis, saw how he anticipated problems and found alternatives that averted crisis in the first place. She knew she could enhance that skill in herself and, if she survived, carry it forward in whatever new life she would create for herself afterward. After she achieved her driven mission to find Jacob before he was destroyed—and if she survived.

She thought about the last time she had seen Jacob, running from the savages, the same ones she was hoping to meet up with somehow. To make a fair trade . . . if they understood that.

She was applying a very quaint interpretation to that concept, she realized, and the reality was that it would be defined in the end by something deep down that most did not understand, an instinct that ran through everything around her—survival, with all negotiations bound together by hope on both sides of the bargain.

Understanding what the other side needed was the real problem.

And in this situation, she had brought material goods and gold, but doubted that was what the aborigines really were after. Was it hope for something beyond material gain? What was it they really wanted?

She shook her head and realized that a very simple set of hopes was the only bright thing that Marté had brought—with word that Jacob really might be at Three Spirits. For that, at least, she was thankful.

For a brief night, it had allowed her to nod asleep in an exhausted heap, briefly, but deeply with dreams about finding her family, as perfectly imperfect as they were together, the way they were the day before it was destroyed.

◇◇◇◇◇

Jojo knew she was worried.

"These two have not made a move, Missus Evers. Yet. But Marté is thinking about it."

"Do you believe they will rob us?" Emmy asked.

"No. They don't know what we carry. Marté thinks we are more valuable to them just as we are because he will try to become an adviser to the Northerners if they are there—to give them an advantage."

"What type of advantage, Jojo?"

"He is thinking that when all offers have been put on the table, if an exchange does occur, if Jacob is there, he can find us for the Northerners and they can take Jacob back, kill me, and take you and Sarah."

Emmy was quiet.

Jojo continued, "Marté is thinking he will get something from this and maybe it is safer to wait to see. Besides, he has whiskey to sell, and that will take up much of his time. It is after the exchange that will be the most dangerous. Getting you all back alive."

They spoke no more for several hours.

Late that afternoon they were joined by a party in three other small cedar dugouts.

"Tsimshian," said Jojo, who spoke to them briefly as they moved alongside and kept pace for a short distance before peeling off into a tributary.

Because he had wrapped Emmy and Sarah in blankets, covered their heads with reed knit hats, and darkened their faces with mud, they were not noticed, or at least the other canoeists paid no attention to them.

"They said Three Spirits is only a long half-day from here," Jojo said, watching Marté and Cull pull to shore, presumably to camp. "We will be there in the morning if we make our camp here, but if we keep moving, we will be there after dark tonight.

Emmy watched Marté and Cull far up ahead.

Jojo turned to her.

"That is what I think we should do," he said. "Let Marté think we are camping downstream and then move ahead in the dark."

He looked up into the sky.

"No moon tonight. That is good, but we will need to be careful."

They pulled ashore and started as if to make camp.

Five hours later, quietly, carefully still-paddling against a slowly moving current, Jojo, Emmy, and Sarah passed the sleeping killers and moved upstream.

Within five more hours, they could see campfires and massive long houses.

They had entered Three Spirits.

CHAPTER THIRTY-FIVE

✕✕✕✕

Anah and Jacob

Jacob tried to move, but when he did, the ropes that cinched his hands and feet together behind his back just got tighter, hurting him more.

He did not know where he was, and the cold ground seemed to move under him, undulating so that he felt like he would fall from the floor into the sky above.

As he opened his eyes, he saw objects lying next to him. They were familiar, but he did not know why. Was that his eagle's beak? His ball of string? He heard barking and curse words and a coarse rattle.

Then his father came to him. He saw his shadow go by, and he held his breath. He wanted to call out for Isaac, but Isaac's shadow just stayed there, behind him, shouting, out of reach.

And then his father was gone.

And when Jacob opened his eyes again, the things he had seen next to his face were gone too.

◇◇◇◇◇

Anticipating that Jacob would resist traveling, Klixuatan had again drugged the boy. Even then, perhaps because of a tenacious determination to remain in control, Jacob had resisted the drowsy submission that occurred with most captives when given the concoction. Instead, the drug made him delirious and combative.

Anah had Klixuatan bind the boy but would not let him increase the dose because he had seen other captives stop breathing when so treated. As he was, powerful as a little defiant wolverine, Jacob was too valuable as a possible source of power to waste.

So they kept him tightly bound again. And after the shaman and his woman tied Jacob's feet and then his hands behind his back, Anah came to him with something to counter the boy's own magic.

They spread out the contents that Jacob had in his pockets the night they had captured him. They had intentionally allowed him to keep these objects, watching for when he became dependent on them as grounding memories— and when they knew the boy was going to them to find reassurance, they stole them away.

Then, when they knew he was in the murky depths of his drugged delirium, they laid the objects out again next to his face.

Next, they brought out the spirit to break him, if they could.

Anah had skinned and tanned the face and scalp of Isaac and wore it now as a mask. Standing behind the boy, he gestured for Klixuatan to keep the boy turned away. And then he began gesturing with big, bold, sweeping movements—a caricature of what Anah presumed would have been those of the boy's father.

The cool leather of the bearded mask and hair formed to his face easily, and as soon as he put it on, Anah felt powerful. He knew that some of the magic of the white tyee was here for him now.

He sang and bellowed out white tyee words: "Hey!" "Me!" "You!" "Me-you!" "Mine" "Bastard" "Keep" "Me" "Powder" for several minutes and then stopped, hovering over the boy.

Then he backed out of the shelter.

Klixuatan watched Jacob that night. He told Anah that Jacob lay motionless but with a rapid pulse that told the shaman they had found the way to control him.

◇◇◇◇

They traveled in four small Kwakiutl canoes carrying their slaves south along the inland coast to the mouth of the river that would bring them east toward the Tsimshian. Except for Jacob, who remained bound, drugged, and hidden, each canoe held two warriors and two captives, all paddling so they moved swiftly.

On the second day upriver, they passed the totems of Ksi Amawaal's summer camp, and by the fourth day, they saw signs of Three Spirits where the Tsimshian stayed during the winter.

The camp was filled with people, and Anah knew that most were not Tsimshian. Many were drunk. The trading would be easy, he thought. And he wanted to see this Ksi Amawaal and how he got his way.

CHAPTER THIRTY-SIX

◇◇◇◇

Pickett

The British have not yet dispositioned their forces, but my sources tell me that their move is imminent. Per your orders, we are now moved and are ensconcing into the best and highest ground available.

—1858 Report by Captain George E. Pickett to General William S. Harney, Commander U.S. Army, Oregon Territory

They would attempt to take this easy beach, he had decided. It presented a gentle slope with hard-packed sand. The Brit marines would run up it quickly once landed, so he had to commandeer the highest perch above and, from that promontory, would lob an artillery barrage to impede their progress.

Gossip and spies had told him the Brits were indeed preparing for a takeover, ostensibly to protect the rights of the twenty English subjects who lived on the island, but everyone knew that was a Douglas ruse. He wanted San Juan Island for its strategic value, as did the U.S. Government.

But the Brits would not get it without a stubborn fight from Captain George Pickett.

Although he was not to provoke an attack nor fire the first shot, Pickett had his orders. General Harney had dispatched Pickett to hold the island at all costs, even if it meant war between the two nations.

The cold south wind pushed over the long spine that ran from this well-situated parapet to the tip of the island, and even in the murky remains of this day, Pickett could see the entire field of future combat.

He saw where the Brit frigates likely would drop anchor, positioning their guns for devastating broadsides against his troops and whatever position he had staked out. Sound carried well in the quiet of the early morning, so he imagined he could hear the faint clank of chains and the rubbing squeak of ropes on pulleys as their landing boats made their way down to the water.

He heard the shouts of their marine captains ordering the disciplined disposition of their hard men. These would not be children like the Mexican cadets or the peasants conscripted into uniform that he had faced in Veracruz and Churubusco, scurrying backward, brave but undisciplined in their rout. They would be seasoned and mean-hearted Royal Marines.

They would most certainly land, take their losses, and determinedly push his equally determined but much smaller company of men down and away from this position.

Both sides would suffer.

He pulled his slicker closer as the wind bit into his neck. He wished he were in Mexico again.

After an hour of mapping and marking, Pickett called up Lieutenant Henry Martyn Robert from the beach below. "I believe this is the best place to be, Henry. Can your howitzers hit the beach from here?"

Robert, only one year out of West Point, shook his head, then looked again through his field glass to be certain.

"No, Captain. We will likely need to land some of the thirty-two-pounders from the Massachusetts. Before it moves away to get out of reach of their frigates. If the reports are correct, they are sending three big ships."

Robert was often hesitant but punctilious and almost always right. Pickett simply nodded his head slowly. He knew he would be outgunned and outnumbered. He was determined not to be outdone.

As he watched his lieutenant walk back down to the south beach to await the landing of more supplies, Pickett said aloud to himself, "Let them come. We'll make another bloody Bunker Hill of it."

Pickett drifted for a bit. He found himself back in Virginia, where even now, in this early March, color was beginning to show through on crocus-covered afternoons. He saw himself riding down a long lane and paying his respects to some fine young woman and her parents, securing a place and position for himself out of uniform, a dandy gentleman of means.

At last.

She would be a red-haired filly or a black Irish high-bred dame.

He closed his eyes and, for a brief moment, tasted the minted cool juleps that quelled the heaviness of Richmond summer afternoons, so far away from the cutting bite of the whiskey from Frisco that he and so many others in his command had as a meager resort to the cold and boredom of the Northwest. Even here on verdant San Juan, only a few miles by sea from the supplies and excitement of Victoria, he envisioned no relief.

So he pulled his slicker even closer and bowed his head slightly to let the light rain fall off the brim of his cap.

And then he thought of Emmy Evers.

She was there in his dream, walking right by him, turning her head ever so slightly, telling him she knew he was there, watching her every step and nuanced gesture. His heart began running double-time, and he felt it deeply pounding up through his neck and into his face. He could feel that his face was flushed, and he opened his eyes, and she was there and then she was not.

And he wondered if she needed him; he wanted her to need him, but she would never be his and would dismiss him for his arrogant presumptuousness. So, in his dream, she just went on, and he was back in the rain, which was in his shirt and on his back now.

It was not a good place to die.

CHAPTER THIRTY-SEVEN

◇◇◇◇

Ksi Amawaal

K si Amawaal Sityaawt Gatgyet was widely known to be a very wealthy tyee, so many saw his widely broadcast invitation to this potlatch as a great opportunity—for the longstanding tradition in the region was that potlatch guests received gifts, and a tyee's wealth and power were measured by how much he gave away.

In the entire Northwest, Ksi Amawaal was the most magnanimous of all the chieftains. And when the Americans spoke of their presidents or the Brits about Victoria, the Tsimshian sneered because their tyee could not be surpassed in their minds. Thus, clan chiefs arrived from areas as far away as the Queen Charlottes and Nootka, many curious and many envious.

To one accustomed to tribal confrontation and pro-
tectionism, or to a European concept of ostentation, the
wealth displayed by the Tsimshian at Three Spirits was
astounding, and most wondered how they had achieved
and maintained it. The answer was straightforward. Ksi
Amawaal had created a well-maintained, neutral platform
for trade, affording protection to everyone who entered.
And at this potlatch, every one of the guests brought along
goods that might be exchanged in a common market that
would develop throughout the encampments.

The Tsimshian were healthy, numerous, well armed,
and protective of that peace because Ksi Amawaal had
long ago shown them how they would prosper if they could
act as intermediaries and facilitators rather than as com-
batants. And observing the disruption to customs and the
uniqueness of his tribe's heritage that always ensued after
the arrival of even the most well-meaning of interlopers,
he tactfully kept missionaries out.

Thus, Ksi Amawaal's people had avoided some plagues
that had beset tribes closer to the coast. He had also learned to
keep his tribe away from the pain of the scourges by listening
to gossip from traders and quarantining anyone who appeared
for trading during the pestilence. And when the opportunity
arose to give cowpox pus to immunize his tribe, he had taken
the first inoculation as a demonstration of its power.

Jojo had presented himself as a lone emissary from his
father MaNuitu 'sta, on behalf of Emmy, whom he kept
hidden with Sarah, encamped deep in the cedar woods to
the north of Three Spirits.

When Ksi Amawaal had heard Jojo's eloquent description of Emmy's quest, he understood immediately what he

had to do to protect the women and wealth that would come from a skillful negotiation with the Northerners.

Alerted by Tsimshian runners who had the ability to move through their woods much faster than canoes traversed up the river, Ksi Amawaal knew the renegades were approaching, dressed as Kwakiutl. He had distaste for headhunters because of the havoc they continued to bring to white victims, and because the Brits and Americans, who could not distinguish one tribe from another, often brought indiscriminate retribution to many tribes, including his own. Ksi Amawaal knew of several misdirected lynchings that had been the consequence of predatory raids on white settlers. The Americans were even less discerning than the Brits, it seemed, so he knew he had to keep his people wary of both white tribes.

And as much as he would have liked to strike the raiders down as they moved in disguise into the Three Spirits, he would need to see the negotiation proceed in order to affect an open trade between the supplicant and sellers.

It was not his way to see blood spilled on Tsimshian rivers because that only dampened profitable exchange and brought bad luck. So Ksi Amawaal waited. And in the hours before the Northerners moved in, he discussed terms with Jojo; negotiated with several other tyees about slaves, tools, and contraband; and prepared his camp for the many feasts that would continue over the next few days.

The whiskey that Marté brought, however, complicated the affair, and by the time Anah arrived, many of the Tsimshian guardians were incapacitated. It would be a very dangerous negotiation.

CHAPTER THIRTY-EIGHT

<><><>

Jojo, Anah and Ksi Amawaal

Jojo took a circuitous route back to the encampment where Emmy and Sarah waited with the gold, doubling back several times to look for tracks other than his own.

He found a stranger's footprints on the second pass and knew that someone was following. So he moved far away from Emmy back into the Three Spirits.

When he found a small stream, he backtracked in his own footsteps to a heavily branched tree. Using a long, sturdy branch, he vaulted over a bramble thicket and hid in the underbrush waiting for the tracker.

He finally showed.

It was Cull, making his way carefully, both knives drawn.

Jojo watched the huge man tracking in the long afternoon shadows of the forest, his head tilted to the ground with his blind eye turned upward.

Jojo held his breath as he watched Cull pass slowly down toward the stream. He knew if he were to have to fight Cull, he would have to move constantly to the man's left blind side, but he also surmised that Cull had survived as long as he had by being very adept at killing with the two long ugly blades and knew many tricks that had surprised many unfortunate men.

Jojo cocked his second pistol carefully.

After ten minutes, Cull returned from the stream, inspecting the tracks. He stopped near the tree and looked right up the trunk into the dense foliage to where Jojo had considered hiding.

Jojo held his breath.

Finally, Cull turned away from the tree, spit, and sheathed his knives. He departed back toward the main camps.

Cull had likely given up because, in the waning light, his one eye had not seen the mark from the vaulting pole Jojo had used. But it was evident to Jojo that his tracker was experienced, and he would have to be very careful. He knew Cull would have found him had he tracked earlier in the day.

Jojo emerged and carefully followed Cull for a half mile to be certain the man was truly departing. He then swiftly moved back through the woods and found Emmy and Sarah.

He told them about Cull and said he had learned the Northerners had arrived in camp, and had brought several

slaves with them, including a young white boy. But he
didn't know if was Jacob.

Seeing Emmy and Sarah's excitement at the news, he
tried to calm them and make them understand the danger
they were now in.

"I will need to move you from here now and bring you
closer in to Ksi Amawaal."

"What was his decision?" Emmy asked, hoping Jojo
had been correct about the Tsimshian tyee.

"As I thought, he has agreed to be the negotiator in
return for half of the gold. He does not want anything else
and does not want any disruption to the potlatch."

Seeing Emmy's hopes rising, Jojo continued. "As soon
as he has concluded the negotiation, however, Missus
Evers, we are on our own and will need to move to the
canoes and leave before Marté or the Northerners find us."

"Do the Northerners know we are here?" Emmy
asked. "I don't know why, but Marté has not told them
yet; otherwise, there would have been Haida looking for
you with Cull."

Emmy and Sarah both nodded.

"If I return with Jacob, we will need to move farther
upstream and wait for this weather to turn bad again."

"Why?" Sarah asked.

Jojo saw Emmy's eyes widen when he mentioned Jacob
again, but knew she did not understand his plan either.

"If Marté tells them about us — and he *will* at some
point — then the Northerners will come looking for us.
If they know about us before the negotiation, they will
spread out through this forest looking for you. If Jacob is
there and Marté tells them *after* the negotiation, and Ksi

Amawaal is successful, the Haida will come looking for us to take Jacob back."

Jojo could see that Emmy understood now.

"They will expect us to try to escape west, down the river to Fort Simpson. When some time has passed, they should give up, and we will leave the canoes and move by land back to the fort."

"And if you do not bring Jacob back?" Emmy asked hesitantly.

"Then Ksi Amawaal failed in the negotiations, or he is not among the captives." Jojo looked down, then back up at Emmy.

"Or Jacob is dead."

◇◇◇◇◇

The words struck Emmy in the gut and her heart at the same time. She recovered her composure and jutted her chin forward to contain a desperate urge to weep.

Then, with a bravado, she said, "And if he *is* there and Ksi Amawaal fails in his negotiations. Then what?"

The intensity of her stare must have given her away, for Jojo shook his head.

"Following them would be very dangerous, Mrs. Evers. They will be looking for us anyway, and we could fall right into their hands."

Their gazes locked, hers determined and his beseeching.

Finally, Jojo sighed and then nodded. "If he is there, I will do my best to win him back for you."

◇◇◇◇◇

On the next morning, it began to rain hard, so many people stayed inside their shelters and long houses. That continued most of the day, and by mid-afternoon, many were drunk on Marté's liquor.

Shortly before dark, Anah, heralded by Klixuatan and leading the tethered gifts of two adolescent slaves, presented himself as "Taxcilsi' Na," a Kwakiutl tyee, to the Tsimshian chieftain.

Ksi Amawaal's younger brother received them and waived the entourage into the long house.

Anah seemed stunned by the wealth displayed—beautiful furs and sculptures, delicately stitched wall hangings, abundant food, and many beautiful metal hammerings.

A few minutes later, Ksi Amawaal, bedecked in a multicolored and feathered ceremonial gown, entered from a side portal accompanied by five other tyees from Tsimshian and Bella Coola clans, all of whom were also beautifully dressed.

By comparison, the Northerners had only their tattoos and shell labrets with simple clothing designed for rapid travel.

Ksi Amawaal bade them all to sit facing each other on long ornately carved and sanded cedar plank benches. In the murkiness of the smoke-filled room, Anah and Ksi Amawaal measured each other. Neither blinked. Then Klixuatan stepped forward and addressed Ksi Amawaal in the Tsimshian dialect.

◇◇◇◇◇

Jojo, who had entered with Ksi Amawaal's group but kept to the rear of the contingent, studied Anah's entourage intently. The shaman's pronunciation and accent were so bad that it made Jojo smile at his clumsiness. It almost made him forget, for a moment, that the old man, like everyone in his group, was a brutal killer.

"Mighty Ksi Sityaawt Amawaal, I speak for my leader Taxcilsi' Na, in giving you praise for being a powerful tyee. He gives you these strong young women as a tribute to you and your family and your daughter who is joining you with the Bella Coola."

As Jojo watched, it was apparent that Anah did not understand everything his shaman was saying, but Ksi Amawaal did.

He bowed to Anah, and Anah bowed slightly back. Klixuatan went on.

"We are here to trade, with your blessing, with other tyees or Tsimshian and Bella Coola who might have need," Klixuatan indicated the slaves, "for what we bring."

Ksi Amawaal nodded, then looked toward the door.

Klixuatan turned to one of the younger men in the Northerners' company who stepped outside and then reentered with eight tethered captives. Jacob was the last to be led in the door.

Jojo recognized him immediately and saw that Ksi Amawaal did as well.

The negotiation proceeded just as Jojo had predicted to Emmy. For all eight of the captives, Ksi Amawaal first offered a variety of gifts, including the items that Emmy and Jojo had ferried up the river.

Klixuatan, without conferring with Anah, immediately rejected that offer.

Then Ksi Amawaal conferred with his younger brother and two of the Tsimshian tyees. He turned back to Anah and offered the equivalent of two hundred U.S. gold dollars for all the captives.

That caused Klixuatan to pause and confer with Anah, who held back even then, rejecting the offer.

Ksi Amawaal feigned disappointment but again consulted with his tyees.

Ksi Amawaal turned to Klixuatan and held up four fingers, doubling the offer.

Anah looked over his slaves and shook his head again.

On cue, Ksi Amawaal turned one more time to his conferees, then, after a brief discussion, back to Klixuatan. He pointed to Jacob and held up four fingers.

Jojo held his breath during the long pause that ensued. He recognized that when Anah and Klixuatan saw this offer, they knew immediately that Ksi Amawaal had perceived the value of Jacob.

Jojo expected more haggling, but instead the Northerners shook their heads, stood up, and walked out of the negotiation, taking their captives with them.

Jojo had not anticipated this reaction. Did Anah and Klixuatan believe Jacob had some special magic? Unfortunately, Ksi Amawaal's bargaining had confirmed their fears. Perhaps they believed selling Jacob would confer to someone else a power they did not yet understand but needed to harness.

◇◇◇◇

Anah made his way back to his encampment, apoplectic at the encounter. Screaming loudly to Klixuatan, he instructed the shaman to bind Jacob again and then attempt to sell the remaining captives for as much gold as he could get from whomever was willing in the entire encampment.

They would depart when the shaman had traded enough to purchase the weapons and cannons Anah needed for the coming raiding season.

As Anah watched Klixuatan fumble with Jacob's ropes, he began bellowing at the sky.

◇◇◇◇

And it was in this state of distraught agitation that René Marté and Eben Cull found Anah.

Marté had held back on approaching the Northerners, anticipating that if he could not succeed in bringing Emmy and Sarah to them before the negotiation, he would be better served by tracking Emmy afterward and returning with three captives instead of two.

Unfortunately for Marté, he did not understand the relationship between Anah and Jacob and thus had not expected the negotiation to fail. When Marté told Anah he had travelled with Jojo and Emmy and knew they were the negotiators behind Ksi Amawaal's ploy, Anah became silent. He started chanting to himself.

Klixuatan and the other Northerners quietly backed away behind Marté. And then, in one swift motion, Anah drew his knife and leaped high at Cull, plunging his blade deeply into the man's neck and downward into his chest.

As Cull collapsed, Anah whirled and pulled his blade across Marté's throat.

Marté fell across Cull.

Wiping his knife on Marté's back, Anah stood and then spit on their bodies.

Later that afternoon, Klixuatan returned with gold and other goods he had traded in exchange for the seven other captives. They struck camp and began preparations to move westward.

Safely hidden, Jojo watched them load their canoes and throw the trappers' remains into the river.

CHAPTER THIRTY-NINE

◇◇◇◇

Jojo

Jojo, Emmy and Sarah followed the four canoes from a safe distance, and fortunately, because the rain was constant now, visibility upstream was limited.

By the way the Northerners moved swiftly downstream, Jojo knew they were eager to depart the Tsimshian stronghold before anyone discovered who they really were. He knew Anah likely had what he wanted and almost certainly had assumed that Ksi Amawaal would behave as he, Anah, would have behaved himself, keeping the gold and killing the whites.

The river was moving swiftly now, and the ice had all but melted. They soon passed the shoal where they had escaped the bear. Thirty miles farther downstream, Jojo pulled them ashore to rest.

He moved into the woods and, a few miles down-stream, found the Northerners encamped, all nine in their party huddled around one fire. Jojo watched for over an hour until all the men had moved under the canoes to sleep.

"I can see Jacob. There are no other captives, he told Emmy and Sarah on his return.

"How is he?" they both asked.

"He is not moving."

"What do you mean? Is he sick?"

"He is gagged and tied and is being carried by the shaman."

Jojo saw Emmy draw in a deep breath, then, as Sarah pulled close to her, lift up her head and recover.

"What is your plan, Jojo?" Emmy asked.

"We will need to follow them for another day. They are moving fast, and they will be close to Fort Simpson in less than two days. Tomorrow night we will move ahead past them and get soldiers from the fort to intercept them."

"What if they move inland to avoid the fort?" asked Emmy hesitantly. "We will miss them then."

Jojo nodded, considering the pain he heard in Emmy's voice. He did not have an answer for her.

The next morning, they moved slowly down the stream, until Jojo pulled them aside a half-mile above the Haida camp and reconnoitered again.

Inspecting the ashes left from the fire on the shore, he knew the raiders had left at least an hour beforehand.

They followed again carefully, pulling aside frequently to allow Jojo to scout for a trap and prevent a blunder into Anah's camp. The second night, he returned to Emmy and Sarah after three hours.

"They moved downstream much closer to the fort than I thought they would," he told them. "They have moved their canoes up to the woods and are preparing to portage them and bypass the fort starting in the morning. That will slow them down, but we do not have time to wait until they are asleep and get to the fort in our canoe. I can get past them to the fort, but it will have to be on foot. Alone. You must wait here with Sarah for me to return."

"And if they leave before you get back?" Emmy asked.

Jojo saw a fierce woman staring intensely at him.

"You must stay here," he said. "You must wait for me to return with the soldiers. You will be safe here."

Emmy and Sarah both were crying.

"How is Jacob now?" Sarah asked anxiously.

"He is drugged, most likely. I think that is why he is not moving. And they have him tethered to a tree," Jojo said.

He saw his words were not reassuring to the women. "They are drinking whiskey. Much whiskey. They think they are safe from the Tsimshian. They are very drunk now. They will not be up early. I will be back in time, Missus Evers."

Five minutes later, in the midst of another downpour and in black, cold darkness, Jojo departed for his run to the fort. He ached from the run, and the relentless rain had seeped through his sealskin, penetrating enough that his arms and legs were starting to numb.

As he pushed himself quietly through the forest, hoping he was far enough away to skirt the camp with some safety but close enough to the sound of the river to keep his bearings, he thought about the futility of it all if he did not succeed in his run to the fort—if he was too late, if Jacob was dying, or if Jacob was worse off because of the brutality of his experience by Anah.

Jojo thought about that ignorant, insane rogue, of Anah's arrogance he had witnessed during the man's negotiation with Ksi Amawaal, and the warrior's cold, smooth murder of Marté and Cull. He thought about how some of the tribes he'd encountered during his travels with his father were savage and uncontrolled, but remembered that MaNuitu 'sta had taught him those tribes that had endured long enough to develop a culture around families had learned ways to control their young men and women.

But Anah was such a dominating monster, Jojo surmised that he really had never been controlled in any way by whomever had raised him. No comeuppance, no responsibility to anything other than unbridled passion. There was a failure in that clan's culture, and the very thing that likely had given it strength — the far-reaching terrifying reputation of Anah — almost certainly had caused the clan to rot from the inside out.

Jojo had seen that by how all of the other men in his party watched Anah move and deferred to his slightest gestures. He was like a mean, rogue bear heading a pack of hungry dogs.

Jojo wondered whether Anah was an evil, unkillable, unstoppable spirit.

The rain stopped; he could again hear the audible marks of his movement and realized he was making too much noise. He slowed down, then stopped and listened.

No other sounds.

It started to rain again, so he ran for several more minutes until he came to the break in the woods where he was certain the Northerners were likely to portage away from the river.

He then stopped and listened again, waiting for the rain to quiet.

It finally did.

Nothing.

He was about to move again when he heard it—behind him the muffled snapping of soggy twigs being broken by footsteps.

Had he been discovered?

He cocked the pistol under his sealskin, unlatched his knife in its sheath, and stopped. Listened.

No more sounds from the direction of the encampment, but there definitely was something coming through the brush off to his right.

Animal? It was too dark to make out anything. Too much time lost. He had to run now, and as he did so, he felt a bitter terror at the thought of being overtaken by one of the Northerners, possibly Anah himself, and then being cut down short. Failing.

He threw down the pistol—too much to risk on wet powder—then ran as fast as he could. There would be no time for a fight, in any case. If a Northerner sentry was pursuing him, his only chance was to make straight for the fort. And then he would have to avoid being shot down at the fort's gates by a sleepy soldier sentry.

He wondered if he would survive.

Running harder now, he pulled his knife out of its sheath and smiled at the irony of it all.

CHAPTER FORTY

◇◇◇◇◇

Emmy and Anah

Emmy was exhausted. Still, she lay awake most of the night waiting.

When she did nod off, she drifted into the day and saw herself facing the Northerners, spiriting Jacob away from them. Then she and Isaac were together again. He was disagreeing with where they should go with Jacob, and their son was confused, and she heard the Northerners coming back to her home on Whidbey again.

This time she told Isaac, who was hurt, to lie down and hide because *she* would take care of Jacob.

Then the Northerners were pounding at the door again, and Rowdy her dog was trying to help, and the children were safe, and Isaac was safe.

She startled awake, regained her bearings, and pulled out Isaac's pocket watch. It was five in the morning, and Jojo had not returned.

She could contain herself no longer. She turned to Sarah and gently woke her.

"Sarah, I have to see what is happening to Jacob. You must remain here and wait for Jojo. When he comes, tell him I am moving closer to the Haida. Tell him I will stay close to the river."

Sarah understood and nodded.

Emmy smeared mud on her face and hands, pulled her sealskin tightly around her body, cinched the belt on her breeches, and moved downstream.

She walked carefully, and by early light, after a one-hour trek along a deer path that bordered the river, she found the camp.

All the men were still asleep under the canoes they had moved fifty yards up from the river in preparation to portage past the stretch of river that bordered the fort.

Jacob was off to the side, tied to a tree, just as Jojo had described.

The sight of her boy, alive after three months, overwhelmed Emmy, and she began to weep silently. Then she shook herself and regained her composure, watching for a few more minutes.

No one was stirring. They might not awaken for a few more hours, she reasoned. If she could get Jacob before they moved inland and carry him back upstream, they could meet up with Jojo when he returned. If she waited, they might move away into an area where she was certain the soldiers would not follow. Then she would lose Jacob again. Perhaps forever.

She waited five more minutes. No sign of Jojo. The warriors still were not stirring.

She decided.

Holding her breath and fighting the urge to run directly to her son, Emmy moved in measured steps, knowing that one foot caught on the underbrush might awaken the sleeping captors.

She became dizzy and forced herself to stop; take a deep, quiet breath; and let the pounding in her chest subside. With Jacob so close to her, the deliberateness of this caution, with each agonizing, careful step, was punishingly cruel, she thought to herself.

And then, when she got close enough to make out his features, she saw he was gagged, uncovered, soaking wet, and slumped over. And for a painful, sinking moment, pushing her hopes down toward the abyss of despair, she saw that Jacob wasn't moving, and she thought she had failed—that her little boy was dead.

But then he sighed and her heart began pounding again.

With contained, focused, and agile movement, Emmy untied him. He was barely conscious.

She kept the gag in his mouth, pulled him up, and threw his small body over her shoulder, noting to herself that he had lost weight since he had been taken.

She turned and started to move away from the camp, quickly, so that she almost walked directly into two long stakes jutting out at the river's edge. In the early dawn light breaking through the trees, she saw that the poles had heads on them: Marté and Cull.

She shuddered and moved upstream.

◇◇◇◇

Anah had slept fitfully, despite drinking heavily that night. He was not accustomed to whiskey and had always preferred to watch others lose their composure when they drank it. He could take advantage then.

But on this night, he had felt anxious and was still angry that Marté had not come to him with information that would have given him an advantage over Ksi Amawaal. He had gold from the sale of his slaves, enough to buy two cannons from the French, who did not accept slaves as currency anymore. They would sell him the weapons willingly because they hated the Brits and knew how much trouble Anah was likely to cause them.

Anah had enough for purchase of a good quantity of powder and canistered grape shot as well, which would devastate any attackers should anyone be foolish enough to fight him.

In a wild stupor from the liquor that night, he had lurched over to the wolverine boy and saw that he was starting to wake up from the drugs that Klixuatan had administered. He was regaining his strength.

Anah hollered over to Klixuatan to give the boy another dose, and after the old shaman did so, Anah slipped on the skinned-face mask of Jacob's father.

When the drug achieved its hallucinatory effect, Anah would dance and control him again, countering the curse from Isaac's father.

But the whiskey and fatigue of the day swept over Anah, and he passed out drunk, still wearing the grisly face of Isaac.

That night he dreamed of his elusive friend, Death. It saw him wearing the powerful mask and stopped. It stopped for him and was turning for him finally, waiting. They would be allies after all.

Anah was the first to waken that morning, and as he stood unsteadily to urinate by the stream, he looked over to where the little wolverine was tethered.

He had escaped!

And then he heard sounds from the west and saw four long boats of red-coated soldiers moving upriver. The boy had escaped and had taken his power with him.

Hollering an alarm over to Klixuatan, Anah looked to the ground to see where the little wolverine had gone. Despite the rain-soaked ground, he could make out deep, small footprints moving away from the tethers and down toward the beach.

He followed. He would need the boy.

Behind him, Anah heard Klixuatan groggily waking the other men and the hollering of the soldiers in the oncoming boats. They had seen the encampment.

Anah moved down to the river and followed the tracks upstream until he came to a long stretch of beach. He saw Jacob draped over the shoulder of what looked like a small man carefully wending his way over the wide, rock-covered beach.

Was it Death, carrying away his power?

◇◇◇◇◇

Emmy had moved as quickly as she could along the low riverbank, avoiding catching herself on exposed tree roots or twisting her ankles on the large rocks polished round by the river. She had traversed a half mile when she heard hollering from downriver, several rounds of rifle shots, and then more hollering.

When she turned, in the distance she saw red-coated soldiers coming ashore, firing into the woods. And then in the foreground, only fifty yards away, she saw someone walking unsteadily over the smooth stones, following her.

He had a knife drawn.

She lay Jacob down and stepped in front of him to protect him. She would fight the man.

But the man moved directly to Jacob and swung at her with his knife.

Emmy ducked, but the blade sliced through her parka, cutting into her left shoulder, and she lost her balance and fell.

Pushing herself back up, she heard herself scream, "Get away from him!"

But the man ignored her and stooped down toward her son. As the figure pulled Jacob up and onto his shoulder, he turned and faced her.

It was Isaac!

But then Emmy realized it *wasn't* her husband. The facial mask of Isaac on the man had been pulled tightly back, and she recognized the blond beard and the smooth, straight, silky hair . . . but peering through the eye slits were two evil, hard, obsidian black coals burning straight from hell. This was the specter, the one that had followed her in nightmares for months, the monster that had destroyed her family and changed her life forever.

The man raised his knife to Jacob's throat as a warning to Emmy. Then he turned and started to walk away.

Following them, she shouted, "Put him down!"

The man kept walking, ignoring her.

As he increased his pace, she shouted again, "Put him down, you bastard!"

He stopped and turned. He stared at her defiantly, and as the lower part of the mask flapped away in the morning wind, Emmy could see him grinning triumphantly.

It was a grisly sneer that sent a furious chill deep down into her core and immediately reawakened the encompassing wretched and miserable despair she had suffered at this man's hands.

A cold, calm clarity settled onto her that was right and just and perfect for this moment. From less than ten feet away, Emmy drew out the pepperbox. She pulled the trigger and put a bullet squarely through the smiling haunt-mask of Isaac and into the forehead of the savage.

CHAPTER FORTY-ONE

Sarah

Jojo had found Jacob's keepsakes, recovered from Klixuatan's purse, which the savage had used to hex her brother and had given them to Sarah.

Presciently, Sarah had carried several things on the trip that both she and Jacob had shared, like the arrow head they had pried from the remains of a fossilized skull bone of some large animal, found in the plowed ground of their parents' farm; and several items that only he would know, little treasures she took out of his trouser pockets and his bureau from home after the attack: a polished burr, a brass button, a blue-brown steely marble, a spent ticket from their trip to Victoria, several pieces of rounded sand-buffed colored glass.

To the items recovered by Jojo, she added the ones she had brought from home, put all the keepsakes into his hands, and let him finger them one by one. Then she put them all into his pocket and kissed him.

When Jacob was returned to her, she cradled him in her arms and told him she would never let him go again. She would take care of him. She would take care of him, her little brother. Could he hear her? Was it too late? Would he ever snuggle with her as he had just a few months before? It would take time to see whether he had been broken; she would work on that, she promised herself.

From these events, Sarah wondered about her own frailty in the face of it all. Her home, and the security she had felt here, had been forever changed. Could she ever find that again? And her inner being had been assaulted as well, she knew. As strong as she believed herself to be, she foresaw herself over the next few years likely ebbing, doubting from time to time, fraying a bit, surprising the framed image of tranquility, an emulation of her mother's behavior, which she wished to project and protect for herself, like when a stone is dropped into the still pond that a modest person should rely upon as one's only mirror. She would keep guard for that.

She wondered what Jacob would see when looking there with her, while waiting for the return to soft reflections off tranquil water — if, indeed, that ever came. She wondered, with all that had occurred, whether he would avoid ever again letting go of the security he would certainly now need, holding on tightly to those precious little things she had found and preserved to help bring him back.

And would he come back?

It would take time, she decided. It would take time.

CHAPTER FORTY-TWO

<><><>

Pickett and Emmy

The shelling from the two Brit frigates began at six o'clock in the morning, just as Pickett had sat down for his breakfast with his staff. The incoming shells, striking the beach 500 yards east of his camp, reverberated with enough force that coffee mugs flew from their laps and set a few younger officers into a frantic tizzy.

Pickett did not lose his composure, however. He had been under fire many times, in Mexico and then from Apache and Kiowa small arms in the badlands of Texas. He had the well-proportioned and measured understanding of danger that can only develop when one is being targeted for death.

He watched the earth spraying up, following each report, and realized immediately that the Brits were simply attempting to intimidate him with their gunnery exercise. So he sat back down, ordered his coffee mug to be refilled, and waited for their range practice to cease.

It kept up for an hour, finishing dramatically with a full barrage from the HBMS *Tribune's* and the HBMS *Satellite's* port eight-pounders, all twenty of them. And then he heard the Brit marines' laughter from both ships, rolling across the water as a mocking peripety to their display.

It made him furious at the bastards.

The next morning, the barrage started again and continued every day for the next few days, not on the clock but rather on cue with the pouring of his staff's breakfast coffee.

Pickett knew they would be tested by the Brits like this in the same manner as he had seen schoolyard bullies taunt smaller children into flight or futile fight. So he waited calmly for three more days, and then, on the fourth, moved his camp with as much solemn dignity as he could display over to the windy south side of the long spit, out of reach from their sneering morning provocation.

It was on that day that he received the note. It was from Mrs. Emmy Evers. She had chartered a passage to the island and was waiting for him twelve miles away at the harbor they called Roche. Would he meet her there the next day to receive a package she wished to personally deliver?

He did not sleep that night at all, and, as he lay awake in the tent, blustered about by a heavy southerner gale, he tried to reconstruct his feelings the last time they had seen each other. How was she?

He had read in a Victoria newspaper two months ago that a woman, who had preferred to keep her anonymity, had survived an arduous journey and had succeeded in rescuing her son from a band of vicious Northerner aborigines. Word of that feat had spread down the coast, and he had speculated it could only have been Emmy.

But there had been no word from her, and the silence had convinced him he was sadly mistaken. She must have perished.

But now that he knew she was alive, he realized it could only have been her! What would she say? What would she be like?

He needed to know. He was up at five the next morning and waited for another cannonade. But none came. So at nine o'clock, containing himself no longer, he ordered his mount and rode west unaccompanied by an orderly.

Upon her arrival, Emmy had booked lodging for one day with an American couple who maintained a small house overlooking a protected cove shared by two other families, one British and the other loyal to neither country.

As she awaited Pickett, she wondered if he would respond, and when she found herself hoping, she thought again about the propriety of this encounter, curious as to what family and friends might think.

But she reminded herself that she had finally decided she did not really care what anyone thought. Something had compulsively drawn her to Pickett, and she still did not know what it was.

She needed his counsel, she told herself. And she wanted to finish a conversation that had been initiated on the day they had inspected cattle together on Whidbey.

As she watched Pickett ride up in the distance on his strong gray mare, with swelling happiness she thought about the freeing finality of her situation.

The week after she had arrived home with Jacob, she had arranged for a quiet ceremony at Isaac's grave. Attended only by Jim Thomas who dug into the grave and his wife Princess Susan who sang a quiet dirge, Emmy buried Isaac's remains—the mask she had stripped from Anah—with the rest of his poor body.

And then it was finished.

She stopped dreaming about him that week, and when word came down about the confrontation on San Juan one week later, she decided she would make this trip. And she decided it was nobody's business.

Watching him approach, she stepped out onto the porch and walked down to the beach below. She noted that Pickett had the same carry as she had seen the day she met him, slightly self-conscious but with a flair that superseded that flaw.

The canter of his horse said something about the rider, revealing a dimension she could not discern from his conversation or in the letter he had first written her. It was a gallant form of communication by him, and it made her heart race, a response reinforced with each toss of his proud mare's head.

As he drew up, Pickett paused for a moment, then he swooped down off his horse, pushed his cape aside, slowly dropped his field cap, and bowed deeply in the French manner.

When she offered her hand, he pulled it to his lips and kissed it gently.

"My deepest respects for you, Mrs. Evers. My profound, deepest respects and admiration for all that I now know you have endured."

"Thank you, Captain Pickett," she said, swallowing her words out of a desperate need to control herself. "I have attempted to keep these travails from the gossip of the community. It seems I have failed."

"I do not believe you fail in any endeavor, Emmy," he said, smiling, but obviously holding himself from saying more.

She nodded, not at his assertion, but in approval of his use of her first name.

She plucked up her courage. "May I call you 'Pickett George'?" she asked with a sly smile.

He straightened, and, from his surprised expression, she saw he realized that she knew much about him.

"You may, Emmy. You may," he said.

◇◇◇◇◇

They walked along the beach for hours until the light started to fade, past the pounding surf in a misting rain, and shared with each other what they had endured during the past several months.

By comparison, his ordeal was slight, he knew. The stories Emmy conveyed were overwhelming to him, as hardened as he believed himself to be. In fact, a few times he had to turn away lest he show emotions that were not befitting a man of his age.

She asked his counsel about the turmoil that definitely was increasing in the East between the states over slavery. She wondered about whether a confrontation was likely to erupt between the opposing cultures of the North and South, each advocating passionately for its position—one side in favor of imposing a civil solution to the affront to human rights represented by the enslavement of others, the other side defending its rationalized position to preserve an economic infrastructure that had existed for generations.

"My father has written. My mother is very ill. With all that is happening, the threat of war, how safe will my children be if I to return with them to my home in Boston?"

"I believe you will be safe there, Emmy."

"And what will become of you, Captain Pickett? How would you, as an educated man, place your bets on the next few years?"

He shook his head. He didn't have an answer.

How closely tied to his heart would his decisions be, she wondered?

⟨XXXX⟩

Pickett was quiet as they walked, for Emmy's questions about his future decisions were ones he had pondered over the past several months.

He knew he would likely move to where his heart brought him rather than where convenience seduced. He understood the value of passion as an underpinning to everything that ultimately mattered, to everything that defined one's legacy, and to the difference he would or would not make in this life.

But what of Emmy?

He looked at the sturdy and beautiful woman who walked beside him and wondered how she might fare and whether she ever could fit into those travels.

He had seen much, and as he thought about her, thought of the wiles and courage necessary to survive in a cold, brutal world, he sensed she would endure and likely flourish.

She did not need to be protected, and that realization was a comfort and a disappointment to him all at once, bred as he was to believe that being a hero and rescuer was a noble reason for a man's existence and ample enough foundation for a durable love.

He did not have answers for Emmy.

And he understood, with some sadness, it wasn't time to make those decisions. He was duty bound for now, so hoping for a future with her in any case would be far-fetched and out of his control.

So, he was silent, and they walked on.

◇◇◇◇◇

They stayed together there for the balance of the day and then, on the next day, she returned home. On the morning she left, she presented him with the inlaid box that contained his Belgian Mariette six-barrel pepperbox. It was the last time they saw each other.

CHAPTER FORTY-THREE

✕✕✕✕

Emmy

Emmy looked over the rail, looked at the dock below, and then up at Port Townsend, framed by the deep green forests and blue mountaintops of the Olympics.

It was warming now, and enough blue patched through the clouds that, it seemed, she saw the land again in a way she had not since the time she had first arrived so many years ago. She would round the Horn again, going against every vow she had made after that first awful journey, and present her children to her family in Boston for the first time.

She wondered whether she would ever return again, here where so much was buried now. Isaac's body was finally at rest, she knew. She hoped his soul finally had moved on and melded with the land that he had believed was his own.

She looked north and thought of George Pickett again. She had heard he had faced down the Brits up on the San Juan and that General Winfield Scott himself had trekked across the Panama isthmus to take over and attend to the disengagement of the hostilities.

She wondered how Pickett George would fare in a world of men who thought themselves and their business and causes so important. She had written to him once since her visit there. She wished that noble, sad man great luck in this desperate world.

She thought of Jojo and how brave he had been and how grateful he was to receive from her the ability to read. She believed the leverage such a commodity would provide to him was a fair exchange after all.

They found his father, MaNuitu 'sta, gravely ill when they returned, but Jojo had been able to read to him before the old tyee died. She knew she had fulfilled an important promise to MaNuitu 'sta—for the time being the best she could do in return for all he had done.

She wondered if she should do more for Jojo, perhaps help in his education?

Would she ever return here? Would her children come back here someday, to this raw and savage land that seduced one with its beauty but tested one so severely with its moodiness? The terrible changes in seasons constantly reminded her she was alive but mortal. She wondered what it would be like if she were to live in a climate where the seasons were less dramatic. Would that cause her to become tepid and complacent and forget about death? Would that be fair?

And what should she tell her family in Boston? What should she write about her own thoughts and memories? What could she preserve for others that would be an adequate mark for her time, her family's suffering, and everything she felt so deeply?

All so real and yet, all so unreal.

All so painful, and all so much at rest now. All at rest . . . and with her duty done.

Could she ever come back? Could she ever will herself into that time and make things right somehow, the way they had been before Isaac had been killed? So much was buried here. But so many people were arriving now and building over it all that soon it would not matter what rested here from before.

The reality, she knew, as she reflected on her journey here in this big Northwest, is that our finite time in life does not allow us to really go back. The biographies and autobiographies, based on the exploration and interpretation of the notes we have saved and the markings shaken loose from the corners where we have tucked them, most often stay unwritten. Thus, the memories and mementos become encumbrances, if not for us, then for the family, friends, and strangers who must clean up afterward. Instead of them being loving presences with fragrances that grace a room, they become pale pieces of paper with words that no longer echo and move mountains and souls. A pity, she thought. But there was still much to see in this life, and that was good.

She would accept that and move on.

EPILOGUE

⟨⟨⟩⟩

Isaac, Anah

Out of darkness . . . and suddenly he was a leaf on the porch pushed across with the yellow and orange ones, blowing across the stoop of this home that was his. It was west to east, this wind from the strait below, and he couldn't be angry with it as he had in the past for pushing him so, because then he was part of it, this wind.

Now he finally understood why it had howled when it found tunnels to whistle itself through. He finally understood that it was a joyous cry because the sound gave him a voice that lasted for just a bit as he buffeted about.

He found a place, a little tube from a broken bottle stem, and he dove into it, and its glass walls vibrated, and he heard the echo of the yearning whistle, a whoop and a warning, and as he swirled up out of it, he was borne up again and he was flying high above what had been his home but no longer was. And as he swooped above, he was in control, and by leaning to the right, he soared high above the beachhead and homestead and saw it all, with its time passing below, all the elements, waiting for their time to fly like him.

He hovered out above the sliver-moon bay, above the tall, empty ship with ragged sails, and as he landed on its mossy deck, he found scratches on the walls left by sad creatures in sad pain. He hopped along the gangway and saw the drops of blood, long dried and faded, that told some other tale that he could no longer remember.

In an empty, dusty room below, next to a broken chair, he found a globe of glass, and inside was a snowing scene with a bright shiny pin inside. He picked it up in his beak and pushed himself aloft and out above the dead ship.

He took himself to a shoreline where he saw a rocky beach to drop his prize, burst it, and get the shiny pin. And as he let go, as he had always done so cleverly, something came from out of nowhere, and his catch was gone. And he was wandering again, and his shore and ship and moon were gone, and he was in darkness without a bearing.

AUTHOR'S NOTES

Widow Walk is a historical adventure novel depicting real and fictionalized characters and events.

Isaac and Emmy Evers. The fictionalized characters of both Isaac and Emmy Evers of Widow Walk is partly derived from the 1857 diary entries of Isaac and Emily Ebey.

Like so many other enterprising speculators in this turbulent era, Isaac had emigrated from the Midwest with his skills to California in search of quick fortune. He found none. Luckless and frustrated, he turned his entrepreneurial hopes to the Oregon territory.

When he arrived in the Puget Sound area in 1850, fewer than 1,500 white settlers had settled there. With the discovery of gold on the Fraser River in 1858, all of that changed and a great booming migration began, with settlers moving northward by ship into the region from California and overland from the Midwest.

After surveying areas like Lake Washington and Whidbey Island, Ebey energized that migration by writing effusive letters to friends and relatives, encouraging them to emigrate "before the good land is all taken."

In 1852, possibly guided to Whidbey Island by Si'ahl, the man later to be known as **Chief "Seattle,"** Isaac Ebey re-established an abandoned claim on 640 acres of the fertile prairie now known as *Ebey's Plateau.* There, he and his first wife, Rebecca, developed a prosperous farm that serviced the needs of the military and civilian populations in Bellingham and Port Townsend. After Rebecca died in 1854, Isaac remarried to a durable woman named Emily.

Ebey participated in the establishment of the territorial government in the southern area of Puget Sound and suggested the name "Olympia" for the Tumwater location that subsequently became the territorial capital. In his duties as a tax collector and regional magistrate, he traveled extensively and immediately understood the importance of San Juan Island as a strategic opportunity for the United States.

His exhortations to the territorial government recommending it move settlers onto San Juan Island helped the United States' case for its claim to the island against Britain. Greatly disturbed by the constant threat of predation and conflict, in 1856 he outfitted a company of volunteers to fight in the Indian wars in Eastern Washington and was widely praised for his help in subduing native tribes.

The fatal cannonade by the **U.S.S.** *Massachusetts* on encamped natives at Port Gamble is thought to have provoked the attack on Ebey and his family and his brutal murder and beheading by Northerners prompted the settlers and military in the region to intensify their precautions, as well as their rationalization of the random lynching of numerous Native Americans. Sightings of long boats parading Ebey's "tyee" (chieftan) head were reported for weeks afterwards.

Blockhouses still stand, preserved on Whidbey and San Juan Islands attesting to the very real threat of pillage, rape and murder by marauding "Northerners," a term used for miscellaneous clans from indigenous regional native tribes. Although no one single group is likely responsible for the legendary headhunting and slaving, clans from the southern tip of Alaska, western British Columbia and the Queen Charlotte Islands (now called Haida Gwaii) were blamed for most of the predation against white settlers and coastal native villages. Many tribes along the coast have stories of conflict with them.

Northerner slaving raids, which reputedly savaged the Pacific Coast all the way to northern California, continued until steam-powered vessels replaced many of the naval ships patrolling the region.

Collection of exquisite Haida Argillite carvings and coastal native artistry began in the late sixteenth century and continues to this day.

The **Emmy Evers** of *Widow Walk* is a composite character, derived from the readings of Emily Ebey's diary as well as the reminiscences of many other strong-hearted pioneer women of that time — a time when most men believed that women had neither rights nor wherewithal.

Anah Nawitka is a composite character, drawn from accounts of several notorious clan leaders with whom the

British and Americans contended in their appropriation of "aboriginal" lands.

Conflict between the cultures was inevitable, with ample provocation and rationalization for each side's escalation of violent retributive actions. James Douglas, the aggressive and enterprising former Hudson's Bay Company director and first governor of British Columbia, used the same tactics in taking land as had his British counterparts in taking New Zealand aboriginal land.

Isaac Stevens, the first Washington territorial Governor, advocated the "extinction" of Native Americans.

Antoine Bill and **René Marté** are composite characters of "Metís" - a mixed "breed" of French Canadian and indigenous native parentage, who participated in the exploration, trading, trapping and interpretative needs for the British and American explorers.

Ma'Nauita 'sta, Jojo, and **Ksi' Amawaal** are composite characters of well-known, peaceful entrepreneurial native leaders in the British Columbia region.

Christian missionary work, particularly that of the Jesuits throughout the Pacific Northwest, is well documented. The character of Marano Levy is a fictionalized version of a legendary wandering Hebrew man who purportedly travelled the region looking for the lost tribes of Israel.

Captain George Edward Pickett, a West Point graduate and Mexican War hero, was stationed in Bellingham from 1855 to 1860. Ordered by Brigadier General William S. Harney to San Juan Island to pre-empt a British claim to that strategically important territory, Pickett made a show of it and subsequently was described by local journalists as a "fighting gamecock."

His comments to the press purportedly were "Let 'em come. We'll make another bloody Bunker Hill of it."

Pickett's stubborn, well-publicized stand off intensified the confrontation, and for a short while there was wild speculation in the region that another war with the British was imminent. **General Winfield Scott** was dispatched by President James Buchanan to San Juan Island to de-escalate what was being called "The Pig War," because the shooting of a Hudson's Bay official's pet pig by an American settler was the provocation used by Douglas to ostensibly "protect the rights of British citizens" on San Juan.

The dispute was finally settled in mediation by Kaiser Wilhelm in 1872.

At the outbreak of the U.S. Civil War, Pickett resigned his commission in the US Army and returned to his native Virginia to join the Confederate Army where he quickly achieved promotions, fame and notoriety. At Gettysburg, his division spearheaded the fateful march, now known as "Pickett's Charge'" against a well-entrenched Union Army.

Major General George Pickett was described posthumously by one of his Union army adversaries, General George McClellan, as "the best fighting infantry commander on either side" of the War Between the States.

The Sunnyside Cemetery on **Whidbey Island** overlooks the farmstead owned by Isaac and Emmy. It contains the remains of Isaac and others in the Ebey family, as well as settlers who first farmed the fertile land. However, one story purports that the grisly scalp and skin mask from Isaac's head was never returned to rest in that grave.

The site of the Ebey massacre remains much as it was in 1858 and many of the Whidbey locals think of it as haunted. On moonlit nights it is purported that the ghost of a woman can be seen walking the plateau.

WIDOW WALK

Acknowledgments

To
Allen Hurt and Nick Kazan
For constructive inspiration

To
Barbara Bourdeau, John Aylward, Rosemary Ambrosia
Bradley, Carmen Bartl, Wayne Bliss,
Paul Auerbach, Greg Brown, Celine Cimino, Shawn
Comerford, Joe Curiel, John DeDakis, Nina Ferrari, Neil
Gonzalez, S.P. Hays, Dorbe Holden, Scott James, Abby
Kitten, Angela LaSalle, Francesca LaSalle, Mo Matthiesen
Weber, Dave McClinton, Tina Minnick, Kimberly Moore,
Randy Mott, Mary Mulcare, Archana Murthy, Kelsye
Nelson, Carey Pelto, Thomas Polizzi, Paul Racey, Sherry
Roberts, Tony Roberts, Lance Rosen, Tom Skerritt,

Laura Smith, Sandy Porrier Smith, Sue Taylor and Theresa
Tavernero
For encouragement and comments

And to
Mike Vouri, a Pacific Northwest Historian; The
Washington State Historical Society; and the Pacific
Northwest Native American tribal storytellers
For historical context and perspective

WIDOW WALK

Book Discussion Guide

1. *Widow Walk* has been compared to *Last of the Mohicans* and *Cold Mountain*. How is this story similar to those historical fictional works?

2. Emmy Evers in *Widow Walk* has been compared to other fictional women like Scarlet O'Hara in *Gone With the Wind*. How is Emmy alike and how is she different than Scarlett and other strong female protagonists in literature?

3. In 1858 only 5,000 non-native settlers had moved to the Pacific Northwest. It is estimated that over a thirty times that number of aboriginal ("First Nation") people lived along the coast at that time. Imagine that you were a non-native settler or a First Nation inhabitant. How would you behave if you saw strangers arrive at your home?

4. Conflict between the new settlers and First Nation peoples was inevitable and sometimes became violent. Expansion of population into new territories was important to both the U.S. and Britain. Was the "jingoism," as manifested in the mid-nineteenth century American and European history, beneficial or destructive?

5. Based on how Christian missionary activity is depicted in *Widow Walk,* how do you assess its impact and/or effectiveness?

6. The responses of the white governments and native peoples to the massacres as depicted in *Widow Walk* were frequently harsh. In your opinion, were they justified?

7. What is a "Potlatch" and why was it important to the Pacific Northwest First Nation tribes? Why did the white governments and missionaries eventually outlaw the Potlatch? How is the Potlatch as now re-established in the twentieth and twenty first century different than the tradition as originally celebrated? Is this good or bad?

8. What is a totem and what is its importance to Pacific Northwest First Nations peoples? What is the significance of the animals depicted in *Widow Walk*? Who is Raven God in the Pacific Northwest native lore? Are there similarities between these archetypes and those found in other cultures?

9. Imagine your family is expecting the birth of another child during the mid-nineteenth century in Pacific Northwest. How would you prepare for this event? Why did so

many women die during and after childbirth in the nineteenth and early twentieth century?

10. Can the actions of Anah against white settlers and other tribes as depicted in *Widow Walk* be interpreted as sociopathic, predatory or justifiable? What, in your opinion, is the relationship between managing sociopathic behavior and the vibrancy of an economy?

About the Author

A physician, sculptor, award-winning filmmaker, and author, Gar LaSalle has been honored widely in the medical and fine arts communities for his leadership and creativity.

LaSalle's 1976 award winning feature length documentary, *Diary of a Moonlighter* premiered nationally on PBS and was the first-ever film about the new specialty of Emergency Medicine.

His two award-winning historical fiction novels. *Widow Walk*, published in 2014 by Greenleaf won multiple awards including the Eric Hoffer Award for Literature, the eLit Silver Medal, the IndieReaders Award for Best Novel, and the San Francisco Book Festival Grand Jury Prize for General Fiction.

Isthmus, published in 2015 by Avasta Press, the first sequel in the series, was a finalist for the PNWWA Nancy Pearl award for literature.

Widow Walk has been optioned by Heyou Media Inc. for a feature film.

http://www.garlasalle.com/about/bio/

ISTHMUS

THE SECOND BOOK IN THE AWARD-WINNING WIDOW WALK SAGA

It is 1860 and revolution is erupting throughout the world over universal emancipation. Civil war looms in the Unites States. In the midst of it all, a young woman is moving back to Boston with what is left of her family, devastated and bankrupted by savage, tragic events that occurred less than a year ago in the Pacific Northwest.

They traverse a hostile terrain on the new Panama isthmus railroad, the most modern transportation in the world. From inside their coach they watch the humid forest, a different type of green from what they knew up north, slipping fast past, a warm verdant blur. Looking down the aisle they see an uncomfortable array of fellow travelers, an international mix of characters whom they will get to know all too well . . . each with hidden hopes and dreams . . . predators and victims, desperadoes and hangmen, widows and widow makers. A convenient ride through the jungle. An inconvenient assault. A run for their lives.

This new edition of *Isthmus*, first published in 2016, was a finalist for the Pacific Northwest Writers Association Nancy Pearl Award for excellence in fiction.

Available at Amazon, Solipsispublishing.com, and GarLaSalle.com

THE FAIRNESS OF BEASTS

THE THIRD BOOK IN THE ACCLAIMED WIDOW WALK SAGA.

It is 1862. A massive Union army is invading the verdant peninsula of Virginia to take Richmond and end the Civil war. Amidst this conflict, a young woman's wounded lover stands in harm's way. To rescue him, she must risk everything she holds dear and cross enemy lines. The fate of her young family hangs in the balance, as does that of the entire nation. The risk she takes turns out to test her heart beyond anything she could have imagined.

Available at Amazon, Solipsispublishing.com, and GarLaSalle.com

CPSIA information can be obtained
at www.ICGtesting.com
Printed in the USA
LVHW090208301219
642035LV00001B/57/P